ISBN 978-1-331-34584-8
PIBN 10177271

TREVLYN HOLD;

OR,

SQUIRE TREVLYN'S HEIR.

TREVLYN HOLD;

OR,

SQUIRE TREVLYN'S HEIR.

BY THE

AUTHOR OF "EAST LYNNE," "DANESBURY HOUSE," &c.

IN THREE VOLUMES.

VOL. I.

LONDON:

TINSLEY BROTHERS, 18, CATHERINE ST., STRAND,
1864.

[The right of Translation is reserved.]

LONDON

BRADBURY AND EVANS, PRINTERS, WHITEFRIARS.

CONTENTS.

CHAPTER I.

CHAPTER X.

CHAPTER XI.

CHAPTER XII.

CHAPTER XIII.

CHAPTER XIV.

CHAPTER XV.

CHAPTER XVI.

CHAPTER XVII.

CHAPTER XVIII.

CHAPTER XIX.

CHAPTER XX.

TREVLYN HOLD.

CHAPTER I.

THE SCARLET CRAVAT.

THE fine hot summer had faded into autumn, and the autumn would soon be fading into winter. All signs of the harvest had disappeared. The farmers had gathered the golden grain into their barns; the meads looked bare, and the partridges hid themselves in the stubble left by the reapers.

Perched on the top of a stile which separated one field from another, was a boy of some fifteen years. Several books, a strap passed round to keep them together, were flung over his shoulder, and he sat throwing stones into a pond close by, softly whistling as he did so. The stones came out of his pocket. Whether stored there for the purpose to which they were now being put, was best known to himself. He was a slender, well-made boy, with finely-shaped features, a clear complexion, and eyes dark and earnest. A refined face ; a good face—and you have not to learn that the face is the outward index of the mind within. An index that never fails, for those gifted with the power to read the human countenance.

Before him, at a short distance, as he sat on the stile, lay the village of Barbrook. A couple of miles beyond the village was the large town of Barmester. But you could get to the town without taking the village *en route*. As to the village itself, there were several ways of reaching it. There was the path through the fields, right in front of the stile where that school-boy was sitting ; there was the green and shady lane (knee-deep in mud sometimes) ; and there were two high roads. To look at the signs of vegetation around (not that the vegetation was of the richest kind), you would not suspect that the barren and bleak lands of coal fields lay so near. But four or five miles away in the opposite direction—that is, behind the boy and the stile—the coal pits flourished. Farm-houses were scattered within view, had the young gentleman on the stile chosen to look at them ; a few gentlemen's houses, and many cottages and hovels. To his left hand, glancing over the field and across the upper road —the road which did not lead to Barbrook, but to Barmester—on a slight eminence, rose the fine but old-fashioned mansion called Trevlyn Hold. Bearing rather to the right at the back of him was the less pretensious, but comfortable dwelling, called Trevlyn Farm. Trevlyn Hold, formerly the property and residence of Squire Trevlyn, had passed, with that gentleman's death, into the hands of Mr. Chattaway, who now lived in it; his wife having been the squire's second daughter. Trevlyn Farm was tenanted by Mr. Ryle; and he now sitting on the stile was Mr. Ryle's eldest son.

There came, scuffling along the field-path from the village, a wan-looking, under-sized girl, as fast as her dilapidated shoes permitted her. The one shoe was tied on with a piece of rag; the other, being tied on with nothing, came off perpetually, thereby impeding her progress. She had nearly gained the pond, when a boy considerably taller and stronger than the one on the stile came flying down the field from the left, and planted himself in her way.

"Now then, you little toad! Do you want another buffeting?"

"Oh, please, sir, don't stop me!" she cried, beginning to sob unnecessarily loud. "Father's a dying, and mother said I was to run and tell them at the farm. Please let me go by."

"Did I not order you yesterday to keep out of

these fields?" asked the tall boy. "There's the lane and there are the roads open to you; how dare you come here? I promised you I'd shake the inside out of you if I caught you here again, and now I'll do it."

"I say," called out at this juncture the lad on the stile, "you keep your hands off her."

The child's assailant turned sharply round at the sound. He had not seen that anybody was there. For one moment he relaxed his hold of the girl, but the next appeared to think better of it, and began to shake her. She turned her face, quite a sight with its tears and its dirt, towards the stile.

"Oh, Master George, make him let me go! I'm a hasting on to your house, Master George. Father, he's lying all white upon the bed; and mother said I was to come off and tell of it."

George leaped off the stile, and advanced. "You let her go, Cris Chattaway!"

Cris Chattaway turned his anger upon George. "Mind your own business, you beggar! It is no concern of yours."

"It is, if I choose to make it mine. Let her go, I say. Don't be a coward."

"What's that you call me?" asked Cris Chattaway. "A coward? Take that."

He had picked up a hard clod of earth, and

dashed it in George Ryle's face. The boy was
not one to stand a gratuitous blow, and Mr. Christopher, before he knew what was coming, found
himself on the ground. The girl, released, flew to
the stile and scrambled over it head foremost.
George stood his ground, waiting for Cris to get
up ; he was less tall and strong, but he would not
run away.

Christopher Chattaway slowly gathered himself
up. He *was* a coward; and fighting, when it
came to close quarters, was not to his mind,
Stone-throwing, or water-squirting, or pea-shoot-
ing—any safe annoyance that might be carried
on at a distance—he was an adept in ; but hand-
to-hand fighting—Cris did not relish that.

"See if you don't suffer for this, George Ryle !"

George laughed good-humouredly, and sat down
on the stile as before. Cris was dusting the earth
off his clothes.

"You have called me a coward, and you have
knocked me down. I'll put it in my memorandum book, George Ryle."

"Put it," equably returned George. "I never
knew any *but* cowards set upon girls."

"I'll set upon her again, if I catch her using
this path. There's not a more impudent little
wretch in all the parish. Let her try it, that's
all."

" She has a right to use this path as much as I have."

"Not if I choose to say she shan't use it. *You* won't have the right long."

" Oh, indeed !" said George. " What is to take it from me ? "

" The squire says he shall cause this way through the fields to be closed."

" *Who* says it ?" asked George, with marked emphasis—and the sound grated on Chris Chattaway's ear.

" The squire says so," he roared. " Are you deaf ? "

" Ah," said George. " But Mr. Chattaway can't close it. My father says he has not the power."

" *Your* father !" contemptuously rejoined Cris Chattaway. " He would like his leave asked, perhaps. When the squire says he shall do a thing, he means it."

" At any rate, it is not done yet," was the significant answer of George. " Don't boast, Cris."

Cris had been making off, and was some distance up the field. He turned to address George.

"You know, you beggar, that if I don't go in and polish you off, it's because I can't condescend to tarnish my hands. When I fight, I like to fight with gentlepeople." And with that he turned tail, and decamped quicker than before.

"Just so," shrieked out George. "Especially if they wear petticoats."

A sly shower of earth came back in answer. But it happened, every bit of it, to stear clear of him, and George kept his seat and his equanimity.

"What has he been doing now, George ?"

George turned his head; the question came from some one close behind him. There stood a lovely boy of some twelve years old, his beautiful features set off by dark blue eyes and silky curls of bright auburn.

"Where did you spring from, Rupert ?"

"I came down by the hedge. You did not hear me. You were calling after Cris. Has he been beating you, George ?"

"Beating me !" returned George, throwing back his handsome face with a laugh. "I don't think he would like to try that on, Rupert. He could not beat me with impunity, as he does you."

Rupert Trevlyn laid his cheek on the top rail of the stile, and fixed his eyes on the clear blue of the evening sky—for the sun was drawing towards its setting. He was a sensitive, romantic, strange sort of boy; gentle and loving by nature, but given to violent fits of passion. People said he inherited the latter from his grandfather, Squire Trevlyn. Others of the squire's descendants had inherited the same. Under happier auspices, Rupert might have learnt to subdue these bursts of passion. Had he possessed a kind home and loving friends, how different might have been his destiny!

"George, I wish my papa had lived!"

"The whole parish has need. to wish that," returned George. "I wish you stood in his shoes! That's what I wish."

"Instead of Uncle Chattaway. Old Canham says I ought to stand in them. He says he thinks I shall, some time, because justice is nearly sure to come uppermost in the end."

"Look here, Rupert!" gravely returned George Ryle. "Don't you go listening to old Canham. He talks nonsense, and it will do neither of you good. If Chattaway heard but a tithe of what he sometimes says, he'd turn him from the lodge, neck and crop, in spite of Miss Diana. What *is*, can't be helped, you know, Rupert."

"But Cris has no right to inherit Trevlyn over me."

"He has the right of law, I suppose," answered George; "at least, he will have it. Make the best of it, Ru. There are lots of things that I have to make the best of. I got a caning yesterday for another boy, and I had to make the best of that."

Rupert still looked up at the sky. " If it were not for Aunt Edith," quoth he, " I'd run away."

" You little stupid ! Where would you run to ? "

" Anywhere. Mr. Chattaway gave me no dinner to-day."

" Why not ? "

" Because Cris carried a tale to him. But it was false, George.'

" Did you tell Chattaway it was false ?"

" Yes. But where's the use ? He always believes Cris before me."

" Have you had no dinner ? "

Rupert shook his head. " I snatched a bit of bread off the tray as they were carrying it through the hall, and a piece of fat that Cris left on his plate. That's all I had."

" Then I'd advise you to make double quick haste home to your tea," said George, jumping over the stile, " as I am going to do to mine."

He, George, ran swiftly across the back fields towards his home. Looking back when he was well on his way, he saw the lad, Rupert, still leaning on the stile with his face turned upward.

Meanwhile the little tatterdemalion of a girl had scuffled along to Trevlyn Farm—a very moderate-sized house, with a rustic porch covered with jessamine, and a large garden, more useful than ornamental, intervening between it and the high road. The garden path, leading to the porch, was straight and narrow; on either side rose alternately cabbage-rose-trees and hollyhocks. Gooseberries, currants, strawberries, raspberries; apple, plum, and other plain fruit trees, grew amidst vegetables of various sorts. A productive garden, if not an elegant one. At the side of the house was the fold-yard palings and a five-barred gate, dividing it from the public road, and at the back of the house were situated the barns and other out-door buildings.

From the porch the entrance led direct into a room, half sitting-room, half kitchen. It was called " Nora's room." Nora generally sat in it; George and his brother did their lessons in it; the real kitchen being at the back. A parlour opening from this room on the right, whose window looked into the fold-yard, was the general sitting-room of the family. The best sitting-room, a really handsome apartment, was on the other side of the house. As the girl scuffled up to the porch, an active, black-eyed, talkative little woman, of five or six-and-thirty, saw her approach from the window of the best kitchen. It was Nora. What with the child's ragged frock and tippet, her broken straw bonnet, her slipshod shoes, and her face smeared with dirt and tears,

she looked wretched enough. Her father, Jim
Sanders, was the carter to Mr. Ryle. He had
been at home ill the last day or two; or, as
the phrase ran in the farm, was " off his
work."

"If ever I saw such an object!" was Nora's
exclamation. " How *can* her mother keep her in
that state? Just look at that Letty Sanders, Mrs.
Ryle!"

Sorting large bunches of sweet herbs on a table
at the back of the room, was a tall, upright woman.
Her dress was plain, but her manner and bearing
bespoke the lady. Those familiar with the district would have recognised in her handsome, but
somewhat masculine face, a likeness to the well-
formed, powerful features of the late Squire
Trevlyn. She was that gentleman's eldest daughter, and had given mortal umbrage to her family
when she quitted Trevlyn Hold to become the
second wife of Mr. Ryle. George Ryle was not
her son. She had but two children: Trevlyn, a
boy two years younger than George; and a little
girl of eight, named Caroline.

Mrs. Ryle turned round, and glanced at the
garden path and at Letty Sanders. " She *is* an
object! See what she wants, Nora."

Nora, who had no patience with idleness and
its signs, opened the door with a fling. The girl

halted a few paces off the porch, and dropped a curtsey.

" Please, father be dreadful bad," began she· " He be lying on the bed and he don't stir, and he have got nothing but white in his face ; and, please, mother said I was to come and tell the missus, and ask her for a spoonful o' brandy."

" And how dare your mother send you up to the house in this trim ?" demanded Nora.   " How many crows did you frighten as you came along ?"

" Please," whimpered the child, " she haven't had time to tidy me to-day, father's been so bad, and t'other frock was tored in the washin'."

" Of course," assented Nora.   " Everything is ' tored' that she has to do with, and it never gets mended.   If ever there was a poor, moithering, thriftless thing, it's that mother of yours.   She has got no needles and no thread, I suppose, and neither soap nor water ? "

Mrs. Ryle came forward to interrupt the colloquy.   " What is the matter with your father, Letty ?   Is he worse ?"

Letty dropped at least ten curtseys in succession.   " Please, 'm, it's his inside as have been bad again, but mother's afeared he's dying.   He has fell back upon the bed, and he don't stir nor breathe.   She says, will you please send him a spoonful o' brandy ?"'

"Have you brought anything to put it in?" inquired Mrs. Ryle.

"No, 'm."

"It's not likely," chimed in Nora. "Meg Sanders wouldn't think to send so much as a cracked teacup. Shall I put a drop in a bottle, and give it to her?" continued Nora, turning to Mrs. Ryle.

"No," replied Mrs. Ryle. "I must know what's the matter with him before I send brandy. You go back to your mother, Letty. Tell her I shall be going past her cottage presently, and will call in."

The child turned and scuffled off. Mrs. Ryle resumed to Nora—

"Should it be another attack of inward inflammation, brandy would be the worst thing he could take. He drinks too much, does Jim Sanders."

"His inside's like a yawning barrel—always waiting to be filled," remarked Nora. "He'd drink the sea dry if 'twas running with beer. What with his drinking, and her untidiness, small wonder that the children are in rags. I am surprised the master keeps him on!"

"He only drinks by fits and starts, Nora. His health will not let him do more."

"No, it won't," acquiesced Nora. "And I misdoubt me but this bout may be the ending of him. That hole was not dug for nothing."

"Nonsense," said Mrs. Ryle. "Find Treve, will you, Nora; and get him ready."

"Treve," a young gentleman given to have his own way, and to be kept very much from school on account of "delicate health," a malady more imaginary than real, was found somewhere about the farm, and put into visiting condition. He and his mother were invited to take tea at Barbrook. In point of fact, the invitation had been for Mrs. Ryle only; but she could not bear to stir anywhere without her darling boy Trevlyn.

They had barely departed when George entered. Nora had then got the tea on the table, and was standing cutting slices of bread-and-butter.

"Where are they all?" asked George, depositing his books upon a small sideboard at the back.

"Your mamma and Treve are off to tea at Mrs. Apperley's," replied Nora. "And the master, he rode over to Barmester this afternoon, and is not back yet. Sit down, George. Would you like a taste of pumpkin pie?"

"Try me," responded George. "Is there any?"

"I saved it you from dinner," said Nora, bringing forth a plate of pie from a closet. "It is not over much. Treve, his stomach is as craving for pies as Jim Sanders's is for beer; and Mrs. Ryle, she'd give him all he wanted, if it cleared the dish. He——. Is that somebody calling?' she broke off, running to the window. "George, it's Mr. Chattaway! Go and see what he wants."

A gentleman on horseback had reined in close to the gate: a spare man, rather above the middle height, with a pale, leaden sort of complexion, small, cold light eyes, and mean-looking features. George ran down the garden path.

"Is your father at home, George?"

"No. He is gone to Barmester."

A scowl passed over Mr. Chattaway's brow. "That's the third time I have been here this week, and cannot get to see him. Tell your father, George, that I have had another letter from Butt, and that I'll trouble him to attend to it. Tell your father I will not be pestered with this business any longer, and if he does not pay the money right off, I'll make him pay it."

Something not unlike an ice-shaft shot through George Ryle's heart. He knew there was trouble between his house and Mr. Chattaway; that his father was, in pecuniary matters, at Mr. Chattaway's mercy. Was this move, this message, the result of his recent encounter with Cris Chattaway? A hot flush died his face, and he wished —for his father's sake—that he had let Mr. Cris alone. For his father's sake he was now ready

to eat humble pie to Mr. Chattaway, though there
never lived a boy less inclined to eat humble pie
in a general way than was George Ryle. He
went close up to the horse and raised his honest
eyes fearlessly.

"Has Christopher been complaining to you,
Mr. Chattaway?"

"No. What has he to complain of?"

"Not much," answered George, his fears subsid-
ing. "Only I know he does carry tales."

"Were there no tales to carry he could not
carry them," coldly remarked Mr. Chattaway. "I
have not seen Christopher since dinner-time. It
seems to me that you are always trying to suspect
him of something. Take care that you deliver
my message correctly, sir."

Mr. Chattaway rode away, and George returned
to his pumpkin pie. He had scarcely eaten it—
with remarkable relish, for the cold dinner which
he took with him to school daily was little more
than a lunch—when Mr. Ryle entered. He came
in by the back door, having been round to the
stables to leave his horse. He was a tall, fine
man, with light curling hair, mild blue eyes, and
a fair countenance pleasant to look at in its honest
simplicity. George delivered the message left by
Mr. Chattaway.

"He left me that message, did he?" cried Mr.

Ryle, who, if he could be angered by one thing, it was on this very subject—Chattaway's claims against him. "He might have kept it in until he saw me himself."

"He bade me tell it you, papa."

"Yes; it is no matter to Chattaway how he browbeats me and exposes my affairs. It is what he has been at for years. Is he gone home?"

"I think so," replied George. "He rode that way."

"I'll stand it no longer, and I'll tell him so to his face," continued Mr. Ryle. "Let him do his best and his worst."

Snatching up his hat, Mr. Ryle strode out of the house, disdaining Nora's invitation to tea, and leaving on the table his neck shawl, a large square of soft scarlet merino, which he had worn to Barmester. Recently suffering from sore throat, Mrs. Ryle had induced him to put it on when he rode out that afternoon.

"Look there!" cried Nora. "He has left his scarlet cravat."

Snatching up the neckerchief, she ran after Mr. Ryle, catching him when he was half-way down the path. He took it from her with a hasty movement, more, as it seemed, to be rid of the importunity than as though he wanted it for use, and went along swinging it in his hand. But he did not attempt to put it on.

"It is just like the master," grumbled Nora to George. "He has had that warm woollen thing on for hours, and now goes off without it! He'll get his throat bad again. There's some men would go about naked, for all the care they take of their health, if it wasn't for the fear that folks might stare at them."

"I am afraid," said George, "papa's gone to have it out with Mr. Chattaway."

"And serve Chattaway right if he is," returned Nora. "It is what the master has threatened this many a day."

CHAPTER II.

THE HOLE IN THE GARDEN PATH.

LATER, when George was working assiduously at his lessons and Nora was sewing, both by the help of the same candle—for an array of candles all alight at once was not more common than other luxuries in Mr. Ryle's house—footsteps were heard approaching the porch, and a modest knock came to the door.

"Come in," called out Nora.

A very thin woman, in a washed-out cotton gown, with a thin face to match, and inflamed eyes, came in, curtseying. It was an honest face, a meek face; although it looked as if it got a meal about once a week.

"Evening, Miss Dickson; evening, Master George. I have stepped round to ask the missis whether I shall be wanted on Tuesday."

"The missis is out," said Nora. "She has been talking of putting off the wash to the week after, but I don't know that she will. If

you sit down a bit, Ann Canham, maybe she'll
be in."

Ann Canham seated herself respectfully on the
edge of a remote chair. And Nora, who liked
gossiping above every earthly thing, began to talk
of Jim Saunders's illness.

" He has dreadful bouts, poor fellow!" observed
Ann Canham.

" But six times out of the seven he brings
them on through his own fault," tartly returned Nora. "Many and many a time I have
told him he'd do for himself, and now I think
he has done it. This bout, it strikes me is his
last."

" Is he so ill as that?" exclaimed Ann Canham.
And George looked up from his exercise book with
surprise.

" I don't know that he is," said Nora;
" but——"

With the word " but," Nora broke suddenly off.
She dropped her work, leaned her arms upon the
table, and bent her head towards Ann Canham in
the distance.

" We have had a strange thing happen here,
Ann Canham," she continued, her voice falling to
a mysterious whisper; " and if it's not a warning
of death, never you believe me again. This
morning——. George, did you hear the dog in

the night ? " she again broke the thread of her discourse to ask.

" No," answered George.

" Boys sleep sound," she remarked to Ann Canham. " You might drive a coach and six through their room, and not wake them. His chamber's back, too. Last night the dog got round to the front of the house," she continued, " and there he was, all night long, sighing and moaning like a human creature. You couldn't call it a howl ; it had too much pain in its sound. He was at it all night long ; I couldn't sleep for it. The missis says she couldn't sleep for it. Molly heard it at times, but dropped off to sleep again ; those hard-worked servants are heavy for sleep. Well, this morning I was up first, the master next, Molly next ; but the master, he went out by the back way, and saw nothing. By-and-by, I spied something out of this window on the garden path, as if somebody had been digging there ; so I went out. Ann Canham, it was for all the world like a grave !—a great hole, with the earth of the path thrown up on either side of it. That dog had done it in the night ! "

Ann Canham, possibly feeling herself inconveniently aloof from the company when graves became the topic, surreptitiously drew her chair nearer the table. George sat, his pen arrested ;

his large eyes, wide open, were turned on Nora—
not with a gaze of fear, however—more one of
merriment.

"A great big hole, about twice the length of
our rolling-pin, and wide in proportion, all hol-
lowed and scratched out," went on Nora. "I
called the cow-boy, and asked him what it looked
like. 'A grave,' says he, without a minute's hesitation. Molly came out, and they two filled it in
again, and trod the path down. The marks of it
have been plain enough to be seen all day. The
master has been talking a long while of having
that path gravelled, but it has not been done."

"And the hole was scratted out by the dog?"
proceeded Ann Canham, unable to overget the
wonder.

"It was scratted out by the dog," emphatically
answered Nora, using the same phraseology in her
earnestness. "And everybody knows what it's a
sign of—that there's death coming to the house,
or to somebody belonging to the bouse. Whether
it's your own dog that scratches it, or whether
it's somebody else's dog comes and scratches it, no
matter; when a hole is made in that manner, it's
a sure and certain sign that a real grave is about
to be dug. It may not happen once in fifty years
—no, not in a hundred; but when it does come,
it's a warning not to be neglected."

"It's odd how the dogs can know!" remarked Ann Canham, meekly.

"Those dumb animals have an instinct within them that we can't understand," said Nora. "We have had that dog ever so many years, and he never did such a thing before. Rely upon it that it's Jim Sanders's warning. How you stare, George!"

"Well I may stare, to hear you," was George's answer. "How can you put faith in such rubbish, Nora?"

"Just hark at him!" exclaimed Nora to Ann Canham. "Boys are half heathens. I'd not laugh in that irreverent way, if I were you, George, because Jim Sanders's time is come."

"I am not laughing at that," said George; "I am laughing at you. Look here, Nora: your argument won't hold water. If the dog had meant to give notice that he was digging a hole for Jim Sanders, he would have dug it before his door, wouldn't he, not before ours? There is no reason in it."

"Go on! go on!" cried Nora, sarcastically. "It's no profit to argue with disbelieving boys. They'd stand it out to your face that the sun never shone."

Ann Canham rose from her chair, and put it back to its place with much humility. Indeed, humility of manner and temperament was her chief characteristic. "I'll come round in the morning, and know about the wash, if you please, ma'am," she said to Nora. "Father, he'll be wanting his supper, and will wonder where I'm a-staying."

She departed. Nora gave George a lecture upon disbelief and irreverence in general, but George was too busy with his books to take much notice of it.

The evening went on. Mrs. Ryle and Trevlyn returned, a diminutive boy the latter, with dark curls and a handsome face.

"Jim Sanders is considerably better," remarked Mrs. Ryle. "He is all right again now, and will be at work again in a day or two. It must have been a sort of fainting fit he had this afternoon, and his wife got frightened. I told him to rest to-morrow, and come up the next day, if he felt strong enough."

George turned to Nora, his eyes dancing, "What of the hole now?" he asked.

"Wait and see," snapped Nora. "And if you are impertinent, George, I'll never save you pie or pudding again."

Mrs. Ryle went into the contiguous sitting-room, but came back speedily when she found it in darkness and untenanted. "Where's the master?" she exclaimed. "Surely he is home from Barmester!"

"Papa has been home ages ago," said George. "He's gone up to the Hold."

"Up to the Hold;" repeated Mrs. Ryle in great surprise, for there was something like deadly feud between Trevlyn Hold and Trevlyn Farm.

"George explained; telling of Mr. Chattaway's message, and the subsequent proceedings upon it. Nora added her word, that "as sure as fate, he was having it out with Chattaway." Nothing else would keep him at Trevlyn Hold.

But Mrs. Ryle knew that her husband, meek-spirited, easy-natured, was not one to "have it out" with anybody, even with his enemy Chattaway. He might say a few words, but it was all he would say, and the interview would be sure to end almost as soon as begun. She took off her things, and Molly carried the supper-tray into the parlour.

But still there was no Mr. Ryle. Ten o'clock struck, and Mrs. Ryle grew, not exactly uneasy, but curious, as to what could have become of him. What *could* he be stopping for at the Hold?

"It wouldn't surprise me to hear that his throat has been taken so bad he can't come back," said Nora. "Closing up, or something. He unwound his scarlet cravat from his neck, and went away swinging it in his hand, instead of giving his neck the benefit of it. There's John Pinder waiting all this while in the kitchen."

"Have you finished your lessons, George?" asked Mrs. Ryle, perceiving that he was putting his books away.

"Every one," answered George.

"Then you shall go up to the Hold, and walk home with your papa. I cannot think what he can be staying for."

"Perhaps he has gone somewhere else?" said George.

"No," said Mrs. Ryle. "He would neither go anywhere else, nor, I think, stop at Chattaway's. This is Tuesday evening."

An argument all conclusive. Tuesday evening was invariably devoted by Mr. Ryle to his farm accounts, and he never suffered anything to interfere with that evening's work. George threw his cap on his head, and started on his errand.

It was a starlight night, cold and clear, and George went along whistling. A quarter of an hour's walk along the turnpike road brought him to Trevlyn Hold. The road rose gently the whole of the way, for the land was higher at Trevlyn Hold than at Trevlyn Farm. A white gate, by the side of a lodge, opened to the shrubbery or avenue—a dark walk, wide enough for two carriages to pass abreast, with the elm trees nearly meeting over head. The shrubbery, wound up to a lawn, which stretched before the windows of the house : an old-fashioned, commodious, stone-built house, with gables to the roof, and a handsome flight of steps before the entrance hall. George ascended the steps and rang the bell.

" Is papa ready to come home ?" he asked, not very ceremoniously, of the servant who answered it.

" The man paused, as though he scarcely understood. " Mr. Ryle is not here, sir," was the answer.

" How long has he been gone ?" resumed George.

" He has not been here at all, sir, that I know of. I don't think he has."

" Just ask, will you ?" said George. " He came here to see Mr. Chattaway. It was about five o'clock."

The man went away and came back. " Mr. Ryle has not been here, sir. I thought he had not."

George wondered. Could he be out somewhere with Chattaway ? " Is Mr. Chattaway at home ?" he inquired.

" Master is in bed," said the servant. " He came home to-day about five, or thereabouts, not feeling well, and he went to bed as soon as tea was over."

George turned away. Where could his father have gone to, if not to Mr. Chattaway's? Where was he to look for him? As he passed the lodge, Ann Canham was locking the gate, she and her father being its keepers. It was a whim of Mr. Chattaway's that the large gate should be locked at night; but not until after ten. Foot passengers could go in by the small gate at its side.

"Have you seen my father anywhere, since you left our house this evening?" he asked.

"No, I have not, Master George."

"I can't think where he can be. I thought he was at Chattaway's, but they say he has not been there."

"At Chattaway's! He'd not go there, would he, Master George?"

"He started to go there this afternoon. It's very odd where he can have gone! Good night, Ann Canham."

"Master George," she interrupted, "do you happen to have heard how it's going with Jim Sanders?"

"Oh, he is better," said George.

"Better!" slowly repeated Ann Canham. "Well, I hope he is," she added, in a tone of much doubt. "But, Master George, I didn't like what Nora told us. I can't bear them tokens from dumb animals. I never knew them fail."

"Jim Sanders is all right, I tell you, Ann Canham," said heathen George. "Mamma has been there, and he is coming to his work the day after to-morrow. Good night."

"Good night, sir," answered Ann Canham, in her usual humble fashion, as she retreated within the lodge. And George went through the gate, and stood there in hesitation, looking up and down the road. But it was apparently of no use to go elsewhere in the uncertainty; and he turned back towards home, wondering much.

What had become of Mr. Ryle?

CHAPTER III.

CHATTAWAY'S BULL.

THE stars shone bright and clear overhead as George Ryle walked down the slight descent of the smooth turnpike road, wondering what could have become of his father. Any other night but this, Tuesday, his mind might have raised no marvel about it; but George could not remember the time when Tuesday evening had been devoted to anything but the farm accounts. John Pinder, who acted as a sort of bailiff, had been waiting in the kitchen some hours with his weekly memorandums, to go through them as usual with his master; and George knew that his father would not willingly keep the man waiting.

George went along whistling a tune; he was fond of whistling. About midway between Trevlyn Hold and his own house, the sound of some other tune being whistled struck upon his ear, marring the unity of his own. A turn in the road brought a lad into view, wearing a smock frock. It was the waggoner's boy at Trevlyn Hold. He ceased whistling when he came up to George, and touched his hat in a rustic fashion.

"Have you seen anything of my father, Bill?"

"Not since this afternoon, Master George," was the answer. "I see him then. He was a-turning into that there field of our'n, just above here, next to where the bull be. A-going up to the Hold, mayhap; else what should he a do there?"

"What time was that?" asked George.

The boy tilted his hat to scratch his head; possibly in the hope that the action might help him in his elucidation of the time asked for. "'Twas afore the sun setted," said he, at length, "I am sure o' that. He had got some'at red in his hand, and the sun gloamed on it enough to set one's eyes a-dazzling."

The boy went on his way; George stood and thought. If his father had turned into the field indicated, there could be no doubt that he was hastening to Mr. Chattaway's. The crossing of this field and the one contiguous to it, both of them of large dimensions, would bring a passenger out close to Trevlyn Hold, cutting off, perhaps, two minutes of the high road, which wound round the fields. But the fields were scarcely ever so favoured, on account of the bull. This bull had

been a subject of much contention in the neighbourhood, and was popularly called " Chattaway's
bull." It was a savage animal, and had once got
out of the field and frightened several people
nearly to death. The neighbours said Mr. Chattaway ought to keep him in his shed, under
safe lock and key. Mr. Chattaway said he should
keep him where he pleased: and he generally
pleased to keep him in the field. This barred it
to pedestrians; and Mr. Ryle must undoubtedly
have been in hot haste to reach Trevlyn Hold for
him to choose that dangerous route.

A hundred fears darted through George Ryle's
mind. He was more thoughtful, it may be said
more imaginative, than boys of his age in general
are. George and Cris Chattaway had once had a
run from the bull, and only saved themselves by
desperate speed. Venturing into the field one
day when the animal was apparently grazing
quietly in a remote corner, they had not anticipated his making an onset at them. George
remembered this; he remembered the terror
excited when the bull had broken loose. Had
his father been attacked by the bull?—perhaps
killed?

His heart beating, his life-blood bounding,
George retraced his steps, and turned into the
first field. He hastened across it, glancing keenly

on all sides—as keenly, at least, as the night allowed him. Not in this field would be the danger, since it was an interdicted field to the bull; and George gained the gate of the other, and stood looking into it.

Apparently it was quite empty. The bull was probably safe in his shed then, in Chattaway's farm-yard. George could see nothing—nothing save the short grass stretched out in the starlight. He threw his eyes in every direction of the extensive plain, but he could not perceive his father, or any trace of him. "What a simpleton I am," thought George, "to fear such an out-of-the-way thing could have happened! Papa must——"

What was that? George brought his sentence to an abrupt conclusion, and held his breath. A sound, not unlike a groan, had smote upon his ear. And there it came again! "Holloa!" shouted George, and cleared the gate with a bound. "What's that? Who is it?"

A moan answered him; a succession of moans; and George Ryle hastened to the spot, guided by the sound. It was but a little way off, down along by the hedge separating the two fields. All the undefined fear, which George, not a minute ago, had felt inclined to treat as a vagary of an absurd imagination, was indeed but a dread

prevision of the terrible reality. Mr. Ryle lay
in a narrow, deep, dry ditch : and, but for that
friendly ditch, he had probably been gored to
death on the spot.

"Who is it?" asked he feebly, as his son bent
over him, trying to distinguish what he could in
the darkness. "George?"

" O papa! what has happened ?"

. "Just my death, lad."

It was a sad tale. One that is often talked of
in the place, in connection with Chattaway's bull.
In crossing the second field—indeed, as soon as
he entered it—Mr. Ryle was attacked by the
furious beast, and tossed into the ditch, where he
lay helpless. The people said then, and say still,
that the scarlet cloth he carried excited the anger
of the bull.

George raised his voice in a loud shout for help,
hoping it might reach the ears of the boy whom
he had recently encountered. "Perhaps I can
get you out, papa," he said. "Though I may not
be able myself to get you home."

"No, George; it will take stronger help than
yours to get me out of this."

"I had better go up to the Hold, then. It is
nearer than our house."

"George, you will not go to the Hold," said Mr.
Ryle authoritatively. "I will not be beholden for

help to Chattaway. He has been the ruin of my peace, and now his bull has done for me."

George bent down closer. There was no room for him to get into the ditch; it was very narrow. "Papa, are you shivering with cold?"

"With cold and pain. The frost strikes keen upon me, and my inward pain is great."

George instantly took off his jacket and waist-coat, and laid them gently on his father, his tears dropping fast and silently in the dark night. "I'll go home for help," he said, speaking as bravely as he could. "John Pinder is there, and we can call up one or two of the men."

"Ay, do," said Mr. Ryle. "They must bring a shutter, and carry me home on it. Take care you don't frighten your mamma, George. Tell her at first that I am a little hurt and can't walk home; break it to her in a way so that she may not be alarmed."

George flew away. At the end of the second field, staring over its space from the top of the gate near the high road, stood the boy, Bill, whose ears George's shouts had reached. He was not a very sharp-witted lad, and his eyes and mouth opened with astonishment to see George Ryle come flying along in his shirt sleeves.

"What's a-gate?" asked he. "Be that there bull got loose again?"

"Bill, you run down for your life to the second field," panted George, seizing upon him in his desperation. "In the ditch, a few yards along the hedge to the right, there's my father lying. You go and stop by him, until I come back with help."

"Lying in the ditch!" repeated Bill, unable to gather his ideas upon the communication. "What's a-done it, Master George? Drink?"

"Drink!" indignantly retorted George. "When did you know Mr. Ryle the worse for drink? It's Chattaway's bull; that's what has done it. Make haste down to him, Bill. You might hear his groans all this way if you listened."

"Is the bull there?" asked Bill, as a measure of precaution.

"I have seen no bull. The bull must have been in his shed hours ago. Stand by him, Bill, and I'll give you sixpence to-morrow."

They separated different ways. Tears falling, brain working, legs flying, George tore down the road, wondering how he should fulfil the injunction of his father not to frighten Mrs. Ryle in the telling of the news. Molly, very probably looking after her sweetheart, was standing at the fold-yard gate as he passed it. George made her go into the house the front way and whisper to Nora to come out; to tell her that "somebody" wanted to speak to her. Molly, a good-natured girl, obeyed;

but so bunglingly did she execute her commission, that not only Nora, but Mrs. Ryle and Trevlyn came flocking out wonderingly to the porch. George could only go in then.

"Don't be frightened, mamma," he said, in answer to their shower of questions, "Papa has had a fall, and—and says he cannot walk home. Perhaps his ankle's sprained."

"What has become of your jacket and waistcoat, you naughty boy?" cried out Nora, laying hold of George as if she meant to shake him.

"Don't, Nora. They are safe enough. Is John Pinder still in the kitchen?" continued George, escaping from the room.

Trevlyn ran after him. "I say George, have you been fighting?" he asked. "Is your jacket torn to ribbons?"

George drew the boy into a dark angle of the passage. "Treve," he whispered, "if I tell you something about papa, you won't cry out?"

"No, I won't cry out," answered Treve.

"We must get a stretcher of some sort up to him, to bring him home. I am going to consult John Pinder. He —— "

"Where is papa?" interrupted Treve.

"He is lying in a ditch in the large meadow. Chattaway's bull has attacked him. I am not sure but he will die."

The first thing Treve did, *was* to cry out. A great shriek. George clapped his hand before his mouth. But Mrs. Ryle and Nora, who were full of curiosity, both as to George's jacketless state, and George's news, had followed them into the passage, and were standing by. Treve began to cry.

"He has got dreadful news about papa, he says," sobbed Treve. "He thinks he's dead."

It was all over. George must tell now, and he could not help himself. "No, no, Treve, you should not exaggerate," he said turning to Mrs. Ryle in his pain and earnestness. "There is an accident, mamma ; but it is not so bad as that."

Mrs. Ryle retained perfect composure ; very few people had ever seen *her* ruffled. It was not in her nature to be so, and her husband had little need to give George the caution that he did give him. She laid her hand upon George's shoulder and looked calmly into his face. "Tell me the truth," she said in a tone of quiet command. "What is the injury ?"

"I do not know it yet —— "

"The truth, boy, I said," she sternly interposed.

"Indeed, mamma, I do not yet know what it is. He has been attacked by Chattaway's bull."

It was Nora's turn now to shriek. "By Chattaway's bull ?" she uttered.

"Yes," said George. "It must have happened immediately after he left here at tea-time, and he has been lying ever since in the ditch in the upper meadow. I covered him over with my jacket and waistcoat; he was shivering with cold and pain."

While George was talking, Mrs. Ryle was acting. She sought John Pinder and issued her orders clearly and concisely. Men were got together; a mattress with secure holders was made ready; and the procession started under the convoy of George, who had been made put on another jacket by Nora. Bill, the wagoner's boy, had been faithful, and was found by the side of Mr. Ryle.

"I'm glad you be come,' was the boy's salutation. "He have been groaning and shivering awful. It set me on to shiver too."

As if to escape from the shivering, Bill ran off, there and then, at his utmost speed across the field, and never drew breath until he reached Trevlyn Hold. In spite of his somewhat stolid properties, he felt a sort of pride in being the first to impart the story there. Entering the house by the back, or farm-yard door—for farming was carried on at Trevlyn Hold as well as at Trevlyn Farm——he passed through sundry passages to the well-lighted hall. There he seemed to hesitate at his temerity, but at length gave an awkward knock at the door of the general sitting-room.

A commodious and handsome room. Lying back in an easy chair was a pretty and pleasing woman, looking considerably younger than she really was. Small features, a profusion of curling auburn hair, light blue eyes, a soft, yielding expression of countenance, and a gentle voice, were many of them adjuncts of a young woman, rather than of one approaching middle age. A stranger, entering, might have taken her for a young unmarried woman; and yet she was the mistress of Trevlyn Hold, the mother of that great girl of sixteen at the table, now playing at backgammon and quarrelling with her brother Christopher. Mistress in name only. Although the wife of its master, Mr. Chattaway, and the daughter of its late master, Squire Trevlyn; although she was universally called *Madam* Chattaway—as it had been customary from time immemorial to designate the mistress of Trevlyn Hold—she was in fact no better than a nonentity in it, possessing little authority, and assuming less. She has been telling her children several times that their hour for bed has passed; she has begged them not to quarrel; she has suggested that if they will not go to bed, Maude should; but she may as well have talked to the winds.

Miss Chattaway possesses a will of her own. She has the same insignificant features, the pale leaden complexion, the small but sly and keen light eyes, that characterise her father. She would like to hold undisputed sway as the house's mistress; but the inclination has to be concealed; to be kept under; for the real mistress of Trevlyn Hold may not be displaced from power. She is sitting at the back there, at a table apart, bending over her desk. A tall, majestic lady, in a stiff green silk dress and an imposing cap, in person very like Mrs. Ryle. It is Miss Trevlyn, usually called Miss Diana, the youngest daughter of the late squire. You would take her to be ten years older at least than her sister, Mrs. Chattaway, but in point of fact she is that lady's junior by a year. Miss Trevlyn is, to all intents and purposes, the mistress of Trevlyn Hold, and she rules with a firm sway its internal economy.

"Maude, you should go to bed," Mrs. Chattaway had said for the fourth or fifth time.

A graceful girl of thirteen turned her dark, violet-blue eyes and her pretty light curls round to Mrs. Chattaway. She had been leaning on the table watching the backgammon. Something of the soft, sweet expression visible in Mrs. Chattaway's face might be. traced in this child's; but in her, Maude, it was blended with greater intellect.

"It is not my fault, Aunt Edith," she gently said. "I should like to go. I am tired."

"Will you be quiet, Maude!" broke from Miss Chattaway. "Mamma, I wish you'd not be so tiresome, worrying about bed! I don't choose Maude to go up until I go. She helps me to undress."

Poor Maude looked sleepy. "I can be going on, Octave," she said to Miss Chattaway. "I can be saying my prayers."

"You can hold your tongue and wait where you are, and not be ungrateful," was the response of Octavia Chattaway. "But for my papa's kindness, you'd not have a bed to go to. Cris, you are cheating! that was not double-six!"

It was at this juncture that the awkward knock came to the door. "Come in!" called out Mrs. Chattaway.

Either her soft voice was not heard, for Cris and his sister were loud just then, or else the boy's modesty did not allow him to respond. He knocked again.

"See who it is, Cris," came forth the ringing, decisive voice of Miss Trevlyn.

Cris did not choose to obey. "Open the door, Maude," said he.

Maude did as she was bid : she had little chance allowed her in that house of doing otherwise.

Opening the door, she saw the boy standing there. "What is it, Bill?" she asked in some surprise.

"Please, is the squire in there, Miss Maude?"

"No," answered Maude. "He is gone to bed: he is not well."

This appeared to be a poser for Bill, and he stood to consider. "Is Madam in there?" he presently asked.

"Who is it, Maude?" came again in Miss Trevlyn's commanding tones.

Maude turned her head. "It is Bill Webb, Aunt Diana."

"What does he want?"

Bill stepped in then. "Please, Miss Diana, I came to tell the squire the news. I thought he might be angry of me if I did not come, seeing as I knowed of it."

"The news?" repeated Miss Diana, looking imperiously at Bill.

"Of the mischief what the bull have done. He have gone and gored Farmer Ryle."

The words arrested the attention of all. They came forward, as with one impulse. Cris and his sister, in their haste to quit their backgammon, upset the board.

"*What* do you say, Bill?" gasped Mrs. Chattaway, with a white face and faltering tongue.

"It's true, ma'am," said Bill. "The bull set on

him this afternoon, and tossed him into the ditch. Master George found him there a short while a-gone, groaning awful."

There was a sad pause. Maude broke the silence with a sob of pain, and Mrs. Chattaway, in her consternation, laid hold of the arm of the boy. "Bill, I—I—hope he is not much injured!"

"He says as it's his death, ma'am," answered Bill. "John Pinder and others have brought a bed, and they be carrying of him home on it."

"What brought Mr. Ryle in that field?" asked Miss Diana.

"He told me, ma'am, as he was a-coming up here to see the squire, and took that way to save time."

Mrs. Chattaway fell a little back. "Cris," said she to her son, "go down to the farm and see what the injury is. I cannot sleep in the uncertainty. It may be fatal."

Cris tossed his head. "You know, mother, I'd do anything almost to oblige you," he said, in his smooth accent, which seemed to carry a false sound with it, "but I can't go to the farm. Mrs. Ryle might insult me: there's no love lost between us."

"If the accident happened this afternoon, how was it that it was not discovered when the bull was fetched in from the field to his shed to-night?'

cried Miss Trevlyn, speaking as much to herself as to anybody else.

Bill shook his head. "I dun know," he replied. "For one thing, Mr. Ryle was right down in the ditch and could'nt be seen. And the bull, maybe, had went to the top o' the field then, Miss Diana, where the groaning wouldn't be heard."

"If I had but been listened to!" exclaimed Mrs. Chattaway, in a wailing accent. "How many a time have I asked that the bull should be parted with, before he did some irreparable injury. And now it has come!"

CHAPTER IV.

LIFE ? OR DEATH ?

MR. RYLE was carried home on the mattress, and laid on the large table in the sitting room, by the surgeon's directions. Mrs. Ryle, clear of head and calm of judgment, had sent for medical advice even before sending for her husband. The only available doctor for immediate purposes was Mr. King. He lived near, about midway between the farm and the village. He attended at once, and was at the house before his patient. Mrs. Ryle had sent also to Barmester for another surgeon, but he could not arrive just yet. It was by Mr. King's direction that the mattress and he who lay upon it was lifted on to the large table in the parlour.

"Better there; better there," acquiesced the sufferer, when he heard the order given. "I don't know how they'd get me up the winding stairs."

Mr. King, a man getting in years, was left alone

with his patient.   The examination over, he came forth from the room and sought Mrs. Ryle, who was waiting for the report.

"The internal injuries are extensive, I fear," he said. "They lie chiefly here "—touching his chest and right side.

"Will he *live*, Mr. King?" she interrupted. "Do not temporise, but let me know the truth. Can he live?"

"You have asked me a question that I cannot yet answer," returned the surgeon. "My examination has been superficial and hasty : I was alone in making it, and I knew you were anxiously waiting. With the help of Mr. Benage, we may be able to arrive at some more decisive opinion.- I do fear the injuries are great."

Yes, they were great ; and nothing could be done, as it seemed, to remedy them or alleviate the pain. Mr. Ryle lay on the bed helpless, giving vent to his regret and anguish in somewhat homely phraseology. It was the phraseology of the simple farm house; that to which he had been accustomed ; it was not likely he would change it now. By descent gentlemen, he and his father had been content to live as plain farmers only, in speech as well as in work.

He lay there groaning, lamenting his impru-dence, now it was too late, in venturing within the reach of that dangerous animal. The rest waited anxiously and restlessly the appearance of the surgeon. For Mr. Benage of Barmester had a world-wide reputation, and such men seem to bring comfort with them. If anybody could apply healing remedies to the injuries and save his life, it was Mr. Benage,

George Ryle had taken up his station at the garden gate. His hands clasping it, his head lying lightly on its iron spikes at the top, he was listening for the sound of the gig which had been dispatched to Barmester. Nora at length came out to him.

" You'll catch cold, George, stopping there in the keen night air."

" The air won't hurt me to-night. Listen, Nora! I thought I heard something. They might be back by this."

He was right. The gig was bowling swiftly up, containing the well-known surgeon and the messenger that had been dispatched for him. The surgeon, a little man, quick and active, was out of the gig before it had well stopped, passed George and Nora with a nod, and entered the house.

A short while and the worst was known. There would be but a few more hours of life for Mr. Ryle.

Mr. King would remain, doing what he could to comfort, to soothe pain. Mr. Benage must return to Barmester, for he was wanted there; and the horse was put to the gig again to convey him. Some refreshment was offered him, but he declined it. Nora waylaid him in the garden as he was going down it to the gig, and caught him by the arm.

" Will the master see to-morrow's sun, sir ? "

" It's rising, he may. He will not see its setting."

Can you picture to yourselves what that night was, for the house and its inmates? In the parlour, gathered round the table on which lay the dying man, were Mrs. Ryle, George and Trevlyn, the surgeon, and sometimes Nora. In the room outside was collected a larger group: John Pinder, the men who had borne him home, and Molly; with a few others whom the news of the accident had brought together.

Mrs. Ryle stood close to her husband. George and Trevlyn seemed scarcely to know where to stand, or what to do with themselves; and Mr. King sat in a chair in the recess of the bay window. They had placed a pillow under Mr. Ryle's head, and covered him over with blankets and a counterpane; a stranger would judge him to be lying on a bed. He looked grievously wan and the surgeon administered something to him in a glass from time to time.

"Come here, boys," he suddenly said; "come close to me."

They approached close, as he said, and leaned over him. He took a hand of each. George swallowed down his tears in the best way that he could. Trevlyn looked scared and frightened.

"Children, I am going. It has pleased God to cut me off in the midst of my career, just when I had the least thoughts of death. I don't know how it will be with you, my dear ones, or how it will be with the old home. Chattaway can sell up everything if he chooses; and I fear there's little hope but he'll do it. If he'd let your mother stop on, she might keep things together, and get clear of him in time. George will be growing up more of a man every day, and he may soon learn to be useful in the farm, if his mother thinks well to keep him on it. Maude, you'll do the best for them? For him, as well as for the younger ones?"

"I will," said Mrs. Ryle.

"Ay, I know you will. I leave them all to you, and you'll act for the best. I think it's well that George should be upon the farm, as I am taken from it; but you and he will see. Treve, you must do the best you can at whatever station you are called to. I don't know what it will be. My boys, there's nothing before you but to work. Do you understand that?"

"Fully," was George's answer. Treve seemed too bewildered to give one.

"To work with all your might; your shoulders to the wheel. Do your best in all ways. Be honest and single-hearted in the sight of God; work for Him while you are working for yourselves, and then He will prosper you. I wish I had worked for Him more than I have done!"

A pause, broken only by the heavy sobs of George, who could no longer control them.

"My days seem to have been made up of nothing but struggling, and quarrelling, and care. Struggling to keep my head above water, and quarrelling with Chattaway. The end seemed a far-off vista, ages away, something like heaven seems. And now the end's come, and heaven's come—that is, I must set out upon the journey that leads to it. I misdoubt me but the end comes to many in the same sudden way; cutting them off in their carelessness, and their sins. Do not you spend your days in quarrelling, my boys; just be working on a bit for the end, while there's time given you to do it. I don't know how it will be in the world I am about to enter. Some fancy that when once we have entered it, we shall see what is going on here,

in our families and homes. For that thought, if
for no other, I'd ask you to try and keep right.
If you were to go wrong, think how it would
grieve me ! I should always be wailing out that
I might have trained you better, and had not.
O children ! it is only when we come to lie here
that we see all our shortcomings. You'd not like
to grieve me, George ? "

"O papa, no !" said George, his sobs deepening.
"Indeed I will try to do my best. I shall be
thinking always that perhaps you are watching
me."

"There's One greater than I always watching
you, George. And that's God. Act well in his
sight ; not in mine. Doctor, I must have that
stuff again. I feel a queer sinking in my inside."

Mr. King rose, poured some drops into a wine-
glass of water, and administered it. The patient
lay a few moments, and then took his sons' hands,
as before.

"And now, children, for my last charge to you.
Reverence and love your mother. Obey her in all
things. George, she is not your mother by blood,
but you have never known another, and she has
been to you as such. Listen to her always, and
she will lead you aright. If I had listened to her,
I shouldn't be lying where I am now, with my side
stove in. A week or two ago I wanted to get the

character of that out-door man from Chattaway.
'Don't go through the field with the bull in it,'
she said to me before I started. 'The bull won't
hurt me,' I answered her. 'He knows me as well
as he knows his master.' 'Thomas, don't trust
him,' she said to me again. 'Better keep where
he *can't* touch you.' Do you remember it,
Maude ?"

Mrs. Ryle simply bowed her head in reply.
That she was feeling the scene deeply there could
be little doubt; but emotion she would not
show.

"Well, I heeded what your mother said, and
went up to Chattaway's by the roadway, avoiding
the fields," resumed Mr. Ryle. "This last afternoon, when I was going up again and had got to
the field gate, I turned to it, for it cut off a few
steps of the way, and my temper was up. When
people's tempers are up, they don't stop to go a
round; if there's a long way and a short way,
they'll take the shortest. I thought of what she'd
say, as I swung in, but I didn't let it stop me. It
must have been that red neckerchief that put him
up, for I was no sooner over the gate than he
bellowed out savagely and butted at me. It was
all over in a minute; I was in the ditch, and he
went on, bellowing and tossing and tearing at the
cloth. If you go to-morrow, you'll see it in shreds

about the field. Children, obey your mother; there'll be double the necessity for it when I am gone."

The boys had been obedient hitherto. At least, George had. Trevlyn was too much indulged to be perfectly so. George promised that he would be so still.

"I wish I could have seen the little wench," resumed the dying man, the tears gathering on his eyelashes. "But may-be it's for the best that she's away, for I'd hardly have borne to part with her. Maude! George! Treve! I leave her to you all. Do the best you can by her. I don't know that she'll be spared to grow up, for she's but a delicate little mite: but that will be as God pleases. I wish I could have stopped with you all a bit longer—if it's not sinful to wish contrary to God's will. Is Mr. King there?"

Mr. King had resumed his seat in the bay window, and was partially hidden by the curtain. He came forward. "Is there anything I can do for you, Mr. Ryle?"

"I'd be obliged if you'd just write out a few directions. I'd like to write them myself, but it can't be; you'll put down the words just as I speak them. I have not made my will. My wife has said to me often, 'Thomas, you ought to make a will;' and I knew I ought, but I put it off, and put it off, thinking I could do it any time ; but now the end's come, and it is not done. Death surprises a great many, I fear, as he has surprised me. It seems that if I could only have one day more of health, I would do many things that I have left undone. You shall put down my wishes, doctor. It will do as well ; for there's only themselves, and they won't dispute one with the other. Let a little table be brought here, and pen and ink and paper."

He lay quiet while these directions were obeyed, and then began to speak again.

" I am in very little pain, considering that I am going ; not half as much as when I lay doubled in that ditch. Thank God for it ! It might have been, that I could not have left a written line, or said a word of farewell to you. There's sure to be a bit of blue sky in the darkest trouble ; and the more implicitly we trust, the more blue sky there'll be. I have not been what I ought to be, especially in the matter of disputing with Chattaway— not but what it's Chattaway's hardness that has been in fault. But God is taking me from a world of care, and I trust he will forgive all my shortcomings for our Saviour's sake. Is that table ready ? "

" It is all ready," said Mr. King.

" Then you'll leave me alone with the doctor a

short while, dear ones," he resumed. " We shall
not keep you out long."

Nora, who had brought in the things required,
held the door open for them to pass through.
The pinched, blue look that the face, lying there,
was assuming, struck upon her ominously.

" After all, the boy was right," she murmured.
" The hole, scratched before this house, was not
meant for Jim Sanders."

CHAPTER V.

LOOKING ON THE DEAD.

THE morning sun rose gloriously, melting the signs of the early October frost, and shedding its glad beams upon the world. But the beams fall upon dark scenes sometimes; perhaps more often than on bright ones.

George Ryle was leaning on the gate of the fold yard. He had strolled out without his hat, and had bent his head down on the gate in his grief. Not that he was shedding tears now. He had shed plenty during the night; but tears cannot flow always without cessation, even from an aching heart.

Hasty steps were heard approaching in the road, and George raised his head. They were Mr. Chattaway's. He stopped suddenly at sight of George.

"George, what is this about your father? What has happened? Is he dead?"

"He is dying," replied George. "The doctors

are with him. Mr. King has been here all night, and Mr. Benage has just come again from Barmester. They have sent us out of the room; me and Treve. They let mamma stop."

"But how on earth did it happen?" asked Mr. Chattaway. "I cannot make it out. The first thing I heard when I woke this morning, was, that Mr. Ryle had been gored to death by the bull. What brought him near the bull?"

"He was going through the field up to your house, and the bull set on him —— "

"But when? but when?" hastily interrupted Mr. Chattaway.

"It was yesterday afternoon. Papa came in directly after you rode away, and I gave him the message you left. He said he would go up then to the Hold, and speak to you; and he took the field way instead of the road."

"Now, how could he take it? He knew that way was hardly safe for strangers. Not but what the bull ought to have known him."

"He had a scarlet cravat in his hand, and he thinks it was the sight of that which excited the bull. He was tossed into the ditch, and lay there, unfound, until past ten at night."

"And he is badly hurt?"

"He is dying," replied George, "dying now. I think that is why they sent us from the room."

Mr. Chattaway paused in dismay. Though a hard, selfish man, who had taken delight in quarrelling with Mr. Ryle and putting upon him, he did possess some feelings of humanity as well as his neighbours; and the terrible nature of the case naturally called them forth. George strove manfully to keep down his tears; the speaking of the circumstances was almost too much for him, but he did not care to give way before the world, especially before that unit in it, represented by Mr. Chattaway. Mr. Chattaway rested his elbow on the gate and looked down at George.

"This is very shocking, lad. I am sorry to hear it. Whatever will the farm do without him? How shall you all get on?"

"It is the thinking of that which has been troubling him all night," said George, speaking by snatches lest his sobs should burst forth. "He said we might get a living at the farm, if you would let us do it. If you would not be hard," added George, determined to speak out.

"Hard, he called me, did he?" said Mr. Chattaway. "It's not my hardness that has been in fault, George; but his pride. He has been as saucy and independent as if he did not owe a shilling; always making himself out my equal."

"He is your equal, Mr. Chattaway," said George, speaking meekly in his sadness.

"My equal! Working Tom Ryle equal with the Chattaways! A man that rents two or three hundred acres and does half the work on them himself the equal of the landlord that owns them and ever so many more on to them!—the equal of the Squire of Trevlyn Hold! Where did you pick up those notions, George Ryle?"

George had a great mind to say that in point of strict justice Mr. Chattaway had no more right to be the Squire of Trevlyn Hold, or to own those acres, than his father had; not quite so much right, if it came to that. He had a great mind to say that the Ryles were gentlemen, and once owners of what his father only rented now. But George remembered they were in Chattaway's power; that he could sell them up, and turn them off the farm, if he pleased; and he held his tongue.

"Not that I blame you for the notions," Mr. Chattaway resumed, in the same thin unpleasant tone—never was there a voice more thin and wiry in its sound. "It's natural you should have got hold of them from Ryle, for they were his. He was always —— But there! I won't say any more, with him lying there, poor fellow. We'll let it drop, George."

"I do not know how things are, between you and my father," said George, "except that there's money owing to you. But if you will not press us, if you will let mamma stay on the farm, I —— "

"That's enough," interrupted Mr. Chattaway. "Never you trouble your head, George, about business that's above you. Anything that's between me and your father, or your mother, either, is no concern of yours; you are not old enough for interference yet. I should like to see him. Do you think I may go in?"

"We can ask," answered George; some vague and indistinct idea floating to his mind that a death-bed reconciliation might tend to smoothe future difficulties.

He led the way to the house through the fold yard. Nora was coming out at the back door as they advanced to it, her eyes wet.

"Nora, do you think Mr. Chattaway may go in to see my father?" asked George.

"If it will do Mr. Chattaway any good," responded Nora, who never regarded that gentleman but in the light of a common enemy, and could with difficulty bring herself to be commonly civil to him. "It's all over; but Mr. Chattaway can see what's left of him."

"Is he dead?" whispered Mr. Chattaway; while George lifted his white and startled face.

"Yes, he is dead!" broke forth Nora, in a fit

of sobs ; " and perhaps there may be some that
will wish now they had been less hard with him in
life. The doctors and Mrs. Ryle have just come
out, and the women have gone in to put him
straight and comfortable. Mr. Chattaway can go
in also, if he'd like it.''

Mr. Chattaway, it appeared, did not like it. He
turned from the door, drawing George with him.

"George, you'll tell your mother that I am
grieved and vexed at her trouble, and I wish that
beast of a bull had been stuck, before he had done
what he has. You tell her that if there's any
little thing she could fancy from the Hold, to let
Edith know, and she'd be glad to send it to her.
Good-bye lad. You and Treve must keep up, you
know."

He passed out by the fold-yard gate, as he had
entered, and George leaned upon it again with his
aching heart ; an orphan now. Treve and Caroline had their mother left, but he had no one.
It is true he had never known a mother, and Mrs.
Ryle, his father's second wife, had acted to him as
such. She had done her duty by him, as her
duty ; but it had not been in love ; not much in
gentleness. Of her own children she was inordi-
nately fond ; she had not been so of George—
which perhaps was in accordance with human
nature. It had never troubled George much ;

but somehow the fact struck upon his mind now with a sense of intense loneliness. His father had loved him deeply and sincerely ; but—he was gone.

In spite of his heavy sorrow, George was awake to the sounds going on in the distance, the every day labour of life. The cow-boy was calling to his cows ; one of the men, acting for Jim Sanders, was going out with the team. And now there came a butcher, riding up from Barmester, and George knew he had come about some beasts, all unconscious as yet that the master was no longer here to command, or to deal. Work, especially farm work, must go on, although death may have been accomplishing its mission.

The butcher, riding fast, had nearly reached the gate, and George was turning away from it to retire in-doors, when the unhappy thought came startlingly upon him—Who is to see this man ? His father no longer there, who must represent him ?—must answer comers—must stand in his shoes? It brought the fact of what had happened more palpably, more *practically* before George Ryle's mind than anything else had brought it. He stood where he was, instead of turning away. He must rise up superior to his grief that day, and be useful ; he must rise up above his years in the future days, for his step-mother's sake.

"Good morning, Mr. George," cried the butcher, as he rode up. "Is the master about?"

"No," answerd George, speaking as steadily as he could. "He—he will never be about again. He is dead."

The butcher took it as a boy's joke. "None of that gammon, young gentleman!" said he with a laugh. "Which way shall I go to find him? He has not laid in bed, and overslep' himself, I suppose?"

"Mr. Cope," said George, raising his grave face upwards—and the expression of it struck a chill to the man's heart—"I should not joke upon the subject of death. My father was attacked by Chattaway's bull yesterday evening, and he has died of the injuries."

"Lawk a mercy!" uttered the startled man. "Attacked by Chattaway's bull! and—and—died of the injuries! Sure-ly it can't be!"

George had turned his face away; it was getting more than he could bear.

"Have Chattaway killed the bull?" was the next question put by the butcher.

"I suppose not."

"Then he is no man and no gentleman if he don't do it. If a beast of mine injured a neighbour, I'd stop him from injuring another, no matter what might be its value. Dear me! Mr.

George, I'd rather have heard any news than this."

George's head was completely turned away now. The butcher roused himself to think of business. His time was short, for he had to be back again in the town before his shop opened for the day.

"I came up about the beasts," he said. "The master as good as sold 'em to me yesterday; it was only a matter of a few shillings split us. But I'll give in sooner than not have 'em. Who is going to carry on the dealings in Mr. Ryle's place? Who can I speak to?"

"You can see John Pinder," answered George. "He knows most about things."

The butcher guided his horse through the fold-yard, scattering the cocks and hens in various directions, and gained the barn. John Pinder was in it, and came out to him; and George escaped in-doors.

It was a sad, weary day. The excitement over, the doctors departed, the gossipers and neighbours dispersed, the village carpenter having come and taken a certain measure, then the house was left to its monotonous quiet; that distressing quiet which tells upon the spirits. Nora's voice was subdued, and Molly went about on tiptoe. The boys wished it was over; that, and many more days to come. Treve fairly broke bounds about twelve, said he could not bear it, and went out amid the men. In the afternoon George was summoned upstairs to the chamber of Mrs. Ryle, where she had remained since the morning.

"George, you shall go to Barmester," she said. "I wish to know how Caroline bears the news, poor child! Mr. Benage said he would call and break it to her; but I cannot get her grief out of my head. You can go over in the gig; but don't stay. Be home by tea-time."

It is more than probable that George felt the commission as a relief, and he started as soon as the gig was ready. As he went out of the yard, Nora called after him to mind how he drove. Not that he had never driven before; but Mr. Ryle, or some one else, had always been in the gig with him. Now he was alone; and it served to bring his loss again more forcibly present to him.

He reached Barmester, and saw his sister Caroline, who was staying there on a visit. She was not overwhelmed with grief; not by any means; on the contrary, she appeared to have taken the matter coolly and lightly. The fact was, the little girl had no definite ideas on the subject of death. She had never been brought into contact with it, and could not at all realise the fact told her, that she would never see papa again. Better for the little heart perhaps that it was so, enough of sorrow comes with later years; and Mrs. Ryle may have judged wisely in deciding to keep the child where she was until after the funeral.

When George reached home, he found Nora at tea alone. Master Treve had chosen to take his with his mamma in her chamber. George sat down with Nora. The shutters of the window were closed, and the room was bright with fire and candle; but to George all things were dreary.

"Why don't you eat?" asked Nora, presently, perceiving that the plate of bread and butter remained untouched.

"I'm not hungry," replied George.

"Not hungry? Did you have tea at Barmester?"

"I did not have anything," he said.

"Now, look you here, George. If you are going to give way to your grief—— Mercy me! What's that?"

Some one had come hastily in at the door, sending it back with a burst. A lovely girl, in a flowing white evening dress, and blue ribbons in her hair. A heavy shawl, which she had worn on her shoulders, fell to the ground, and she stood there panting, like one who has outrun her breath, her fair curls falling, her cheeks crimson, her dark blue eyes glistening. On the pretty arms, about half way up, were clasped some coral bracelets, and a thin gold chain, bearing a coral cross, rested on her neck. It was Maude Trevlyn, whom you saw at Trevlyn Hold last night. So entirely out of place did she look altogether in that scene, that Nora for once lost her tongue. She could only stare.

"I ran away, Nora,' said Maude, coming forward. "Octave has got a party, but they won't miss me if I stay but a little while. I have wanted to come all day, but they would not let me."

"Who would not?" asked Nora.

"Not any of them. Even Aunt Edith. Nora, is it *true?* Is it true that he is dead?" she reiterated, her pretty hands clasped together in emotion, and her great blue eyes glistening with tears as they were cast upwards at Nora's, waiting for the answer.

"Oh, Miss Maude! you might have heard it was true enough up at the Hold. And so they have got a party, have they! Some folks in Madam Chattaway's place might have had the grace to put it off, when their sister's husband was lying dead!"

"It is not Aunt Edith's fault. You know it is not, Nora. George, you know it. She has been crying several times to-day; and she asked long and long ago for the bull to be sent off. But he was not sent. O George, I am so sorry! I wish I could have come to see him before he died. There was nobody I liked so well as Mr. Ryle."

"Will you have some tea?" asked Nora.

"No, I must not stop. Should Octave miss me she will tell of me, and then I should be punished. What do you think? Rupert displeased Cris in some way, and Miss Diana sent him to bed out of all the pleasure. It is a shame!"

"It is all a shame together, up at Trevlyn Hold—all that concerns Rupert," said Nora, not, perhaps, very judiciously.

"Nora, where did he die?" asked Maude, in a whisper. "Did they take him up to his bedroom when they brought him home?"

"They carried him in there," said Nora, pointing to the sitting-room door. "He is lying there now."

"Nora, I want to see him," she continued.

Nora received the intimation dubiously. "I don't know whether you had better," said she, after a pause.

"Yes, I must, Nora. What was that about the dog?" added Maude. "Did he scratch out a grave before the porch?"

"Who told you anything about that?" asked Nora, sharply.

"Ann Canham came and told it at the Hold. Was it so, Nora?"

Nora nodded. "A great hole, Miss Maude, nearly big enough to lay the master in. Not that I thought it was a token for *him*; I thought of Jim Sanders. And some folks laugh at these warnings!" she added, in a burst of feeling. "There sits one," pointing to George.

"Well, never mind it now, Nora," said George, hastily. Never was there a boy less given to superstition; but, somehow, with his father lying where he was, he did not care to hear much about the mysterious hole.

Maude moved towards the door. "Take me in to see him, Nora," she pleaded.

"Will you promise not to be frightened?" asked Nora. "Some young people can't endure the sight of a dead person."

"Why should I be frightened?" returned Maude. "He cannot hurt me."

Nora rose in acquiescence, and took up the candle. But George laid his hand on the little girl.

"Don't go, Maude. Nora, you must not let her go in. It—it—she might not like it. It would not be right."

Now, of all things, Nora had a dislike to be dictated to, especially by those whom she called children. She saw no reason why Maude should not look upon the dead if she had a mind to do so, and she gave a sharp word of reprimand to George, all in an undertone. How could they speak loud, entering into that presence ?

"Maude, Maude'" he whispered. "I would advise you not to go in."

"Yes, yes, let me go, George!" she pleaded. "I should like to see him once again. I did not see him for a whole week before he died. The last time I ever saw him was one day in the copse, and he got down some hazel nuts for me. I never thanked him," she added, the tears streaming from her eyes ; " I was in a hurry to get home, and I never stayed to thank him. I shall always be sorry for it. I must see him, George."

Nora was already in the room with the candle. Maude advanced on tip-toe, her heart beating, her breath held with awe. She halted at the foot of the table, looked eagerly upwards, and saw—— What was it that she saw ?

A white, ghastly face, cold and still, with its white bands tied up round it, and its closed eyes. Maude Trevlyn had never seen the dead, and her heart gave a great bound of terror, and she fell away with a loud, convulsive shriek. Before Nora knew well what had occurred, George had her in the other room, his arms wound about her to impart a sense of protection. Nora came out and closed the door, vexed with herself for having allowed her to enter.

"You should have told me you had never seen anybody dead before, Miss Maude," cried she, testily. "How was I to know? And you ought to have come right up to the top before you turned your eyes on it. Of course, glancing up from the foot, they look bad."

Maude was clinging to George, trembling excessively, sobbing hysterically. "Don't be angry with me," she whispered. "I did not think he would be like that."

"O Maude, dear, I am not angry; I am only sorry," he soothingly said. "There's nothing really to be frightened at. Papa loved you very much; almost as much as he loved me."

"I will take you back, Maude," said George, when she was ready to go.

"Yes, please," she eagerly answered. "I should not dare to go alone now. I should be fancying I saw—I saw—you know. That it was looking out to me from the hedges."

Nora folded her shawl well over her again, and George drew her close to him that she might feel his presence as well as see it. Nora watched them down the path, right over the hole which the restless dog had favoured the house with a night or two before.

They went on up the road. An involuntary shudder shook George's frame as he passed the turning which led to the fatal field. He seemed to see his father in the unequal conflict. Maude felt the movement, and drew closer to him.

"It is never going to be out again, George," she whispered.

"What ?" he asked, his thoughts buried deeply just then.

"The bull. I heard Aunt Diana talking to Mr. Chattaway. She said it must not be set at liberty again, or we might have the law down upon Trevlyn Hold."

"Yes; that's all Miss Trevlyn and he care for —the law," returned George, in a tone of pain. "What do they care for the death of my father?"

"George, he is better off," said she, in a dreamy manner, her face turned upwards towards the stars. "I am very sorry; I have cried a great deal to-day over it; and I wish it had never happened; I wish he was back with us; but still he is better off; Aunt Edith says so. You don't know how she has cried."

"Yes," answered George, his heart very full.

"Mamma and papa are better off," continued
Maude. "Your own mamma is better off. The
next world is a happier one than this."

George made no rejoinder. Favourite though
Maude was with George Ryle, those were heavy
moments for him. They proceeded along in
silence until they turned in at the great gate by
the lodge. The lodge was a round building, containing two rooms up and two down. Its walls were
not very substantially built, and the sound of voices
could be heard from inside the window. Maude
stopped in consternation.

"George! George! that is Rupert talking!"

"Rupert! You told me he was in bed."

"He was sent to bed. He must have got out
of the window again. I am sure it is his voice.
Oh, what will be done if it is found out?"

George Ryle swung himself on the top of the
very narrow ledge which ran along underneath the
window, contriving to hold on by his hands and
toes. The inside shutter ascended only three
parts up the window, and George thus obtained a
view of the room above it.

"Yes, it is Rupert," said he, as he jumped down.
"He is sitting there, talking to old Canham."

But the same slightness of structure which
allowed inside noises to be heard without the
lodge, allowed outside noises to be heard within.

Ann Canham had come hastening to the door, opened it a few inches, and stood peeping out. Maude took the opportunity to slip past her into the room.

But no trace of her brother was there. Mark Canham was sitting in his usual invalid seat by the fire, smoking a pipe, his back towards the door.

" Where is he gone ? " cried Maude.

" Where's who gone ? " roughly spoke old Canham, without turning his head. " There ain't nobody here."

" Father, it's Miss Maude," interposed Ann Canham, closing the outer door, after allowing George to enter. " Who be you a taking her for ? "

The old man, partly disabled by rheumatism, put down his pipe, and contrived to turn in his chair. "Ah, Miss Maude! Why who'd ever have thought of seeing you to-night ? "

" Where is Rupert gone ? " asked Maude.

" Rupert? " composedly returned old Canham. " Is it Master Rupert you're asking after ? How should we know where he is, Miss Maude ? "

" We saw him here," interposed George Ryle. " He was sitting on that bench, talking to you. We both heard his voice, and I saw him."

" Very odd ! " said the old man. " Fancy goes a great way. Folks is ofttimes deluded by it."

"Mark Canham, I tell you, we——"

"Wait a minute, George," interrupted Maude. She opened the door which led into the outer room, and stood with it in her hand, looking into the darkness. "Rupert!" she called out, "it is only I and George Ryle. You need not hide yourself."

It brought forth Rupert; that lovely boy, with his large blue eyes and his auburn curls. There was a great likeness between him and Maude; but Maude's hair was lighter.

"I thought it was Cris," he said. "He is learning to be as sly as a fox: though I don't know that he was ever anything else. When I am ordered to bed before my time, he has taken to dodge into the room every ten minutes to see that I am safe in it. Have they missed me, Maude?"

"I don't know," she answered. "I came away, too, without their knowing it. I have been down to Aunt Ryle's, and George has brought me back again."

"Will you be pleased to sit down, Miss Maude?" asked Ann Canham, dusting a chair.

"Eh, but that's a pretty picture!" cried old Canham, gazing at Maude, who had let her heavy shawl slip off, and stood warming her hands at the fire.

Mark Canham was right. A very pretty picture, she, with her flowing white dress, her fair neck and arms, and the blue ribbons in her falling hair. He extended the one hand that was not helpless, and laid it on her wrist.

" Miss Maude, I mind me seeing your mother looking just as you look now. The squire was out, and the young ladies at the Hold thought they'd give a dance, and Parson Dean and Miss Emily were invited to it. I don't know that they'd have been asked if the squire had been at home, matters not being smooth between him and the parson. She was older than you be; but she was dressed just as you be now; and I could fancy, as I look at you, that it was her over again. I was in the rooms, helping to wait, handing round the negus and things. It doesn't seem so long ago! Miss Emily was the sweetest-looking of 'em all present; and the young heir seemed to think so. He opened the ball with Miss Emily in spite of his sisters : they wanted him to choose somebody grander. Ah, me ! and both of 'em lying low so soon after, leaving you two behind 'em ! "

"Mark !" cried Rupert, earnestly casting his eyes on the old man—eyes that sparkled with excitement—" if they had lived, my papa and mamma, I should not have been sent to bed to-

night because there's another party·at Trevlyn
Hold."

Mark's only answer was to put up his hands
with an indignant gesture. Ann Canham was
still offering the chair to Maude. Maude declined
it.

"I cannot stop, Ann Canham. They will be
missing me if I don't return. Rupert, you will
come ?"

"To be mured up in my bed-room, while the rest
of you are enjoying yourselves," cried Rupert.
"They would like to get the spirit out of me; they
have been trying at it a long while."

Maude wound her arm within his. "Do come,
Rupert !" she coaxingly whispered. "Think of the
disturbance if Cris should find you here and
tell !"

"And tell !" repeated Rupert, his tone a mocking one. "*Not* to tell would be impossible to Cris
Chattaway. It's what he'd delight in more than
in gold. I'd not be the sneak Cris Chattaway is
for the world."

But Rupert appeared to think it well to depart
with his sister. As they were going out, old Canham spoke to George.

"And Miss Trevlyn, sir—how does she bear
it ? Forgive me, I'm always a· forgetting ·myself
and going back to the old days. 'Twas but a

week a-gone I called Madam 'Miss Edith' to her face. I should ha' said 'Mrs. Ryle,' sir."

" She bears it very well, Mark," answered George.

Something, George himself could not have told what, caused *him* not to bear it well just then. The tears rushed to his eyes unbidden, and they hung trembling on the lashes. The old man marked it.

"There's one comfort for ye, Master George," he said, in a low tone ; " that he has took all his neighbours' sorrow with him. And as much couldn't be said if every gentleman round about here was cut off by death."

The significant tone was not needed to tell George that the words "every gentleman" was meant for Mr. Chattaway. The master of Trevlyn Hold was, in fact, no greater favourite with old Canham than he was with George Ryle.

"Mind how you get in, Master Rupert, so that they don't fall upon you," whispered Ann Canham, as she held open the lodge door.

" I'll mind, Ann Canham," was the boy's answer. " Not that I should care much if they did," he added, in the next breath. "I am getting tired of it."

She stood and watched them up the dark walk

until a turning in the road hid them from view, and then closed the door. " If they don't take to treat him kinder, I misdoubt me but he'll be doing something desperate, as the dead-and-gone heir, Rupert, did," she remarked, sitting down by her father.

" Likely enough," was the old man's reply, taking up his pipe again. " He have got the true Trevlyn temper, have young Rupert."

" I say, Maude," began Rupert, as they wound their way up the dark avenue, " don't they know you came out.

" They would not have let me come if they had known it," replied Maude. " I have been wanting to go down all day, but Aunt Diana and Octave kept me in. I cried to go down last night when Bill Webb brought the news; and they were angry with me."

" Do you know what I should have done in Chattaway's place, George ? " cried the boy, impulsively. " I should have loaded my gun the minute I heard of it, and shot the beast between the eyes. Chattaway would, if he were half a man."

" It is of no use talking of it, Rupert," answered George, in a sadly subdued tone. " It would not have mended the evil."

" Only fancy their having this rout to-night,

while Mr. Ryle is lying dead!" indignantly resumed Rupert. "Aunt Edith ought to have
interfered for once, and stopped it."

"Aunt Edith did interfere," spoke up Maude.
"She said it must be put off. But Octave would
not hear of it, and Miss Diana said Mr. Ryle was
no blood rela——"

Maude dropped her voice. They were now in
view of the house, of its lighted windows, and
some one, hearing probably their footsteps, came
bearing down upon them with a fleet step. It
was Cris Chattaway. Rupert stole amidst the
trees, and disappeared : Maude, holding George's
arm, bore bravely on, and met him.

"Where have you been, Maude ? The house
has been searched over for you. What brings *you*
here ? " he roughly added to George.

"I came because I chose to come," was George's
answer.

"None of that insolence." returned Cris. "We
don't want you here to-night. Just be off from
this."

Was Cris Chattaway's motive a good one, under
his rudeness ? Did he feel ashamed of the gaiety
going on, while Mr. Ryle, his uncle by marriage,
was lying dead, under circumstances so unhappy ?
Was he anxious to conceal the unseemly proceeding from George ? Perhaps so.

"I shall go back when I have taken Maude to the hall door," said George. "Not before."

Anything that might have been said further by Cris, was interrupted by the appearance of Miss Trevlyn. She was standing on the steps.

"Where have you been, Maude?"

"To Trevlyn Farm, Aunt Diana," was Maude's truthful answer. "You would not let me go in the day, so I have been now. It seemed to me that I must see him before he was put underground."

"To see *him*!" cried Miss Trevlyn.

"Yes. It was all I went for. I did not see my aunt. Thank you, George, for bringing me home," she continued, stepping in. "Good night. I would have given all I have for it never to have happened."

She burst into a passionate flood of tears as she spoke—the result, no doubt, of her previous fright and excitement, as well as of her sorrow for Mr. Ryle's unhappy fate. George wrung her hand, and lifted his hat to Miss Trevlyn as he turned away.

But ere he had well plunged into the dark avenue, there came swift and stealthy steps behind him. A soft hand was laid upon him, and a soft voice spoke, broken by its tears:

"O, George, I am so sorry! I have felt all day

as if it would almost be my death. I think I could have given my own life to save his."

"I know, I know," he answered. "I know how *you* will feel it." And George, utterly unmanned, burst into tears, and sobbed with her.

It was Mrs. Chattaway.

CHAPTER VI.

THE ROMANCE OF TREVLYN HOLD.

IT is impossible to get on without a word of retrospect. The Ryles, gentlemen by descent, had been rich men once, but they were open-handed and heedless, and in the time of George's grandfather, the farm (not called the farm then) passed into the possession of the Trevlyns of the Hold, who had a mortgage on it. They named it Trevlyn Farm, and Mr. Ryle and his son remained on it as tenants; as tenants where they had once been owners.

After old Mr. Ryle's death, his son married the daughter of the curate of Barbrook, the Reverend George Berkeley, familiarly known as Parson Berkeley. In point of fact, the parish knew no other pastor, for its rector was an absentee. Mary Berkeley was an only child; she had been petted, and physicked, and nursed, after the manner of only children; and she grew up sickly as a matter of course. A delicate, beautiful girl in appearance, but not strong. People (who are always fond, you know, of settling everybody else's business for them) deemed that she made a poor match in marrying Thomas Ryle. It was whispered, however, that *he* might have made a greater match for himself, had he chosen—no other than Squire Trevlyn's eldest daughter. There was not so handsome, so attractive a man in all the country round as Thomas Ryle.

Soon after the marriage, Parson Berkeley died —to the intense grief of his daughter, Mrs. Ryle. He was succeeded in the curacy and parsonage by a young clergyman just in priest's orders, the Reverend Shafto Dean. A well-meaning man, but opinionated and self-sufficient in the highest degree, and before he had been one month at the parsonage, he and Squire Trevlyn were at issue. Mr. Dean wished to introduce certain new fashions and customs into the church and parish, Squire Trevlyn held to the old. Proud, haughty, overbearing, but honourable and generous, Squire Trevlyn had known no master, no opposer; *he* was lord of the neighbourhood, and was bowed down to as such. Mr. Dean would not give way, the Squire would not give way; and the little seed of dissension grew and grew, and spread and spread. Obstinacy begets obstinacy. What a slight yielding on either side, a little mutual good feeling, might have been removed at first, became at length a terrible breach, a county's talk.

Meanwhile Thomas Ryle's fair young wife died, leaving an infant boy—George. In spite of her husband's loving care, in spite of her having been shielded from all work and management, so necessary on a farm, she died. Nora Dickson, a humble relative of the Ryle family, who had been partially brought up on the farm, was housekeeper and manager. She saved all trouble to young Mrs. Ryle: but she could not save her life.

The past history of Trevlyn Hold was a romance in itself. Squire Trevlyn had five children: Rupert, Maude, Joseph, Edith, and Diana. Rupert, Maude, and Diana were imperious as their father; Joseph and Edith were mild, yielding, and gentle, as had been their mother. Rupert was of course regarded as the heir, intended to be such: but the property was not entailed. An ancestor of Squire Trevlyn's coming from some distant part—it was said Cornwall—bought it and settled down upon it. There was not a great deal of grass land on the estate, but the coal mines in the distance rendered it valuable. Of all his children, Rupert, the eldest, was the squire's favourite: but poor Rupert did not live to come into the estate. He had inherited the fits of passion characteristic of the Trevlyns; he was of a thoughtless, impetuous nature; and he fell into trouble and ran from his country. He embarked for a distant port, which he did not live to reach. And that left Joseph the heir.

Quite different, he, from his brother Rupert. Gentle and yielding, like his sister Edith, the squire half despised him. The squire would have preferred him to be passionate, and haughty, and overbearing—a true Trevlyn. But the squire had no intention of superseding him in the succession of Trevlyn Hold. Provided Joseph lived, none other would be its inheritor. *Provided.* Joseph—called Joe always—appeared to have inherited his mother's feeble constitution; and she had died early, of decline.

Yielding, however, as Joe Trevlyn was naturally, on one point he did not prove himself so—that of his marriage. He chose Emily Dean; the pretty and loveable sister of Squire Trevlyn's *bête noire,* the obstinate parson. " I'd rather you took a wife out of the parish workhouse, Joe," the squire said, in his vexation and anger. Joe said little in answering argument, but he held to his own choice; and one fine morning the marriage was celebrated by the obstinate parson himself in the church at Barbrook.

The squire and Thomas Ryle were close friends, and the former was fond of passing his evenings

at the farm. The farm was not a productive one.
The land, never of the richest, had become poorer
and poorer: it wanted draining and manuring;
it wanted, in short, money laid out upon it; and
that money Mr. Ryle did not possess. "I shall
have to leave it, and try and take a farm that's
in better condition," he said at length to the
squire.

The squire, with all his faults of passion and
his overbearing sway, was a generous and con-
siderate man. He knew what the land wanted;
money spent on it; he knew Mr. Ryle had not
the money to spend, and he offered to lend it.
Mr. Ryle accepted it, and had two thousand
pounds. He gave a bond for the sum, and the
squire on his part promised to renew the lease
upon the present terms, when the time of renewal
came, and not to raise the rent. This promise
was not given in writing: but none ever thought
to doubt the word of Squire Trevlyn.

The first of Squire Trevlyn's children to marry,
had been Edith: she had married some years
before, Mr. Chattaway. The two next to marry
had been Maude and Joseph. Joseph, as you
have heard, married Emily Dean; Maude, the
eldest daughter, became the second wife of Mr.
Ryle. A twelvemonth subsequent to the death
of his fair young wife Mary, Miss Trevlyn of the

Hold stepped into her shoes, and became the step-mother of the little baby-boy, George. The youngest daughter, Diana, never married.

Miss Trevlyn, in marrying Thomas Ryle, gave mortal offence to some of her kindred. The squire himself would have forgiven it; nay, perhaps have grown to like it—for he never could do otherwise than like Thomas Ryle—but he was constantly incited against it by his family. Mr. Chattaway, who had no great means of living of his own, was at the Hold on a long long visit, with his wife and two little children, Christopher and Octavia. They were always saying they must leave and leave; but they did *not* leave; they stayed on. Mr. Chattaway made himself useful to the squire on business matters, and whether they ever would leave was a question. She, Mrs. Chattaway, was too gentle-spirited and loving to speak against her sister and Mr. Ryle; but Chattaway and Miss Diana Trevlyn kept up the ball. In point of fact, they had a motive—at least, Chattaway had—for making the estrangement between the squire and Mr. Ryle a permanent one, for it was thought that Squire Trevlyn would have to look out for another heir.

News had come home of poor Joe Trevlyn's fading health. He had taken up his abode in the south of France on his marriage : for even

then the doctors had begun to say that a more
genial climate, than this, could alone save the life
of the heir to Trevlyn. Bitterly as the squire
had felt the marriage, angry as he had been with
Joe, he had never had the remotest thought of
disinheriting him. He was the only son left:
and Squire Trevlyn would never, if he could help
it, bequeath Trevlyn Hold to a woman. A little
girl, Maude, was born in due time to Joe Trevlyn
and his wife; and not long after this, there
arrived home the tidings that Joe's health was
rapidly failing. Mr. Chattaway, selfish, mean,
sly, covetous, began to entertain hopes that he
should be named the heir; he began to work on
for it in stealthy earnestness. He did not forget
that, were it bequeathed to the husband of one
of the daughters, Mr. Ryle, as the husband of the
eldest, might be considered to possess most claim
to it; no wonder then that he did all he could,
secretly and openly, to incite the squire against
Mr. Ryle and his wife. And in this he was joined
by Miss Diana Trevlyn. She, haughty and imperious, resented the marriage of her sister with
one inferior in position, and willingly espoused
the cause of Mr. Chattaway as against Thomas
Ryle. It was whispered about; none knew with
what truth, that Miss Diana made a compact
with Chattaway, to the effect that she should

reign jointly at Trevlyn Hold with him and enjoy part of the revenues, did he come into the inheritance.

Before the news came of Joe Trevlyn's death—and it was some months in coming—Squire Trevlyn had taken to his bed. Never did man seem to fade so rapidly as the squire. Not only his health, but his mind failed him; all its vigour seemed gone. He mourned poor Joe excessively: in rude health and strength, he would not have mourned him; at least, he would not have shown that he did; never a man less inclined than the squire to suffer his private emotions to be seen: but in his weakened state of mind and body, he gave way to lamentation for his heir (his *heir*, note you, more than his son) every hour in the day. Over and over again he regretted that the little child, Maude, left by Joe, was not a boy: nay, if it had not been for his prejudice against her mother, he would have willed the estate to her, girl though she was. Now was Mr. Chattaway's time: he put forth in glowing colours his own claims, as Edith's husband; he made golden promises; he persuaded the poor squire, in his wreck of mind and body, that black was white—and he succeeded in his plans.

To the will which had bequeathed the estate to the eldest son, dead Rupert, the squire added a

codicil, to the effect that, failing his two sons,
James Chattaway was the inheritor. But all this
was kept a profound secret.

During the time the squire lay ill, Mr. Ryle
went to Trevlyn Hold, and succeeded in obtaining
an interview. Mr. Chattaway was out that day,
or he had never accomplished it. Miss Diana
Trevlyn was out. All the squire's animosity went
away the moment he saw Thomas Ryle's long
familiar face. He lay clasping his hand, and
lamenting their estrangement ; he told him he
should cancel the two thousand pound bond,
giving the money as his daughter's fortune ; he
said his promise of renewing the lease of the
farm to him on the same terms would be held
sacred, for he had left a memorandum to that
effect amidst his papers. He sent for a certain
box, in which the bond for the two thousand
pounds had been placed, and searched for it,
intending to give it to him then, but the bond was
not there, and he said that Mr. Chattaway, who
managed all his affairs now, must have placed it
elsewhere ; but he would ask him for it when he
came in, and it should be destroyed before he
slept. Altogether, it was a most pleasant and
satisfactory interview.

But strange news arrived from abroad ere the
squire died. Not strange, certainly, in itself ;

only strange because it was so very unexpected. Joseph Trevlyn's widow had given birth to a boy! On the very day that little Maude was twelve months old, exactly three months subsequent to Joe's death, this little fellow was born. Mr. Chattaway opened the letter, and I'll leave you to judge of his state of mind. A male heir, after he had got everything so sure and safe!

But Mr. Chattaway was not a man to be balked. *He* would not be deprived of the inheritance, if he could by any possible scheming retain it, no matter what wrong he dealt out to others. James Chattaway had as little conscience as most people. The whole of that day he never spoke of the news, he kept it to himself, and the next morning there arrived a second letter, which rendered the affair a little more complicated. Young Mrs. Trevlyn was dead. She had died, leaving the two little ones, Maude and the infant.

Squire Trevlyn was always saying, " Oh, that Joe had left a boy; that Joe had left a boy!" And now, as it was found, Joe *had* left one. But Mr. Chattaway kindly determined that the fact should never reach the squire's ears to gladden them. Something had to be done, however, or the little children would be coming to Trevlyn. Mr. Chattaway arranged his plans, and wrote off hastily to stop their departure. He told the squire that Joe's widow had died, leaving Maude ; but he never said a word about the baby boy. Had the squire lived, perhaps it could not have been kept from him ; but he did not live ; he went to his grave all too soon, never knowing that there was a male heir born to Trevlyn.

The danger was over then. Mr. Chattaway was the legal inheritor ; had Joe left ten boys, they could not have displaced him. Trevlyn Hold was his by the squire's will, and could not be wrested from him. The two little ones, friendless and penniless, were brought home to the Hold. Mrs. Trevlyn had lived long enough to name the infant "Rupert," after the old squire and the heir who had run away and died. Poor Joe had always said that if ever he had a boy, it should be named after his brother.

There they had been ever since, these two orphans, aliens in the home that ought to have been theirs ; lovely children, both ; but Rupert had the passionate Trevlyn temper. It was not made a systematically unkind home for them ; Miss Diana would not have allowed that ; but it was a very different home from what they ought to have enjoyed. Mr. Chattaway was at times almost cruel to Rupert ; Christopher exercised upon him all sorts of galling and petty tyranny, as Octave Chattaway did upon Maude ; and the neighbourhood, you may be quite sure, did not fail to talk. But it was not known abroad, you understand, save to one or too, that Mr. Chattaway had kept the fact of Rupert's birth, from the knowledge of the squire.

.. He stood tolerably well with his fellow men, did Chattaway. In himself he was not liked; nay, he was very much disliked; but he was the owner of Trevlyn Hold, and possessed sway in the neighbourhood. One thing, he could not get the title of squire accorded to him. In vain he strove for it; he exacted it from his tenants; he wrote notes in the third person, "Squire Chattaway presents his compliments," &c. ; or, "the Squire of Trevlyn Hold desires," &c., &c., all in vain. People readily accorded his wife the title of Madam—as it was the custom to call the mistress of Trevlyn Hold—she was the old squire's daughter, and they recognised her claim to it, but they did not give that of squire to her husband.

These things had happened years ago, for Maude and Rupert are now aged respectively thirteen and twelve, and all that while had James Chattaway enjoyed his sway. Never, never; no, not even in the still night when the voice of conscience in most men is so suggestive; never giving a thought to the wrong dealt out to Rupert.

And it must be mentioned that the first thing Mr. Chattaway did, after the death of Squire Trevlyn, was to sue Mr. Ryle upon the bond; which he had *not* destroyed, although ordered to do so by the squire. The next thing he did was to raise the rent of the farm to a ruinous price. Mr. Ryle, naturally indignant, remonstrated, and there had been ill-feeling between them from that hour to this; but Chattaway had the law on his own side. Some of the bond was paid off; but altogether, what with the raised rent, and the bond and its interest, and a succession of ill-luck on the farm, Mr. Ryle had been scarcely able to keep his head above water. As he said to his wife and children, when the bull had done its work,—he was taken from a world of care.

CHAPTER VII.

MR. RYLE'S LAST WILL AND TESTAMENT.

ETIQUETTE, touching the important ceremonies of buryings and christenings, is much more observed in the country than in towns. To rural districts this remark especially applies. In a large town, people don't know their next door neighbours, don't care for those neighbours' opinions ; in a small place the inhabitants are almost as one family, and their actions are chiefly governed by that pertinent remark, " What will people say ? " In these little communities, numbers of which are scattered about England, it is held necessary on the occasion of a funeral to invite all kith and kin. Omit to do so, and it would be set down as a premeditated slight ; affording a theme of gossip to the parish for weeks afterwards. Hence Mr. Chattaway, being a connection—brother-in-law, in fact, of the deceased gentleman's wife—was invited to follow the remains of Thomas Ryle to the grave. In

spite of the bad terms they had been upon; in
spite of Mrs. Ryle's own bitter feelings against
Chattaway and Trevlyn Hold generally; in spite
of Mr. Ryle's death having been caused by what
did cause it—Chattaway's bull—Mr. Chattaway
received a formal invitation, in writing, to attend,
as mourner, the remains to the grave. And it
never would have entered into the notion of Mr.
Chattaway's good manners to decline it.

An inquest had been held at the nearest inn.
The verdict returned was "Accidental Death,"
with a deodand of five pounds upon the bull.
Which Mr. Chattaway had to pay.

The bull was already condemned. Not to
annihilation; but to be taken to a distant fair,
and there sold; whence he would be conveyed to a
home in other pastures, where he might possibly
gore somebody else. It was not consideration for
the feelings of the Ryle family which induced Mr.
Chattaway to adopt this step, and so rid the
neighbourhood of the animal; but consideration
for his own pocket. Feeling ran high in the
vicinity; fear also; the stoutest hearts could feel
no security that the bull might not be for having
a tilt at them: and Chattaway, on his part, was
at as little certainty that an effectual silencer
would not be surreptitiously dealt out to the bull
some quiet night. Therefore, he resolved to part

with him ; apart from his misdoings, he was a valuable animal, worth a great deal more than Mr. Chattaway would like to lose ; and the bull was dismissed.

The day of the funeral came, and those bidden to it began to arrive about one o'clock : that is, the undertaker's men, the clerk, and the carriers. Of the latter, Jim Sanders made one. "Better that he had gone than his master," said Nora, in a matter-of-fact, worldly spirit of reasoning, as her thoughts were cast back to the mysterious hole with which she had gratuitously, and the reader will no doubt say absurdly, coupled the fate of Jim. A table of eatables was laid out in the entrance room : cold round of beef, and bread-and-cheese, with ale in cans. To help convey a coffin to church without being plentifully regaled with a good meal first, was a thing that Barbrook had never heard of, and never wished to hear. The select of the company were shown to the large drawing-room, where the refreshment consisted of port and sherry wine, and a plate of " pound " cake. These were the established rules of hospitality at all genteel, well-to-do funerals : wine and pound cake for the gentlefolks ; cold beef and ale for the men. They had been observed at Squire Trevlyn's ; they had been observed at Mr. Ryle's father's ; they had been observed at every substantial funeral within the memory of Barbrook. Mr. Chattaway, Mr. Berkeley (a distant relative of Mr. Ryle's first wife), Mr. King the surgeon, and Farmer Apperley, comprised the assemblage in the drawing-room.

At two, after some little difficulty in getting it into order, the sad procession started. It had then been joined by George and Trevlyn Ryle. A great many spectators had collected to view and attend it. The somewhat infrequency of a funeral of the respectable class, combined with the circumstances attending the death, drew them together : and before the church was reached, where it was met by the clergyman, it had a train half a mile long after it ; mostly women and children. Many dropped a tear for the unhappy fate, the premature death of one who had lived among them, a good master, a kind neighbour.

They left him in his grave, by the side of his long-dead young wife, Mary Berkeley. As George stood at the head of his father's coffin, during the ceremony in the churchyard, the grave-stone with its name was right in front of his eyes ; his mother's name. "Mary, the wife of Thomas Ryle, and only daughter of the Rev. George Berkeley." None knew with what a shivering feeling of loneliness the orphan boy turned from the spot, as the last words of the minister's voice died away.

Mrs. Ryle, in her widow's weeds, was seated in the drawing-room on their return, as the gentlemen filed into it. In Barbrook custom, the relatives of the deceased, near or distant, were expected to congregate together for the remainder of the day; or for a portion of its remainder. The gentlemen would sometimes smoke pipes, and the ladies in their deep mourning sat with their hands folded in their laps, resting on their snow-white handkerchiefs. The conversation was only allowed to run on family matters, prospects, and the like; and the voices were amicable and subdued.

As the mourners entered, they shook hands severally with Mrs. Ryle. Chattaway put out his hand last, and with perceptible hesitation. It was many a year since his hand had been given in fellowship to Mrs. Ryle, or had taken hers. They had been friendly once, and in the old days he used to call her " Maude :" but that was over now.

Mrs. Ryle turned from the offered hand. " No," she said, speaking in a quiet but most decisive tone. " I cannot forget the past sufficiently for that, James Chattaway. On this day it is forcibly present to me."

They sat down. Trevlyn next his mother,
called there by her. The gentlemen disposed
themselves on the side of the table facing the fire,
and George found a chair a little behind : nobody
seemed to notice him. And so much the better;
for the boy's heart was too full to bear much
notice then.

On the table was placed the paper which had
been written by the surgeon, at the dictation of
Mr. Ryle, the night when he lay in extremity.
It had not been unfolded since. Mr. King took
it up; he knew that he was expected to read it.
They were waiting for him to do so.

"I must premise that the wording of this is
Mr. Ryle's," he said. "He expressly requested
me to pen down his *own words*, just as they
issued from his lips. He—— "

"Is it a will?" interrupted Farmer Apperley, a
little gentleman, with a red face and large nose.
He had come to the funeral in top boots; they
constituting his ideas of full dress.

"You can call it a will, if you please," replied
Mr. King. "I am not sure that the law would.
It was in consequence of his not having made a
will that he requested me to write down these
few directions."

The farmer nodded; and Mr. King began to
read.

"In the name of God: Amen. I, Thomas Ryle.

"First of all, I bequeath my soul to God. Trusting that he will pardon my sins, for the sake of Jesus Christ our Saviour. Amen.

"It's a dreadful blow, the cutting of me off by that bull of Chattaway's. The more so, that I am unable to leave things straightforward for my wife and children. They know—at least, my wife does, and all the parish knows—the pressure that has been upon me, through Chattaway coming down upon me as he has done. I have been as a bird with its wings clipped; as soon as I'd try to get up, I was pulled down again.

"Ill luck has been upon me besides. Beasts have died off, and crops have failed; the farm's not good for much, for all the money that has been laid out upon it, and nobody but me knows the labour it has cost. When you think of these things, my dear wife and boys, you'll know why I do not leave you better provided for. Many and many a night have I laid awake upon my bed, fretting, and planning, and hoping, all for your sakes. Perhaps if that bull had spared me to an old age, I might have left you better off.

"I'd like to bequeath the furniture and all that is in the house, and the stock, and the beasts, and all that I die possessed of, to my dear wife,

Maude—but it's not of any good, for Chattaway
will sell up—except the silver tankard, and that
should go to Trevlyn. But for having 'T. R.'
upon it, it should go to George, for he is the
eldest. T. R. stood for my father, and T. R. has
stood for me, and T. R. will stand for Trevlyn.
George, though he is the eldest, won't grudge it
him, if I know anything of his nature. And I
give to George my watch, and I hope he'll keep
it for his dead father's sake. It is only a silver
one, as I dare say you have noticed, doctor; but
it's very good to go, and George can have his
initials engraved on the shield at the back, 'G. B.
R.' And the three seals, and the gold key, I give
to him with it. The red cornelian has our arms
on it; for we had arms once, and my father and I
have generally sealed our letters with them: not
that they have done him or me any good. And
let Treve keep the tankard faithfully, and never
part with it; and remember, my dear boys, that
your poor father would have left you better keep-
sakes had it been in his power. You must prize
these for the dead giver's sake. But there! it's
of no use talking, for Chattaway, he'll sell up,
watch and tankard, and all.

"And I'd like to leave that bay foal to my dear
little Caroline. It will be a rare pretty creature
when it's bigger. And you must let it have the

run of the three-cornered paddock, and I should like to see her on it, sweet little soul !—but Chattaway's bull has stopped it. And don't grudge the cost of a little saddle for her ; and Roger, he can break it in ; and mind you are all true and tender with my dear little wench, and if I thought you wouldn't be, I'd like to have her with me in my coffin. But you are good lads—though Treve he is hasty when his temper's put out—and I know you'll be to her what brothers ought to be. I always meant that foal for Carry, since I saw how pretty it was likely to grow, though I didn't say what was in my mind ; and now I give it to her. But where's the use ? Chattaway, he'll sell up.

" If he does sell up, to the last stick and stone, he'll not get his debt in full. Perhaps not much above the half of it ; for things at a forced sale don't bring their value. You have put down ' his debt,' Mr. King, I suppose ; but it is not his debt. I am on my death-bed, and I say that the two thousand pounds was made a present of to me by the squire on *his* death-bed. He told me it was made all right with Chattaway ; that Chattaway understood the promise given to me, not to raise the rent ; and that he'd be the same just landlord to me that the squire had been. The squire could not lay his hand upon the bond, or he would have given it me then; but he said Chattaway should burn it as soon as he entered, which would be in an hour or two. Chattaway knows whether he has acted up to this; and now his bull has finished me.

"And I wish to tell Chattaway that if he'll act a fair part as a man ought, and let my wife and the boys stop on the farm, he'll stand a much better chance of getting the money, than he would if he turns them off it. I don't say this for their sakes more than for his; but because from my very heart I believe it to be the truth. George has got his head on his shoulders the right way, and I'd advise his mother to keep him on the farm; he'll be getting older every day. Not but that I wish her to use her own judgment in all things, for her judgment is good. In time, they may be able to pay off Chattaway; in time they may be able even to buy back the farm, for I cannot forget that it belonged to my forefathers, and not to the squire. That is, if Chattaway will be reasonable, and let them stop on it, and not be hard and pressing. But perhaps I am talking nonsense, doctor, for he may turn them off, as his bull has turned off me.

"And now, my dear George and Treve, I repeat it to you, be good boys to your mother. Obey her in all things. Maude, I have left all to you in preference to dividing it between you and them, which there's no time for ; but I know you'll do the right thing by them : and when it comes to your turn to leave—if Chattaway don't sell up— I'd wish you to bequeath to them in equal shares what you die possessed of. George is not your son, but he is mine, and—and—perhaps I'd better not say what I was going to say, doctor. Maude, I leave all to you, trusting to your justice to leave all in turn to them in equal portions ; to the three —George, Treve, and Caroline. And, my boys, you be loving and obedient to your mother, and work for her to the best of your ability ; work for her, and work for yourselves. Work while it's day. In that book which I have not read so much as I ought to have read, it says 'The night cometh when no man can work.' When we hear that read in church, or when we get the book out on a Sunday evening and read it to ourselves, that night seems a long, long way off. It seems so far off that it can never hardly be any concern of ours ; and it is only when we are cut off suddenly that we find how very near it is. That night has come for me, through Chattaway's bull ; and that night will come for you before you are aware. So, *work*—and please to score that, doctor. God has placed us in this world to work, and not to be ashamed of it ; and to work for Him as well as for ourselves. It was often in my mind that I ought to work more for God—that I ought to think of Him more; and I used to say, 'I will soon, when a bit of this bother's off my mind.' But the bother was always there, and I never did it. And now the end's come, and I am cut off in the midst through that bull of Chattaway's; and I can see things would have been made easier to me if I *had* done it—score it, doctor—and I say it as a lesson to you, my children.

"And I think that's about all; and I am much obliged to you, doctor, for writing this. I hope they'll be able to manage things on the farm, and I'd ask my neighbour Apperley to give them his advice a bit now and then, for old friendship's sake, until George shall be older, and to put him in a way of buying and selling stock. If Chattaway don't sell up, that is. If he does, I hardly know how it will be. Perhaps God will put them in some other way, and take care of them. And I'd leave my best thanks to Nora, for she has been a true friend to us all, and I don't know how the house would have got along without her. And now I am growing faint, doctor, and I think the end is coming. God bless you all, my dear ones. Amen."

A deep silence fell on the room as Mr. King ceased. He folded up the paper, and laid it on the table near to Mrs. Ryle. The first to speak was Farmer Apperley.

"Any help that I can be of to you and George, Mrs. Ryle, and to all of you, is heartily at your service. It'll be yours with right good will at all times and seasons. The more so, that you know if it had been me cut off in this way, my poor friend Ryle would have been the first to offer to do so much for my wife and boys, and have thought no trouble of it. George, you come over and ask me about things, just as you would ask your father; or send for me up here to the farm; and whatever work I may be at at home, though it was the putting out of a barn as was a-fire, I'd quit it to come."

"And now it is my turn to speak," said Mr. Chattaway. "And, Mrs. Ryle, I give you my promise, in the presence of these gentlemen, that if you choose to remain on the farm, I will not put a hindrance upon it. Your husband thought me hard—unjust; he said it before my face and behind my back. My opinion always has been that he entirely mistook Squire Trevlyn in that last interview he had with him. I do not think it was ever the squire's intention to cancel the bond: Ryle must have misunderstood him altogether: at any rate, I heard nothing of it. As the successor in the estate, the bond came into my possession; and in my wife and children's interest I could not consent to suppress it. Nobody but a soft-hearted man—and that's what Ryle was, poor fellow—would have thought of asking such a thing. But I was willing to give him all facilities for paying it, and I did do so. · No! It was not my hardness that was in fault, but his pride and his nonsense, and his thinking I ought not to ask for my own money——"

"If you bring up these things, James Chattaway, I must answer them," interrupted Mrs. Ryle. "I would prefer not to be forced to do it to-day."

"I do not want to bring them up in an unpleasant spirit," answered Mr. Chattaway; "or to say it was his fault or my fault. We'll let bygones be bygones. He is gone, poor man; and I wish that savage beast of a bull had been in four quarters, before he had done the mischief! All I would now say, is, that I'll put no impediment to your remaining on the farm. We will not go into business details this afternoon, but I will come in any day that you like to appoint, and talk it over. If you choose to keep on the farm at its present rent—it is well worth it—and to pay me interest for the money that's owing, and a yearly sum— as shall be agreed upon—towards diminishing the debt, you are welcome to do it."

Just what Nora had predicted! Mr. Chatta-way loved money too greatly to run the risk of losing part of the debt—as he probably would do if he turned them off the farm. Mrs. Ryle bowed her head in cold acquiescence. She saw no other way open to her, save that of accepting the offer. Very probably Mr. Chattaway knew that there was no other.

"The sooner things are settled, the better," she remarked. "I will name eleven o'clock to-morrow morning."

"Very good; I'll be here," he answered. "And I am glad it is decided harmoniously."

The rest of those present appeared also to be glad. Perhaps they had feared some unpleasant recrimination might take place between Mrs. Ryle and James Chattaway. Thus relieved, they unbent a little, and crossed their legs as if inclined to become more sociable.

"What shall you do with the boys, Mrs. Ryle?" suddenly asked Farmer Apperley.

"Treve, of course, will go to school as usual," she replied. "George —— I have not decided about George."

"Shall I have to leave school?" cried George, looking up with a start.

"Of course you will," said Mrs. Ryle.

"But what will become of my Latin; of **my**

studies altogether?" returned George, in a tone of dismay. "You know, mamma, I——"

"It cannot be helped, George," she interrupted, speaking in the uncompromisingly decisive manner, so characteristic of her; as it was of her sister, Miss Diana Trevlyn. "You must turn your attention to something more profitable than schooling, now."

"If a boy at fifteen has not had schooling enough, I'd like to know when he has had it?" interposed Farmer Apperley, who neither understood nor approved of the strides which education and intellect had made since the time when he was a boy. Very substantial people in his day had been content to learn to read and write and cipher, and to deem that amount of learning sufficient to grow rich upon. As the Dutch professor did, to whom George Primrose wished to teach Greek, but who declined the offer. He had never learned Greek; he had lived, and ate, and slept without Greek; and therefore he did not see any good in Greek. Thus it was with Farmer Apperley.

"What do you learn at school, George?" questioned Mr. Berkeley.

"Latin and Greek, and mathematics, and——"

"But, George, where will be the good of such things to you?" cried Farmer Apperley, not allowing him to finish the catalogue. "Latin and Greek and mathematics! that *is* fine, that is l"

"I don't see much good in giving a boy that style of education myself," put in Mr. Chattaway, before any one else had time to speak. "Unless he is to be reared to a profession, the classics only he fallow in the memory. I hated them, I know that; I and my brother, too. Many and many a caning we have had over our Latin, until we wished the books at the bottom of the sea. Twelve months after we left school we could not have construed a page, had it been put before us. That's all the good learning Latin did for us."

"I shall keep up my Latin and Greek," observed George, very independently, "although I may have to leave school."

"Why need you keep it up?" asked Mr. Chattaway, turning his head to take a full look at George.

"Why?" echoed George. "I like it, for one thing. And a knowledge of the classics is necessary to a gentleman, now-a-days."

"Necessary to what?" cried Mr. Chattaway.

"To a gentleman," repeated George.

"Oh," said Mr. Chattaway. "Do you think of being one?"

" Yes, I do," replied George, in a tone as decisive as any ever used by his stepmother.

This bold assertion nearly took away the breath of Farmer Apperley. Had George Ryle announced his intention to become a Botany Bay convict, Mr. Apperley's consternation had been scarcely less. The same word will bear different constructions to different minds. That of " gentleman " in the mouth of George, could only bear one to the plain and simple farmer.

" Hey, lad ! What wild notions have ye been getting in your head ? " he asked.

" George," spoke Mrs. Ryle almost at the same moment, " are you going to give me trouble at the very onset ? There is nothing for you to look forward to, but work. Your father said it."

" Of course I look forward to work, mamma," returned George, as cheerfully as he could speak that sad afternoon. " But that will not prevent my being a gentleman."

" George, I fancy you may be somewhat misusing terms," remarked the surgeon, who was an old inhabitant of that rustic district, and little more advanced in notions than the rest. " What you meant to say was, that you would be a good, honourable, upright man ; not a mean one. Was it not ? "

"Yes," said George, after an imperceptible hesitation. "Something of that."

"The boy did not express himse lfclearly, you see," said Mr. King, looking round on the rest. "He means right."

"Don't you ever talk about being a gentleman again, my lad," cried Farmer Apperley, with a sagacious nod. "It would make the neighbours think you were going on for bad ways. A gentleman is one who follows the hounds in white smalls and a scarlet coat, and goes to dinners and drinks wine, and never puts his hands to anything, but leads an idle life."

"That is not the sort of gentleman I meant," said George.

"It is to be hoped it's not," emphatically replied the farmer. "A man may do this if he has got a good fat banker's book, George, but not else."

George made no answering remark. To have explained how very different his notions of a gentleman were from those of Farmer Apperley's, might have involved him in a long conversation. His silence was looked suspiciously upon by Mr. Chattaway.

"Where idle and roving notions are taken up, there's only one cure for them!" he remarked, in a short, uncompromising tone. "And that is hard work."

But that George's spirit was subdued, he might have hotly answered that he had taken up neither idle nor roving notions. As it was, he sat in silence.

"I doubt whether it will be prudent to keep George at home," said Mrs. Ryle, speaking generally, but not to Mr. Chattaway. "He is too young to do much good upon the farm. And there's John Pinder."

"John Pinder would do his best, no doubt," said Mr. Chattaway.

"The question is—if I do resolve to put George out, what can I put him to?" resumed Mrs. Ryle.

"Papa thought it best that I should stay on the farm," interposed George, his heart beating a shade quicker.

"He thought it best that I should exercise my own judgment in the matter," corrected Mrs. Ryle. "The worst is, it takes money to place a lad out," she added, looking at Farmer Apperley.

"It does that," replied the farmer.

"There's nothing like a trade for boys," said Mr. Chattaway, impressively. "They learn to get a good living, and they are kept out of mischief. It appears to me that Mrs. Ryle will have enough expense upon her hands, without the cost and keep of George being added to it. What service can so young a boy do the farm?"

"True," mused Mrs. Ryle, agreeing for once with Mr. Chattaway. "He could not be of much use at present. But the cost of placing him out?"

"Of course he could not," repeated Mr. Chattaway, with an eagerness which might have betrayed his motive to suspicion, but that he coughed it down. "Perhaps I may be able to manage the putting him out for you, without cost. I know of an eligible place where there's a vacancy. The trade is a good one, too."

"I am not going to any trade," spoke George, looking Mr. Chattaway full in the face.

"You are going where Mrs. Ryle thinks fit that you shall go," returned Mr. Chattaway, in his hard, cold tone. "If I can get you into the establishment of Wall and Barnes without premium, it will be a first-rate thing for you."

All the blood in George Ryle's body seemed to rush to his face. Poor though they had become in point of money, trade had been unknown in their family, and its sound in George's ears, as applied to himself, was something terrible. "That is a retail shop!" he cried, rising from his seat in a commotion.

"Well?" said Mr. Chattaway.

They remained gazing at each other. George with his changing face, flushing to crimson, fading to paleness; Mr. Chattaway with his composed,

leaden one. His light eyes were sternly directed
to George, but he did not glance at Mr. Ryle.
George was the first to speak.

" You should never force me there, Mr. Chattaway."

Mr. Chattaway rose from his seat, took George
by the shoulder, and turned him towards the
window. The view did not overlook much of the
road to Barbrook, the lower road ; but a glimpse
of it might be caught sight of here and there,
winding along in the distance.

" Boy ! do you remember what was carried
down that road this afternoon—what you followed
next to, with your younger brother ? *He* said
that you were not to cross your mother, but to
obey her in all things. These are early moments
to begin to turn against your father's dying
charge."

George sat down, his brain throbbing, his heart
beating. He did not see his duty very distinctly
before him then. His father certainly had charged
him to obey his mother's bequests, he had left him
entirely subject to her control ; but George felt
perfectly sure that his father would never have
placed him in a retail shop ; would not have
allowed him to enter one.

Mr. Chattaway continued talking, but the boy
heard him not. He was bending towards Mrs.

Ryle, enlarging upon the advantages of the plan in persuasive language. He knew that Wall and Barnes had taken a boy into their house without premium, he said, and he believed he could induce them to waive it in George's case. He and Wall had been at school together; had passed many an impatient hour over the Latin, previously spoken of; and he often called in to have a chat with him in passing. Wall was a ten thousand pound man now; and George might become the same in time.

"How would you like to place Christopher at it, Mr. Chattaway?" asked George, his breast heaving rebelliously.

"Christopher!" indignantly responded Mr. Chattaway. "Christopher's heir to Trev—— Christopher isn't you," he concluded, cutting his first retort short. In the presence of Mrs. Ryle it might not be altogether prudent to allude to the heirship of Cris to Trevlyn Hold.

The sum named conciliated the ear of Mr. Apperley, otherwise he had not listened with any favour to the plan. "Ten thousand pounds! And Wall but a middle-aged man! That's worth thinking of, George."

"I could never live in a shop; the close air, the confinement, would stifle me," said George, with a sort of groan, putting aside for the moment his more forcible objections.

" You'd rather live in a thunder-storm, with the
rain coming down on your head in bucketfuls,"
said Mr. Chattaway, sarcastically.

" A great deal," said George.

Farmer Apperley did not detect the irony of
Mr. Chattaway's remark, or the bitterness of the
answer. " You'll say next, boy, that you'd rather
go for a sailor, and be exposed to the weather
night and day, perched midway atween sky and
water !"

" So I would," was George's truthful answer.
" Mamma l let me stay at the farm !" he cried,
the nervous motion of his hands, the strained
countenance, proving how momentous was the
question to his grieved heart. " You do not
know how useful I should soon become ! And
papa wished it."

Mrs. Ryle shook her head. " You are too young,
George, to be of use. No."

George seemed to turn white ; face, and heart,
and all. He was approaching Mrs. Ryle with an
imploring gesture ; but Mr. Chattaway caught his
arm and pushed him to his seat again. " George,
if I were you, I would not, on this day, cross my
mother."

George glanced at her. Not a shade of love,
of relenting, was there on her countenance. Cold,
haughty, self-willed, it always was ; but more cold,

more haughty, more self-willed than usual now. He turned and left the room, his heart bursting, crossed the kitchen, and passed into the room whence his father had been carried but two hours before.

"Oh, papa! papa!" he sobbed, "if you were but back again!"

CHAPTER VIII.

INCIPIENT REBELLION.

BORNE down by the powers above him, George Ryle could only succumb to their will. Persuaded by the eloquence of Mr. Chattaway, Mrs. Ryle became convinced that the placing out of George in the establishment of Wall and Barnes was the most appropriate thing that could be found for him, the most promising. The great wonder was, that she should have brought herself to listen to Chattaway at all, or have entertained for a moment any proposal emanating from him. There could have been but one solution to the riddle : that of her own anxiety to get George settled in something away from home. Down deep in the heart of Mrs. Ryle, there was seated a deep sense of injury—of injustice—of wrong. It had been seated there ever since the death of Squire Trevlyn, influencing her actions, warping her temper—the question of the heirship of Trevlyn. Her father had bequeathed Trevlyn Hold to

Chattaway; and Chattaway's son was now the heir; whereas, in her opinion, it was her son, Trevlyn Ryle, who should be occupying that desirable distinction. How Mrs. Ryle reconciled it to her conscience to ignore the claims of young Rupert Trevlyn, she best knew.

She did ignore them. She cast no more thought to Rupert in connection with the succession to Trevlyn, than if he had not been in existence· He had been barred from it by the squire's will, and there it ended. But, failing heirs of her two dead brothers, it was *her* son who should have come in. Was she not the eldest daughter? What right had that worm, Chattaway, to have insinuated himself into the home of the squire? into—it may be said—his heart? and so willed over to himself the inheritance?

A bitter fact to Mrs. Ryle; a fact which rankled in her heart by night and by day; a turning from the path of justice which she firmly intended to see turned back again. She saw not how it was to be accomplished; she knew not by what means it could be brought about; she divined not yet how she should help in it; but she was fully determined that it should be Trevlyn Ryle eventually to possess Trevlyn Hold. Never, Cris Chattaway.

A determination immutable as the rock; a

purpose in the furtherance of which she never
swerved nor faltered ; there it lay in the archives
of her most secret thoughts, a part and parcel of
herself, not the less nourished because never
spoken of. It may be, that in the death of her
husband she saw her way to the end somewhat
more clearly ; that his removal was but one
impediment taken from the path. She had never
given utterance to her ambitious hopes for Trevlyn
but once ; and that had been to her husband.
His reception of them was a warning to her never
to speak of them again to him. No son of his,
he said, should inherit Trevlyn Hold while the
children of Joseph Trevlyn lived. If Chattaway
chose to wrest their rights from them, to make his
son Cris the usurper after him, he, Mr. Ryle, could
not hinder it ; but his own boy Treve should never
take act or part in so crying a wrong. So long as
Rupert and Maude Trevlyn lived, he could never
recognise other rights than theirs. From that
time forward Mrs. Ryle held her tongue to
her husband, as she had done to all else ; but
the roots of the project grew deeper and
deeper in her heart, overspreading all its healthy
fibres.

With this great destiny in view for Treve, it
will readily be understood why she did not purpose
bringing him up to any profession, or sending him

out in the world. Her intention was, that Treve should live at home, as soon as his school-days were over; should be the master of Trevlyn Farm, until he could become the master of Trevlyn Hold. And for this reason, and this alone, she did not care to keep George with her. Trevlyn Farm, might be a living for one son; it would not be for two : neither would two masters on it answer, although they were brothers. It is true, a thought at times crossed her whether it might not be well, in the interests of the farm, to retain George. He would soon become useful; he would be trustworthy; her interests would be his; and she felt dubious about confiding all management to John Pinder. But these suggestions were over-ruled by the thought that it would not be desirable for George to acquire a footing on the farm as its master, and then to be turned from it when the time came for the mastership of Treve. As much for George's sake as for Treve's, she felt this; and she determined to place George at something away, where his interests and Treve's would not clash.

Wall and Barnes were flourishing and respectable tradesmen, silk-mercers and linendrapers ; their establishment a large one, the oldest and best conducted in Barmester. Had it been suggested to Mrs. Ryle to place Treve there, she

would have retorted in haughty indignation.   And
yet she was sending George !

What Mr. Chattaway's precise object could be,
in wishing to get George away from home, he
alone knew.   That he had such an object, there
could be no shadow of doubt ; and Mrs. Ryle's
usual clear-sightedness must have been just then
obscured, not to perceive it.   Had his own interests or pleasure not been in some way involved,
Chattaway would have taken no more heed as to
what became of George, than he did of a clod of
earth in that miserable field just rendered famous
by the doings of the ill-conditioned bull.   It was
Chattaway who did it all.   He negotiated with
Wall and Barnes ; he brought news of his success
to Mrs. Ryle ; he won over Farmer Apperley.
Wall and Barnes had occasionally taken a youth
without premium—the youth being expected to
perform an unusual variety of work for the favour,
to make himself conjointly into an apprentice
and a servant-in-general, to be at the beck and
call of the establishment.   Under those conces-
sions, Wall and Barnes had been known to forego
the usual premium ; and this great boon was,
through Mr. Chattaway, offered to George Ryle.
Chattaway boasted of it ; he enlarged upon his
luck to George ; and Mrs. Ryle—accepted it.

And George ?   Every pulse in his body coursed

on in fiery indignation against the measure, every
feeling of his heart rebelled at it. But, of opposition, he could make none : none that served him.
Chattaway quietly put him down ; Mrs. Ryle met
all his remonstrances with the answer that she
had *decided;* and Farmer Apperley laboured to
convince him that it was a slice of good fortune,
which anybody (under the degree of a gentleman
who rode to cover in a scarlet coat and white
smalls) might jump at. Was not Wall, who had
not yet reached his five-and-fortieth year, a ten
thousand pound man ? Turn where George would,
there appeared to be no escape for him ; no refuge.
He must give up all the dreams of his life—not
that the dreams had been of any particular colour
yet awhile—and become what his mind quite
revolted at, what he knew he should never do
anything but dislike bitterly. Had he been a less
right-minded boy, less dutiful, he would have
openly rebelled, have defied Chattaway ; have
declined to obey Mrs. Ryle. But that sort of
rebellion George did not enter upon. The injunction of his dead father lay on him all too forcibly
—" Obey and reverence your mother." And so
the agreement was made, and George Ryle was to
go to Wall and Barnes, to be bound to them for
seven years.

He stood leaning out of the casement window,

the night before he was to enter; his aching brow bared to the cold air, cloudy as the autumn sky. Treve was fast asleep, in his own little bed in the far corner, shaded and sheltered by its curtains: but there was no such peaceful sleep for George. The thoughts to which he was giving vent were not altogether profitable ones; and certain questions which arose in his mind had been better left out of it.

"What *right* have they so to dispose of me?" he asked, alluding, it must be confessed, to the trio, Chattaway, Mrs. Ryle, and Mr. Apperley. "They *know* that if papa had lived, they'd not have dared to urge my being put to it. I wonder what it will end in? I wonder whether I shall have to be at it always? It is *not* right to put a poor fellow to what he hates most of all in life, and what he'll hate for ever and for ever."

He gazed out at the low gloomy line of land lying under the night sky, looking as desolate as he was. "I'd rather go for a sailor!" broke from him in his despair; "I'd rather——"

A hot hand on his shoulder caused him to start and turn. There stood Nora.

"If I didn't say one of you boys was out of bed! What's this for, George? What are you doing?—trying to catch your death at the open window?"

"As good catch my death, for all I see, as live in this world, now," was George's answer.

"As good be a young simpleton and confess to it," retorted Nora, angrily. "What's the matter, George?"

"Why should they force me to that place at Barmester?" cried George, following up his grieved thoughts, rather than replying to Nora's question. "I wish Chattaway had been a thousand miles away first! What business has he to interfere about me?"

"I wish I was queen at odd moments, when work seems to be coming in seven ways at once, and only one pair of hands to do it," quoth Nora.

George turned from the window. "Nora, look here! You know I am a gentleman born: *is* it right to put me to it?"

Nora evaded an answer. She felt nearly as much as the boy did; but she saw no way of escape for him, and therefore would not oppose it.

There was no way of escape. Chattaway had decided it, Mrs. Ryle had acquiesced, and George was conducted to the new house, and took up his abode in it, rebellious feelings choking his heart, rebellious words rising to his lips.

But he did his utmost to beat the rebellion

down. The charge of his dead father was ever before him—to render all duty and obedience to his step-mother—and George was mindful of it. He felt as one crushed under a whole weight of despair; he felt as one who had been rudely thrust from his proper place on the earth : but he did constant battle with himself and his wrongs, and strove to make the best of it. How bitter the struggle was, none, save himself, knew; its remembrance would never die out from his memory.

The new work seemed terrible; not for its amount, though that was great; but for its nature. To help make up this parcel, to undo that; to take down these goods, to put up others. He ran to the post with letters—and that was a delightful phase of his life, compared with the rest of its phases—he carried out big bundles in brown paper; once a yard measure was added. He had to stand behind the counter, and roll and unroll goods, and measure tapes and ribbons, and bow and smile, and say "sir" and "ma'am." You will readily conceive what all this was to a proud boy. George might have run away from it altogether, but that the image of that table in the sitting-room, and of him who lay upon it, was ever before him, whispering to him to shrink not from his duty.

Not a moment of idleness was allowed to George; however the shopmen might enjoy leisure intervals when customers ran slack, there was no interval of leisure for him. He was the new scapegoat of the establishment; often doing the work that of right did not belong to him. It was perfectly well known to the young men that he had entered as a working apprentice; one who was not to be particular what work he did, or its quantity, in consideration of his non-premium terms; and therefore he was not spared. He had taken his books with him, classics and others; he soon found that he might as well have left them at home. Not one minute in all the twenty-four hours could he devote to them: his hands were full of work until the last moment, up to bed-time; and no reading was permitted in the chambers. "Where is the use of my having gone to school at all?" he sometimes would ask himself. He would soon become as oblivious of Latin and Greek as Mr. Chattaway could wish; indeed, his prospects of adding to his stock of learning were such as would have gladdened Farmer Apperley's heart.

One Saturday, when George had been there about three weeks, and when the day was drawing near for the indentures to be signed, binding him to the business for years, Mr. Chattaway rode up in the very costume that was the subject of Farmer Apperley's ire, when worn by those who ought not to afford to wear it. The hounds had met that day near Barmester, had found their fox, and been led a round-about chase, the fox bringing them back to their starting-point, to resign his brush; and the master of Trevlyn Hold, on his splashed but fine hunter, in his scarlet coat, white smalls and boots, splashed also, rode through Barmester on his return, and pulled up at the door of Wall and Barnes. Giving his horse to a street boy to hold, he entered the shop, whip in hand.

The scarlet coat, looming in unexpectedly, caused a flutter in the establishment. Saturday was market-day, and the shop was unusually full. The customers looked round in admiration, the shopmen with envy; little chance was there, thought those hard-worked, unambitious young men, that they should ever wear a scarlet coat, and ride to cover on a blood hunter. Mr. Chattaway, of Trevlyn Hold, was an object of consideration just then. He shook hands with Mr. Wall, who came forward from some remote region; he turned and shook hands condescendingly with George.

"And how does he suit?" blandly inquired

Mr. Chattaway. "Can you make anything of him?"

"He does his best," was the reply of Mr. Wall. "Awkward at present; but we have had others who have been as awkward at first, I think, and who have turned out valuable assistants in the long run. I am willing to take him."

"That's all right, then," said Mr. Chattaway· "I'll call in and tell Mrs. Ryle. Wednesday is the day he is to be bound, I think?"

"Wednesday," assented Mr. Wall.

"I shall be here. I am glad to take this trouble off Mrs. Ryle's hands. I hope you like your employment, George."

"I do not like it at all," replied George. And he spoke out fearlessly, although his master stood by.

"Oh, indeed!" said Mr. Chattaway, with a false-sounding laugh. "Well, I did not suppose you would like it too well at first."

Mr. Wall laughed also, a hearty, kindly laugh. "Never yet was there an apprentice liked his work too well," said he. "It's their first taste of the labour of life. George Ryle will like it better when he is used to it."

"I never shall," thought George. But he supposed it would not quite do to say so; neither would it answer any end. Mr. Chattaway shook hands with Mr. Wall, gave a nod to George, and he and his scarlet coat loomed out again.

. "Will it last my life ?—will this dreadful slaver last my life ?" burst from George Ryle's rebellious heart.

CHAPTER IX.

EMANCIPATION.

On the following day, Sunday, George walked home: Mrs. Ryle had told him he might come and spend the day. All were at church except Molly, and George went to meet them. Several groups were coming along; and presently he met Cris Chattaway, Rupert Trevlyn, and his brother Treve, walking together.

"Where's mamma?" asked George.

"She stepped in-doors with Mrs. Apperley," answered Treve. "She said she'd follow me on directly."

"How do you relish linendrapering?" asked Cris Chattaway, in a chaffing sort of manner, as George turned with them. "Horrid, isn't it?"

"There's only about one thing in this world more horrid," answered George.

"My father said you expressed fears before you went that you'd find the air at the shop stifling," went on Cris, not asking what the one exception might be. " Is it hopelessly so ? "

" Isn't it ! " returned George. " The black hole in Calcutta must have been cool and pleasant in comparison with it."

" I wonder you are alive," continued Cris.

" I wonder I am," said George, equably. " I was quite off in a faint one day, when the shop was at the fullest. They thought they must have sent for you, Cris ; that the sight of you might bring me to again."

" There you go ! " exclaimed Treve Ryle. " I wonder if you two *could* let each other alone if you were bribed to do it ? "

" Cris began it," said George.

" I didn't," said Cris. " I *should* like to see you at your work, though, George ! I'll come some day. The squire paid you a visit yesterday after-noon, he told us. He says you are getting to be quite the polite cut ; one can't serve out yards of calico without it, you know."

George Ryle's face burnt. He knew that Mr. Chattaway had been speaking of him with ridicule at Trevlyn Hold, in connection with his new occu-patiou. " It would be a more fitting situation for you than for me, Cris," said he. " And now you hear it."

Cris laughed scornfully. " Perhaps it might, if

I wanted one. The master of Trevlyn won't need to go into a linendraper's shop, George Ryle."

"Look here, Cris. That shop is horrid, and I don't mind telling you that I find it so, that not an hour in the day goes over my head but I wish myself out of it; but I would rather bind myself to it for twenty years, than be the master of Trevlyn Hold, if I came to it as you will come to it—by wrong."

Cris broke into a shrill, derisive whistle. It was being prolonged to an apparently interminable length, when he found himself rudely seized from behind.

"Is that the way you walk home from church, Christopher Chattaway? Whistling!"

Cris looked round and saw Miss Trevlyn. "Goodness, Aunt Diana! are you going to shake me?"

"Walk along as a gentleman should, then," returned Miss Trevlyn.

She went on. Miss Chattaway walked by her side, not deigning to cast a word or a look to the boys as she swept past. Gliding up behind them, holding the hand of Maude, was gentle Mrs. Chattaway. They all wore black silk dresses and white silk bonnets: the apology for mourning assumed for Mr. Ryle. But the gowns were not new ; and the bonnets were but the bonnets of the past summer, with the coloured flowers taken out.

Mrs. Chattaway slackened her pace, and George found himself at her side. She seemed to linger, as if she would speak with him, unheard by the rest.

"Are you pretty well, my dear?" were her first words. "You look taller and thinner, and your face is pale."

"I shall look paler ere I have been much longer in the shop, Mrs. Chattaway."

Mrs. Chattaway glanced her head timidly round with the air of one who fears she may be heard. But they were alone now.

"Are you grieving, George?"

"How can I help it?" he passionately answered, eeling that he could open his heart to Mrs. Chattaway, as he could to no one else in the wide world. "Is it a proper thing to put me to, dear Mrs. Chattaway?"

"I said it was not," she murmured. "I said to Diana that I wondered Maude should place you there."

"It was not mamma; it was not mamma so much as Mr. Chattaway," he answered, forgetting possibly that it was Mr. Chattaway's wife to whom he spoke. "At times, do you know, I

feel as though I would almost - rather be—–
be——"

"Be what, dear?"

"Be dead, than stop."

"Hush, George!" she cried, almost with a shudder. "Random figures of speech never do good; I have learnt it. In the old days, when——".

She suddenly broke off what she was saying, and glided forward without further notice, catching Maude's hand in hers as she passed, who was then walking by the side of the boys. George looked round for the cause of the desertion, and found it in Mr. Chattaway. That gentleman was coming along with a quick step, one of his younger children in his hand.

The Chattaways turned off towards Trevlyn Hold, and George walked on with Treve. "Do you know how things are going on at home, Treve, between mamma and Chattaway?" asked George.

"Chattaway's a miserable screw," was Treve's answer. "He'd like to grind down the world, and he doesn't let a chance escape him of doing it. Mamma says it's a dreadful sum he has put upon her to pay yearly, and she does not see how the farm will do it, besides keeping us. I wish we were clear of him! I wish I was as big as you, George! I'd work the farm barren, I'd work my arms off, but what I'd get together the money to pay him !"

"They won't let me work," said George. "They have thrust me away from the farm."

"I wish you were back at it; I know that! Nothing goes on as it used to, when you were there and papa was alive. Nora's cross, and mamma's cross; and I have not a soul to speak to. What do you think Chattaway did this week?"

"Something mean, I suppose!"

"Mean! Mean and double mean. We killed a pig, and while it was being cut up, Chattaway marched in. 'That's fine meat, John Pinder,' said he, when he had looked at it a bit; 'as fine as I ever saw. That was a good plan of Mr. Ryle's, the keeping his pigs clean. I should like a bit of this meat; I think I'll take a sparerib; and it can go against Mrs. Ryle's account with me.' With that, he laid hold of a fine sparerib, the finest of the two, and called to the boy who was standing by, and sent him up with it at once to Trevlyn Hold. What do you think of that?"

"Think! That it's just the thing Chattaway would be doing every day of his life, if he could. Mamma should have sent for the meat back."

" And anger Chattaway ? It might be all the worse for us if she did."

" Is it not early to begin pig-killing ?"

" Yes. John Pinder killed this one on his own authority: never so much as asking mamma. She was so angry. She told him, if ever he acted for himself again, without knowing what her pleasure might be, she should discharge him. But it strikes me John Pinder is•fond of doing things on his own head," concluded Treve, sagaciously ; " and that he will do them, in spite of mamma, now there's no master over him."

The day soon passed. George told his mamma how terribly he disliked being where he was placed ; worse than that, how completely unsuited he believed he was to the business. Mrs. Ryle coldly said we all had to put up with what we disliked, and that he would get reconciled to it in time. There was evidently no hope for him ; and he returned to Barmester at night, feeling that there was not.

On the following afternoon, Monday, some one in deep mourning entered the shop of Wall and Barnes, and asked if she could speak to Master Ryle. George was at the upper end of the shop. A box of lace had been accidentally upset on the floor, and he had been called to set it to rights. Behind him hung two shawls, open, and further back, hidden by those shawls, was a private desk, belonging to Mr. Wall. The visitor approached George and saluted him.

"Well, you *are* busy!"

George lifted his head at the well-known voice— Nora's. Her attention appeared chiefly attracted by the box of lace.

"What a mess it is in! And you don't go a bit handy to work, towards putting it tidy."

"I shall never be handy at this sort of work. Oh, Nora! I cannot tell you how I dislike it!" he exclaimed, with a burst of feeling that betrayed its own pain. "I'd rather be with papa in his coffin!"

"Don't talk nonsense!" said Nora.

"It is not nonsense. I shall never care for anything again in life, now they have put me here. It was Chattaway's doings; you know it was, Nora. Mamma never would have thought of it. When I remember that papa would have objected to this for me just as strongly as I object to it for myself, I can hardly *bear* my thoughts. I think how he will be grieved, if he can see what goes on in this world. You know he said something about that when he was dying—the dead retaining their consciousness of the doings here."

"Have you objected to be bound?"

"I have not objected. I don't mean to object.

Papa charged me to obey Mrs. Ryle, and not cross her—and I won't forget that; therefore I shall remain, and do my duty to the very best of my power. But it was a cruel thing to put me to it. Chattaway has some motive for getting me off the farm; there's no doubt of it. I shall stay if—if——"

"Why do you hesitate?" asked Nora.

"Well, there are moments," he answered, "when a fear comes over me whether I *can* bear on, and stay. You see, Nora, it is Chattaway's and mamma's will balancing against all the hopes and prospects of my life. I know that my father charged me to obey mamma; but on the other hand, I know that if he were alive he would be pained to see me here; would be the first to snatch me away. When these thoughts come forcibly upon me, I doubt whether I can stay."

"You must not encourage them," said Nora.

"I don't think I encourage them. But they come in spite of me. The fear comes; it is always coming. Don't say anything to mamma, Nora. I have made my mind up to stop, and I'll try hard to do it. As soon as I am out of my time I'll go off to India, or somewhere, and forget the old life in a new one."

"My goodness me!" uttered Nora. But having no good answering arguments at hand, she thought it as well to leave him, and took her departure.

The day arrived on which George was to be bound. It was a gloomy November day, and the tall chimneys of Barmester rose dark and dull and dismal against the outlines of the grey sky. The previous night had been a hopelessly wet one, and the mud in the streets was ankle-deep. People who had no urgent occasion to be abroad, drew closer to their comfortable firesides, and wished the dreary month of November was over.

George stood at the door of the shop, having snatched a moment to come to it. A slender, handsome boy, he was, with his earnest eyes and his dark chestnut hair, looking too gentlemanly to belong to that shop. Belong to it! Ere the stroke of another hour should have been told on the dial of the church clock of Barmester, he would be bound to it by an irrevocable bond— have become as much a part and parcel of it as the silks that were displayed in its windows, as the shawls which exhibited themselves in all their gay and gaudy colours. As he stood there, he was feeling that no fate on earth was ever so hopelessly dark as his: he was feeling that he had no friend either in earth or heaven.

One, two; three, four! chimed out over the town through the leaden atmosphere. Half-past

eleven ! It was the hour fixed for the signing of
the indentures which would bind him to servitude
for years ; and he, Geòrge Ryle, looked to the
extremity of the street, expecting the appearance
of Mr. Chattaway.

Considering the manner in which Mr. Chattaway had urged the binding on, George had
thought he would be half an hour before the
hour, rather than five minutes beyond it. He
looked eagerly to the extremity of the street, at
the same time dreading the sight he sought for.

"George Ryle !" The call came ringing on
his ears in a sharp, imperative tone, and he
turned in, in obedience to it. He was told to
" measure those trimmings, and card them."

An apparently interminable task. About fifty
pieces of ribbon-trimmings, some scores of yards
in each piece, all off their cards. George sighed
as he singled out one and began upon it—he was
terribly awkward at the work.

It advanced slowly. In addition to the inap-
titude of his fingers for the task, to his intense
natural distaste of it—and so intense was that
distaste, that the ribbons felt as if they burnt his
fingers—in addition to this, there were frequent
interruptions. Any of the shopmen who wanted
help called to George Ryle ; and once he was
told to open the door for a lady who was de-

parting. On that cold, gloomy day, the doors were kept shut.

As the lady walked away, George leaned out, and took another gaze. Mr. Chattaway was not in sight. The clocks were then striking the quarter to twelve. A feeling of something like hope, but vague and faint, and terribly unreal, dawned over his heart. Could the delay augur good for him?—was it possible that there could be any change?

How unreal it was, the next moment proved to him. There came round that far corner a horseman at a hand-gallop, his horse's hoofs scattering the mud in all directions. It was Mr. Chattaway. He reined up at the private door of Wall and Barnes, dismounted, and consigned his horse to his groom, who had followed at the same pace, splashing the mud also. The false, faint hope was over; and George walked back to his cards and his trimmings, like one from whom the spirit has gone out.

A message was brought to him almost immediately by one of the house servants: Squire Chattaway waited in the drawing-room. Squire Chattaway had sent the message himself, not to George; to Mr. Wall. But Mr. Wall was engaged at the moment with a gentleman, and he sent the message on to George. George went up-stairs.

Mr. Chattaway, in his top boots and spurs, stood warming his hands over the fire. He had not removed his hat. When the door opened, he raised his hand to do so; but seeing it was only George who entered, he left it on. He was much given to the old-fashioned use of boots and spurs when he rode abroad.

"Well, George, how are you?"

George went up to the fire-place. On the centre table, as he passed it, lay an official-looking parchment rolled up, a large inkstand with writing materials by its side. George had not the least doubt that the parchment was no other than that formidable document, yclept Indentures.

Mr. Chattaway had taken up the same opinion. He extended his riding-whip towards the parchment, and spoke in a significant tone, turning his eye on George.

"Ready?"

"It is no use attempting to say I am not," replied George. "I would rather you had forced me to be one of the lowest boys in your coal mines, Mr. Chattaway."

"What's this?" asked Mr. Chattaway.

He was pointing now to the upper part of the sleeve of George's jacket. Some ravellings of cotton had collected there unnoticed. George took them off, and put them on the fire.

"It is only a mark of my trade, Mr. Chatta-way."

Whether Mr. Chattaway detected the bitterness of the words—not the bitterness of sarcasm, but of despair—cannot be told. He laughed plea-santly, and before the laugh was over, Mr. Wall came in. Mr. Chattaway removed his hat now, and laid it with his riding-whip alongside of the indentures.

"I am later than I ought to be," observed Mr. Chattaway, as they shook hands. "The fact is, I was on the point of starting, when my manager at the colliery came up. His business was im-portant, and it kept me the best part of an hour."

"Plenty of time; plenty of time," said Mr. Wall. "Take a seat."

They sat down near the table. George, appa-rently unnoticed, remained standing on the hearthrug. A few minutes were spent con-versing on different subjects, and then Mr. Chat-taway turned to the parchment.

"These are the indentures, I presume?"

"Yes."

"I called on Mrs. Ryle last evening. She requested me to say that should her signature be required, as the boy's nearest relative and guar-dian—as his only parent, it may be said, in fact

—she should be ready to affix it at any given time."

" It will not be required," replied Mr. Wall, in a clear voice. " I shall not take George Ryle as an apprentice."

A stolid look of surprise struggled to Mr. Chattaway's leaden face. At first, he scarcely seemed to take in the full meaning of the words. " Not take him ? " he rejoined, staring helplessly.

" No. It is a pity these were made out," continued Mr. Wall, taking the indentures in his hand. " It has been so much time and paper wasted. However, that is not of great consequence. I will be at the loss, as the refusal comes from my side."

Mr. Chattaway found his tongue—found it volubly. " Won't he do ? Is he not suitable ? I—I don't understand this."

" Not at all suitable, in my opinion," answered Mr. Wall.

Mr. Chattaway turned sharply upon George, a strangely evil look in his dull grey eye, an ominous twist in his thin, dry lip. Mr. Wall likewise turned ; but on his face there was a reassuring smile.

And George ? George stood there as one in a dream ; his face changing to perplexity, his eyes strained to wonder, his fingers intertwined with the nervous grasp of emotion.

"What have you been guilty of, sir, to cause this change of intentions?" shouted Mr. Chattaway.

"He has not been guilty at all," interposed Mr. Wall, who appeared to be enjoying a smile at George's bewildered astonishment and Mr. Chattaway's discomfiture. "Don't blame the boy. So far as I know and believe, he has striven to do his best ever since he has been here."

"Then why won't you take him? You *will* take him," added Mr. Chattaway, in a more agreeable voice, as the idea dawned upon him that Mr. Wall had been joking.

"Indeed, I will not. If Mrs. Ryle offered me £1000 premium with him, I should not take him."

Mr. Chattaway's small eyes opened to their utmost width. "And why would you not?"

"Because, knowing what I know now, I believe that I should be committing an injustice upon the boy ; an injustice which nothing could repair. To condemn a youth to pass the best years of his life at an uncongenial pursuit, to make the pursuit his calling, is a cruel injustice, wherever it is knowingly inflicted. I myself was a victim to it."

"My boy," added Mr. Wall, laying his hand on George's shoulder, " you have a marked distaste to the silk mercery business. Is it not so ? Speak out fearlessly. Don't regard me as your master —I shall never be that, you hear—but as your friend?"

"Yes, I have," replied George.

"You think it a cruel piece of injustice to have put you to it: you shall never more feel an interest in life; you'd as soon be with poor Mr. Ryle in his coffin! And when you are out of your time, you mean to start for India or some out-of-the-world place, and begin life afresh!"

George was too much confused to answer. His face turned scarlet. Undoubtedly Mr. Wall had heard his conversation with Nora.

Mr. Chattaway was looking red and angry. When his face did turn red, it presented a charming hue of brick-dust, garnished with yellow. "It is only scamps who take a dislike to what they are put to," he exclaimed. "And their dislike is all pretence."

"I differ from you in both propositions," replied Mr. Wall. "At any rate, I do not think it the case with your nephew."

Mr. Chattaway's salmon colour turned to green. "He is no nephew of mine. What next will you say, Wall?"

"Your step-nephew, then, to be correct," equably rejoined Mr. Wall. "You remember when we left school together, you and I, and began to turn our thoughts to the business of life? Your father wished you to go into the bank as clerk, you know; and mine——"

"But he did not get his wish, more's the luck," again interposed Mr. Chattaway, not pleased at the allusion. "A poor start in life that would have been for the future squire of Trevlyn Hold."

"Pooh!" rejoined Mr. Wall, in a good-tempered, matter-of-fact tone. "You did not look forward then to be exalted to Trevlyn Hold. Nonsense, Chattaway! We are old friends, you know. But, let me continue. I heard a certain conversation of this boy's with Nora Dickson, and it seemed to bring my own early life back to me. With every word that he spoke, I had a fellow feeling. My father insisted that I should follow the same business that he was in; this. He carried on a successful trade for years, in this very house; and nothing would do but I must succeed him in it. I vain I urged my repugnance to it, my dislike; in vain I said I had formed other views for myself; I was not listened to. In those days it was not the fashion for sons to run counter to their fathers' will; at least, such was my experience; and into the business I came. I have reconciled myself to it by dint of time and habit; liked it, I never have; and I have always felt that it was—as I heard this boy express it—a cruel wrong to force me into it. You cannot, therefore, be surprised that I decline so to force another. I will never do it knowingly."

"You decline absolutely to take him?" asked Mr. Chattaway.

"Absolutely and positively. He can remain in the house a few days longer if it will suit his convenience, or he can leave to-day. I am not displeased with you," added Mr. Wall, turning to George and holding out his hand. "We shall part good friends."

George seized it and grasped it, his countenance glowing, a whole world of gratitude shining forth from his eyes as he lifted them to Mr. Wall. "I shall always think you have been the best friend I ever had, sir, next to my father."

"I hope it will prove so, George. I hope you will find some pursuit in life more congenial to you than this."

Mr. Chattaway took his hat and his whip from the table. "This will be fine news for your mother, sir!" cried he severely to George.

"It may turn out well for her," replied George, boldly. "My belief is that the farm never would have got along with John Pinder for its manager."

"You think you would make a better?" said Mr. Chattaway, his thin lip curling.

"I can be true to her, at any rate," said George. "And I can have my eyes about me."

"Good morning," resumed Mr. Chattaway to Mr. Wall, putting out unwillingly the tips of two of his fingers.

Mr. Wall laughed as he grasped them. "I do not see why you should be vexed, Mr. Chattaway. The boy is no son of yours. For myself, all I can say is, that I have been actuated by motives of regard for his interest."

"It remains to be proved whether it will be for his interest," coldly rejoined Mr. Chattaway. "Were I his mother, and this check were dealt out to me, I should send him off to break stones on the road. Good morning, Wall. And I beg you will not bring me here again upon a fool's errand."

George went into the shop, to get from it some few personal trifles that he had left there. He deemed it well to depart at once, and carry, himself, the news home to Mrs. Ryle. The cards and trimmings lay in the unfinished state that he had left them. What a change, that moment and this! One or two of the employés noticed his radiant countenance.

"Has anything happened?" they asked.

"Yes," answered George. "I have been suddenly lifted into elysium."

He started on his way, leaving his things to be sent after him. His footsteps scarcely touched the ground. Not a rough ridge of the road, felt he ; not a sharp stone ; not a hill ; it seemed like a smooth, soft bowling-green. Only when he turned in at the gate did he remember there was his mother's displeasure to be met and grappled with.

Nora gave a shriek when he entered the house. "*George!* whatever brings you here?"

"Where's mamma?" was George's only answer.

"She's in the best parlour," said Nora. "And I can tell you that she's not in the best of humours just now, so I'd advise you not to go in."

"What about?" asked George, taking it for granted that she had heard the news of himself, and that that was the grievance. But he was agreeably undeceived.

"It's about John Pinder. He has been having two of the meads ploughed up, and he never asked the missis first. She *is* angry."

"Has Chattaway been here to see mamma, Nora?"

"He came up here on horseback in a desperate hurry half-an-hour ago ; but she was out on the farm, so he said he'd call again. It was through her going abroad this morning that she discovered what they were about with the fields. She says she thinks John Pinder must be going out of his mind; to take things upon himself, in the way he is doing."

George bent his steps to the drawing-room. Mrs. Ryle was seated before her desk, writing a note. The expression of her face, as she looked up at George between the white lappets of her widow's cap, was resolutely severe. It changed to astonishment.

Strange to say she was writing to Mr. Wall to stop the signature of the indentures, or to desire they might be cancelled if signed. She could not do without George at home, she said; and she told him why she could not.

"Mamma," said George, "will you be angry if I tell you something that has struck me in all this?"

"Tell it," said Mrs. Ryle.

"I feel quite certain that Chattaway has been acting with a motive; that he has some private reason for wishing to get me away from home. That's what he has been working for; otherwise he would never have troubled himself about me. It is not in his nature."

Mrs. Ryle gazed at George steadfastly, as if weighing his words, and presently knitted her brow. George could read her countenance tolerably well. He felt sure she had arrived at a similar conclusion, and that it irritated her. He resumed.

"It looks bad for you, mamma; but you mus not think I say this selfishly. Twenty times I have asked myself the question, Why does he wish me away? And I can only think that he would like the farm to go to rack and ruin, so that you may be driven off it."

"Nonsense, George."

"Well, I can't tell what else it can be."

"If so, he is defeated," said Mrs. Ryle. "You will take your place as master of the farm to-day, George, under me. Deferring to me in all things, you understand; giving no orders on your own responsibility, taking my pleasure upon the merest trifle."

"I should not think of doing otherwise," replied George. "I will do my best for you in all ways, mamma. You will soon see how useful I can be."

"Very well. But I may as well mention one thing to you. When Treve shall be old enough, it is he who will be the master here, and you must resign the place to him. It is not that I wish to set the younger of your father's sons unjustly above the head of the elder. This farm will be a living but for one of you; barely that; and I prefer that Treve should have it; he is

my own son. We will endeavour to find a better
arm for you, George, before that time shall
come."

"Just as you please," said George, cheerfully.
"Now that I am emancipated from that dreadful
nightmare, my prospects look of a bright rose-
colour. I'll do the best I can on the farm, remem-
bering that I do it for Treve's future benefit; not
for mine. Something else will turn up for me, no
doubt, before I'm ready for it."

"Which will not be for some years to come,
George," said Mrs. Ryle, feeling pleased with the
boy's cheerful, acquiescent spirit. "Treve will not
be old enough for —— "

Mrs. Ryle was interrupted. The room door had
opened, and there appeared Mr. Chattaway, showing himself in. Nora never affected to be too
courteous to that gentleman; and on his coming
to the house to ask for Mrs. Ryle a second time,
she had curtly answered that Mrs. Ryle was in the
best parlour (the more familiar name for the drawing-room in the farm-house), and allowed him to
find his own way to it.

Mr. Chattaway looked surprised at seeing
George; he had not bargained for his arriving
at home so soon. Extending his hand towards
him, he turned to Mrs. Ryle.

"There's a dutiful son for you! You hear

what he has done ?—that he has returned on your hands as a bale of worthless goods."

"Yes, I hear that Mr. Wall has declined to take him," was her composed answer. "It has happened for the best. When he arrived just now, I was writing to Mr. Wall, requesting that he might *not* be bound."

"And why ? " asked Mr. Chattaway, in considerable amazement.

"I find that I am unable to do without him," said Mrs. Ryle, her tone harder and firmer than ever ; her eyes, stern and steady, thrown full on Chattaway. "I tried the experiment, and it has failed. I cannot do without one by my side devoted to my interests ; and John Pinder cannot get along without a master."

"And do you think you'll find what you want in him !—in that inexperienced schoolboy ? " burst forth Mr. Chattaway.

"I do," replied Mrs. Ryle, her tone so significantly decisive as to be almost offensive. "He takes his standing from this day, the master of Trevlyn Farm ; subject only to me."

"I wish you joy of him ! " angrily returned Chattaway. "But you must understand, Mrs. Ryle, that your having a boy at the head of affairs will oblige me to look more keenly after my interests."

"My arrangements with you are settled," she said. "So long as I fulfil my part, that is all that concerns you, James Chattaway."

"You'll not fulfil it, if you put him at the head of things."

"When I fail, you can come here and tell me of it. Until then, I would prefer that you should not intrude on Trevlyn Farm."

She rang the bell violently as she spoke, and Molly, who was passing along the passage, immediately appeared, staring and wondering. Mrs. Ryle extended her hand imperiously, the forefinger pointed out.

"The door for Mr. Chattaway."

CHAPTER X.

MADAM'S ROOM.

LEADING out of the dressing-room of Mrs. Chat taway was a moderate-sized, comfortable apartment, fitted up as a sitting-room, its hangings of chintz, and its furniture maple-wood. It was called in the household " Madam's Room," and it was where Mrs. Chattaway frequently sat. Yes; the house and the neighbourhood accorded her readily the title which usage had long given to the mistress of Trevlyn Hold : but they would not give that of "Squire" to her husband. I wish particularly to repeat this. Strive for it as he would, force his personal servants to observe the title as he did, he could not get it recognised or adopted. When a written invitation came to the Hold—a rare event, for the good old-fashioned custom of inviting by word of mouth was mostly followed there—it would be worded, " Mr. and Madam Chattaway," and Chattaway's face turned green as he read it. No, never! He enjoyed the substantial good of being the proprietor of Trevlyn Hold, he received its revenues, he held sway as its lord and master; but its honours were not given to him. Which was so much gall and wormwood to Chattaway.

Mrs. Chattaway stood at this window on that dull morning in November mentioned in the last chapter, her eyes strained outwards. What was she gazing on? On those lodge chimneys?—on the dark and nearly bare trees that waved to and fro in the wintry wind?—on the extensive landscape stretching out in the distance, not fine to-day, but dull and cheerless?—or on the shifting clouds of the grey skies? Not on any of these; her eyes, though apparently bent on all, in reality saw none. They were fixed in vacancy; buried like her thoughts, inwards.

She wore a muslin gown with dark purple spots upon it; her collar was fastened with a bow of black ribbon, her sleeves were confined with black ribbons at the wrist. She was passing a finger underneath one of these wrist-ribbons, round and round, as if the ribbon were tight; in point of fact, it was a proof of her abstraction, and she knew not that she was doing it. Her smooth hair fell in curls on her fair face, and her blue eyes were bright as with a slight touch of inward fever.

Some one opened the door, and peeped in. It wás Maude Trevlyn. Her frock was of the same material as the gown of Mrs. Chattaway, and a sash of black ribbon encircled her waist. Mrs. Chattaway did not turn, and Maude came forward.

"Are you well to-day, Aunt Edith?"

"Not very, dear." Mrs. Chattaway took the pretty young head within her arm as she answered, and fondly stroked the bright curls. "You have been crying, Maude!"

Maude shook back her curls with a smile, as if she meant to be brave; to make light of the accusation. "Cris and Octave went on so shamefully, Aunt Edith, ridiculing George Ryle; and when I took his part, Cris hit me here"—pointing to the side of her face—"a sharp blow. It was stupid of me to cry, though."

"Cris did?" exclaimed Mrs. Chattaway.

"But I know I provoked him," candidly acknowledged Maude. "I'm afraid I got into a passion; and you know, Aunt Edith, I don't mind what I say when I do get into one.. I told Cris that he would be placed at something not half as good as a linendraper's some time, for he'd want a living when Rupert came into Trevlyn Hold."

"Maude! Maude! hush!" exclaimed Mrs. Chattaway in a tone of terror. "You must not say that."

"I know I must not, Aunt Edith; I know it is wrong; wrong to think it, and foolish to say it. It was my temper. I am very sorry."

She nestled close to Mrs. Chattaway, caressing and penitent. Mrs. Chattaway stooped and kissed her, a strangely-marked expression of tribulation, of tribulation shrinking and hopeless, upon her countenance.

"Oh, Maude! I am so ill!"

Maude felt awed; and somewhat puzzled. "Ill, Aunt Edith?"

"There is an illness of mind worse than that of body, Maude; inward trouble is more wearing than outward, child! I feel as though I should sink; sink under my weight of care. Sometimes I wonder why I am kept on earth."

"Oh, Aunt Edith! You——"

A knocking at the room door. It was followed by the entrance of the upper part of a female servant's face. She could not see Mrs. Chattaway; only Maude.

"Is Miss Diana here, Miss Maude?"

"No. Only Madam."

"What is it, Phœbe?" called out Mrs. Chattaway.

The girl came in now. "Master Cris wants to know if he can take out the gig, ma'am?"

"I cannot tell anything about it," said Mrs.

Chattaway. "You must ask Miss Diana. Maude,
see; that is your Aunt Diana's step on the stairs
now."

Miss Trevlyn came in. "The gig?" she repeated. "No; Cris cannot take it. Go and tell
him so, Maude. Phœbe, return to your work."

Maude ran away, and Phœbe went off grumbling, not aloud, but to herself; nobody dared
grumble in the hearing of Miss Trevlyn. She had
spoken in a sharp tone to Phœbe, and the girl did
not like sharp tones when addressed to herself.
As Miss Trevlyn sat down opposite Mrs. Chattaway, the feverish state of that lady's countenance
struck upon her attention.

"What is the matter, Edith?"

Mrs. Chattaway buried her elbow on the sofa-
cushion, and pressed her hand on her face, half
covering it, before she spoke. "I cannot get over
this business," she answered in a low tone. "To-
day—perhaps naturally—I am feeling it more
than is good for me. It makes me ill, Diana."

"What business?" asked Miss Trevlyn.

"This binding out of George Ryle."

"Nonsense," said Miss Diana.

"It is not the proper thing for him, Diana;
you admitted yesterday that it was not. The boy
says that it is the blighting of his whole future
life: and I feel that it is nothing less. I could

not sleep last night for thinking of it. Once I dozed off, and fell into an ugly dream :" she shivered. " I thought Mr. Ryle came to me, and asked whether it was not enough that we had heaped care upon him in life, and then sent him to his death, but we must pursue his son."

" You always were weak, you know, Edith," was the composed rejoinder of Miss Trevlyn. " Why Chattaway should be interfering with George Ryle, I cannot understand ; but it surely need not give concern to you. The proper person to put a veto on his being placed at Barmester, as he is being placed, was Maude Ryle. If she did not see fit to do it, it is no business of ours."

" It seems to me as if he had no one to stand up for him. It seems," added Mrs. Chattaway, with more of passion in her tone, " as if his father must be looking on at us and condemning us from his grave."

" If you will worry yourself over it, you must," was the rejoinder of Miss Trevlyn. " It is very foolish, Edith, and it can do no earthly good. He is bound by this time, and the thing is irrevocable."

" Perhaps that is the reason—because it is irrevocable—that it presses upon me to-day with a greater weight. It has made me think of the past, Diana," she added in a whisper. " Of that other wrong, which I cheat myself sometimes into forgetting; a wrong——"

"Be silent!" imperatively interrupted Miss Trevlyn, and the next moment Cris Chattaway bounded into the room.

"What's the reason I can't have the gig?" he began. "Who says I can't have it?"

"I do," said Miss Trevlyn.

Cris insolently turned from her, and walked up to Mrs. Chattaway. "May I not take the gig, mamma?"

If one thing irritated the sweet temper of Mrs. Chattaway, it was the being appealed to against any decision of Diana's. She knew that she possessed no power; that she was a nonentity in the house; and though she bowed to her dependency, and had no resource but to bow to it, she did not like it to be brought palpably before her.

"Don't apply to me, Cris. I know nothing about things down-stairs; I cannot say, one way or the other. The horses and vehicles are the things in particular that your papa will not have meddled with. Do you remember taking out the dog-cart without leave, and the result?"

Cris looked angry; perhaps the reminiscence was not agreeable. Miss Diana interfered.

"You will *not* take out the gig, Cris.. I have said it."

"Then see if I don't walk! And if I am not home to dinner, Aunt Diana, you can just tell the squire that the thanks are due to you."

"Where is it that you wish to go?" asked Mrs. Chattaway.

"I am going to Barmester. I want to wish that fellow joy of his indentures," added Cris, a glow of triumph lighting his face. "He is bound by this time. I wonder the squire is not back again!"

The squire was back again. As Cris spoke, his tread was heard on the stairs, and he came into the room. Cris was too full of his own concerns to note the expression of Mr. Chattaway's face.

"Papa, may I take out the gig? I want to go to Barmester, to pay a visit of congratulation to George Ryle."

"No, you will not take out the gig," said Mr. Chattaway, the allusion exciting his vexation almost beyond bearing.

Cris thought he might have been misunderstood. Cris deemed that his proclaimed intention would find favour with Mr. Chattaway.

"I suppose you have been binding that fellow, papa, I want to go and ask him how he likes it."

"No, sir, I have not been binding him," thundered Mr. Chattaway. "What's more, he is not going to be bound. He has left it, and is at home again."

Cris gave a blank stare of puzzled wonderment, and Mrs. Chattaway let her hands fall silently upon her lap, and heaved a gentle sigh, as if some great good had come to her.

CHAPTER XI.

LIKE THE SLIPPERS IN THE EASTERN STORY.

NONE of us can stand still in life. Everything rolls on its course towards the end of all things. The world goes on ; its events go on ; we go on, in one universal progress : nothing can arrest itself—nothing can be diverted from the appointed laws of progression.

In noting down a family's or a life's history, it must of necessity occur that periods in it will be differently marked. Years at times will glide quietly on, giving forth little of event in them worthy of record ; while, again, it will happen that occurrences, varied and momentous, will be crowded into an incredibly short space. Events, sufficient one would think to fill up the allotted life of man—threescore years and ten—will follow one another in rapid succession in the course of as many months. Nay, of as many days.

Thus it was with the history of the Trevlyns, and those connected with them. After the lamentable death of Mr. Ryle, the new agreement touching money matters between Mr. Chattaway and Mrs. Ryle, and the settlement of George Ryle in his own home, it may be said in his father's place, little occurred for some years worthy of note. Time seemed to pass on uneventfully. The girls and the boys grew into men and women; the little children into growing-up girls and boys. Cris Chattaway lorded it in his own offensive manner as the squire's son—as the future squire; his sister Octavia was not more amiable than of yore, and Maude Trevlyn was governess to Mr. and Mrs. Chattaway's younger children. Miss Diana Trevlyn had taken care that Maude should be well educated, and she paid the expenses of it from her own pocket, in spite of Mr. Chattaway's sneers. When Maude was eighteen years of age, the question arose, What shall be done with her? " She shall go out and be a governess," said Mr. Chattaway. " Where will be the profit of all her fine education, if it's not to be made use of ? " " No," dissented Miss Diana; " a Trevlyn cannot be sent out in the world to earn her own living : our family have not come to that." "I won't keep her in idleness," growled Chattaway. " Very well," said Miss Diana; " make her governess to your girls, Edith and Emily : it will save the cost of their schooling." And the advice was taken;

and Maude for the past three years now had been governess at Trevlyn Hold.

But Rupert? Rupert was not found to be so easily disposed of. There's no knowing what Chattaway, in his ill-feeling, might have put Rupert to, had he been free to place him as he pleased. If he had not shown any superfluous consideration in the placing out of George Ryle— or rather in the essaying to place him out—it was not likely he would show it to one whom he hated as he hated Rupert. But here Miss Diana stepped in, as she had done with regard to Maude. Rupert was a Trevlyn, she said, and consequently could not be converted into a chimney-sweep or a shoe-black : he must get his living at something more befitting his degree. Chattaway demurred, but he knew better than to run counter to any mandate issued by Diana Trevlyn.

Several things were tried for Rupert. He was placed with a clergyman to study for the Church; he went to an LL.D. to read for the Bar ; he was consigned to a wealthy grazier, to be made into a farmer ; he was posted off to Sir John Rennet, to be initiated into the science of civil engineering. And he came back from all. As one after the other venture was made, so it failed, and a very short space of time would see Rupert returned as ineligible to Trevlyn Hold. Ineligible!

Was he deficient in capacity? No. He was only deficient in that one great blessing, without which life can bring no enjoyment—health. In his weakness of chest and lungs—in his liability to take cold—in his suspiciously delicate frame, Rupert Trevlyn was ominously like his dead father. The clergyman, the doctor of laws, the hearty grazier, and the far-famed engineer, thought after a month's trial that they would rather not take charge of him. He had a fit of illness—it may be better to say of weakness—in the house of each; and they, no doubt, one and all, deemed that a pupil predisposed to disease—it may be almost said to death—as Rupert Trevlyn appeared to be, would bring with him too much of responsibility.

So, times and again, Rupert was returned on the hands of Mr. Chattaway. To describe that gentleman's wrath would take a pen dipped in gall. Was Rupert *never* to be got rid of? It was as the slippers in the well-read Eastern story, which persisted in turning up, their unhappy owner knew not how. From the bottom of the sea—from a grave dug deep in the earth—from a roaring furnace of fire—up came those miserable slippers again and again. And up came Rupert Trevlyn. The boy could not help his ill-health; but you may be sure Mr. Chattaway's favour to

him was not increased. "I shall put him in the
office at Blackstone," said he. And Miss Diana
acquiesced.

Blackstone was the name of the locality where
Mr. Chattaway's mines were situated. An appropriate name, for the place was black enough, and
stony enough, and dreary enough for anything.
A low, barren, level country, its utter flatness
alone broken by the signs of the pits, its uncompromising gloom enlivened only by the ascending
fires which blazed up near the pits at night, and
illumined the country for miles round. The pits
were not all of coal: iron mines and other mines
were scattered with them. On Chattaway's
property, however, there was coal alone. Long
rows of houses, as dreary as the barren country,
were built near: they were occupied by the
workers in the mines. The overseer or manager
for Mr. Chattaway was named Pinder, a brother
to John Pinder, who was on Mrs. Ryle's farm;
but Chattaway chose to interfere very much with
the executive of things himself, and may almost
have been called his own overseer. He had an
office near to the pits, in which accounts were
kept, the men paid, and other items of business
transacted; a low building, of one story only,
consisting of three or four rooms. In this office
he kept one regular clerk, a young man named

Ford, and into this same office he put Rupert Trevlyn. But many and many and many a day was Rupert ailing; weak, sick, feverish, coughing, and unable to go to it. But for Diana Trevlyn, Chattaway might have driven him thither, sick or well. Not that Miss Diana possessed any extraordinary affection for Rupert: she did not keep him at home from love, or from motives of indulgence. But hard, cold, and imperious though she was, Miss Diana owned somewhat of the large open-handedness of the Trevlyns: she could not be guilty of trivial spite, of petty meanness. She ruled the servants with an iron hand; but in case of their falling into sickness or trouble, she had them generously well cared for. So with respect to Rupert. It may be that she regarded him as an interloper; that she would have been better pleased were he removed far away. She had helped to deprive him of his birthright, but she did not treat him with personal unkindness; and she would have been the last to say he must go out to his daily occupation, if he felt ill or incapable of it. She deplored his ill-health; but, the ill-health upon him, Miss Diana was not one to ignore it, to reproach him with it, or to put hindrances in the way of his being nursed.

It was a tolerably long walk for Rupert in a morning to Blackstone. Cris Chattaway, when he chose to go over, rode on horseback ; and Mr. Cris did not unfrequently choose to go over, for he had the same propensity as his father had—that of throwing himself into every petty detail, and interfering unwarrantably. In disposition, father and son were alike—mean, stingy, grasping. To save a sixpence, Chattaway would almost have sacrificed a miner's life. Improvements which other mine owners had introduced into their pits, into the working of them, Chattaway held aloof from. In his own person, however, Cris was not disposed to spare entirely. He had his horse, and he had his servant, and he favoured an extensive wardrobe, and was given altogether to various little odds and ends of self-indulgence.

Yes, Cris Chattaway rode to Blackstone ; with his groom behind him sometimes, when he chose to make a dash ; and Rupert Trevlyn walked. Better that the order of travelling had been reversed, for that walk, morning and evening, was not too good for Rupert in his weakly state. He would feel it particularly in an evening. It was a gradual ascent nearly all the way from Blackstone to Trevlyn Hold, almost imperceptible to a strong man, but sufficiently apparent to Rupert Trevlyn, who would be fatigued with the day's work.

Not that he had hard work to do. The sitting only on the stool at the office tired him. Another thing that tired him—and which, no doubt, was for him excessively pernicious—was the deprivation of his regular meals.   Except on Sundays, or on those days when he was not well enough to leave Trevlyn Hold, he had no dinner : what he got at Blackstone was but an apology for one. The clerk, Ford, who lived at nearly as great a distance from the place as Rupert, used to cook himself a piece of steak at the office grate.   But that the coals were lying about in heaps and cost nothing, Chattaway might have objected to the fire being used for any such purpose.   Rupert occasionally cooked himself some steak ; but he more frequently dined upon bread and cheese, or upon some cold scraps brought from Trevlyn Hold. *It was not often that Rupert had the money necessary to buy the steak,* his supply of that indispensable commodity, the current coin of the realm, being of the most limited extent. Deprived of his dinner, deprived of his tea—tea being generally over when he got back to the Hold—that, of itself, was almost sufficient to bring on the disease feared for Rupert Trevlyn. One of sound constitution, revelling in hearty health and strength, might not have been much the worse for the deprivation in the long run ; but Rupert did not come under the head of that favoured class of humanity.

It was a bright day in that mellow season when the summer is merging into autumn. A few fields of the later sort of grain were lying out yet, but most of the golden store had been gathered into its barns. The sunlight glistened on the leaves of the trees, lighting up their rich tints of brown and red—tints which never come until the season of passing away.

Halting at a stile which led from a lane into a field white with stubble, were two children and a young lady. Not very much of children, either, for the younger of the two must have been thirteen. Pale girls both, with light hair, and just now a disagreeable expression of countenance. They were insisting upon crossing that stile to go through the field: one of them, in fact, was already mounted on it, and they did not like the denial that was being dealt out to them.

"You cross old thing!" cried she on the stile, turning her head to make a face at the lady who was interposing her veto. "You always object to our going where we want to go. What dislike have you to the field, pray, that we may not cross it?"

"I have no dislike to it, Emily. I am but obeying your papa's injunctions. You know he has forbidden you to go on the lands of Mrs. Ryle."

She spoke in a calm tone ; in a sweet, persuasive, gentle voice. She had a sweet and gentle
face, too, with its delicate features, and its large
blue eyes. It is Maude Trevlyn, grown into a
woman. Eight years have passed since you last
saw her, and she is twenty-one. In spite of her
girlish and graceful figure, which scarcely reaches
to the middle height, she bears about her a look
of the Trevlyns. Her head is set well upon her
shoulders, thrown somewhat back, as you may see
in Miss Diana Trevlyn. She wore a grey flowing
cloak, and a pretty blue bonnet.

"The lands are not Mrs. Ryle's," contentiously
retorted the young lady on the stile. "They are
papa's."

"They are Mrs. Ryle's so long as she rents
them. It is all the same. Mr. Chattaway has
forbidden you to cross them. Come down from the
style, Emily."

"I shan't. I shall jump over it."

It was ever thus. Save when in the presence
of Miss Diana Trevlyn, the girls were openly rude
and disobedient to Maude. Expected, though she
was, to teach them, she was yet debarred from the
common authority vested in a governess. And
Maude could not emancipate herself: she must
suffer and submit.

Emily Chattaway put her foot over the top bar

of the stile, preparatory to carrying out her threat of jumping over it, when the near sound of a horse was heard, and she turned her head. Riding along the lane at a quick pace was a gentleman of some three or four-and-twenty years : a tall man, so far as could be seen, who sat his horse well. He reined in when he saw them, and bent down a pleasant face, with a pleasant smile upon it. The sun shone into his fine dark eyes, as he stooped to shake hands with Maude.

Maude's cheeks had turned to crimson. "Quite well," she stammered, in answer to his greeting, losing her self-possession in a remarkable degree. "When did you come home ?"

"Last night. I was away two days only, instead of the four anticipated. Miss Emily, you'll fall backwards if you don't mind."

"No, I shan't," said Emily. "Why did you not stay longer ?"

"I found Treve away when I reached Oxford, so I came back, and got home last night—to Nora's discomfiture."

Maude looked in his face with a questioning glance. She had quite recovered her self-possession. "Why ?" she asked.

George Ryle laughed. "Nora had turned my bed-room inside out. Nothing was in it but the boards, and they were wet. She accused me, in her vexation, of coming back on purpose."

"Did you sleep on the wet boards?" asked Emily.

"No, I slept in Treve's room. Take care, Edith!"

Maude hastily drew Edith Chattaway back. She had gone very near the horse. "How is Mrs. Ryle?" asked Maude. "We heard yesterday she was not well."

"She is suffering very much from a cold. I have scarcely seen her. Maude," he added, leaning down and speaking in a whisper, "are things any brighter?"

Again the soft colour came into her face, and she cast a glance from her dark blue eyes at his. If ever glance spoke of indignation, that did: not indignation at *him;* rather at the state of things in general—a state which he knew well. "What change can there be?" she breathed. "Rupert is ill again," she added, in a louder tone.

"Rupert!"

"At least, he is poorly, and is at home to-day. But he is better than he was yesterday——"

"Here comes Octave," interrupted Emily.

George Ryle put his horse in motion. Shaking hands with Maude, he said a hasty good-bye to the other two, and cantered down the lane, lifting his hat to Miss Chattaway, who was coming up at right angles from the distance.

She was advancing very quickly across the common, behind the fence on the other side of the lane. A tall, thin, bony young woman, looking her full age of four or five-and-twenty, with the same dull, leaden-coloured complexion as of yore, and the disagreeably sly grey eyes. She wore a puce silk paletot, as they are called, made coat fashion, and a brown hat with a black lace falling from its shading brim: an unbecoming costume for one so tall.

"That was George Ryle!" she exclaimed, as she came up. "What brings him back already?"

"He found his brother away when he reached Oxford," was Maude's reply.

"I think he was very rude, not to stop and speak to you, Octave," observed Emily Chattaway. "He saw you coming."

Octave made no reply. She mounted the stile by the side of Emily, and gazed after the horseman, apparently to see what direction he would take when he came to the end of the lane. Patiently watching, her hand shading her eyes from the sun, she saw him turn into another lane, which branched off to the left. Octave Chattaway jumped over the stile, and ran swiftly across the field.

"She's gone to meet him," was the comment of Emily.

It was precisely what Miss Chattaway *had* gone to do. Penetrating through a copse after quitting the field, she emerged from it out of breath, just as George was riding quietly past. He halted and stooped to shake hands with her, as he had done with Maude.

"You are out of breath, Octave. Have you been running to catch me?"

"I need not have run but for your great gallantry in riding off the moment you saw me," she answered, resentment in her tone.

"I beg your pardon. I did not know you wanted me. I was in a hurry."

"It seemed as if you were—by your stopping to speak so long to the children and Maude," she returned, with irony. And George Ryle's answering laugh was a conscious one.

There was an ever perpetual latent antagonism seated in the minds of them both. There was a latent consciousness of it running through their hearts. When George Ryle saw Octave hastening across the common, he knew as surely as though he had been told it, that she was speeding to come up ere he should be gone; when Octave saw him ride away, a sure voice whispered her that he so rode to avoid meeting her; and each felt that

their secret thoughts and motives were known to
the other.   Yes, there was constant antagonism
between them ; if the word may be applied to
Octave Chattaway, who had learnt to value more
highly than was good for her the society of George
Ryle.   Did he so value hers ?   Octave pined out
her heart, hoping for it.   But in the midst of her
unwise love for him ; in the midst of her never-
ceasing efforts to be in his presence, near to him,
anywhere that he was, there constantly arose the
bitter conviction that she was no more to him
than the idle wind ; there arose a bitter consciousness that he did not care for her.

"I wished to ask you about the book that you
promised to get me," she said. "Have you pro-
cured it ?"

"No; and I am sorry to say that I cannot meet
with it," replied George. "I thought of it at
Oxford, and went into every bookseller's shop in
the place, unsuccessfully.   I told you it was
difficult to be had.   I must get them to write to
London for it from Barmester."

"It is an insignificant book. It costs but three-
and-sixpence."

"True.   Its insignificance may be the explanation of its scarcity.   Good afternoon, Octave."

"Will you come to the Hold this evening ?" she
asked, as he was riding away.

"Thank you. I am not sure that I can. My day or two's absence has made me busy."

Octave Chattaway drew back under the cover of the trees, and there halted. She did not retreat until every trace of that fine young horseman whom she was gazing after, had faded from her sight in the distance.

CHAPTER XII.

A NIGHT BELL UNANSWERED.

It is singular to observe how lightly the wearing marks of Time sometimes pass over the human form and face. An instance of this might be seen in Mrs. Chattaway. It was strange that it should be so in her case. Her health was not good, and she certainly was not a happy woman. Illness was frequently her portion; care seemed to follow her perpetually; and it is upon these sufferers of mind and body that Time is fond of leaving his traces. He had not left them on Mrs. Chattaway; her face was fair and fresh as it had been eight years ago; her hair fell in its mass of curls; her eyes were still blue, and clear, and bright.

And yet anxiety was her constant companion. It may be said that remorse never left her. She would sit at the window of her room up-stairs — Madam's room — for hours, apparently contemplating the outer world; in reality seeing nothing.

As she was sitting now. The glories of the bright day had faded into twilight; the sun no longer lit up the many hues of the autumn foliage; the various familiar points in the charming landscape had revealed themselves into one indistinct line of a dusky colour; old Canham's chimneys at the lodge were becoming obscure, and the red light thrown up from the mines was beginning to show itself on the right in the extreme distance. Mrs. Chattaway leaned her elbow on the old-fashioned arm-chair as she sat in it, and rested her cheek upon her hand. Had you looked at her eyes, gazing out so pertinaciously where the past day had been, you might have seen that they had no speculation in them. They were deep in the world of thought.

That constitutional timidity of hers had been nothing but a blight to her throughout her life. Reticence in a woman is good; but not that timorous reticence which is the result of fear; which dare not speak up for itself, even to oppose a wrong. Every wrong inflicted upon Rupert Trevlyn—every unkindness showered down upon him—every pang of sickness, whether of mind or body, which happier circumstances might have spared to him, was avenged over and over again in the person of Mrs. Chattaway. It may be said that she lived but in pain; her life was one perpetual, never-ending aching—aching for Rupert.

In the old days, when her husband had chosen to deceive Squire Trevlyn as to the existence of Rupert, she had not dared to avow the truth, and say to her father, "There is an heir born." She dared not fly in the face of her husband, and say it; and, it may be, that she was too willingly silent for her husband's sake. It would seem strange, but that we know what fantastic tricks our passions play us, that pretty, gentle Edith Trevlyn should have *loved* that essentially disagreeable man, James Chattaway. But so it was. And, while deploring the fact of the wrong dealt out to Rupert—it may almost be said *expiating* it—Mrs. Chattaway never visited that wrong upon her husband, even in thought, as it ought to have been visited. None could realise more intensely its consequences than she realised them in her secret heart. Expiate it? Ay, she expiated it again and again, if her sufferings could only have been reckoned as expiation.

But they could not. *They* were enjoying Trevlyn Hold and its benefits, and Rupert was little better than an outcast on the face of the earth. Every dinner that was put upon their table, every article of expensive attire bought for their children, every mark of honour or substantial comfort which their position brought to them, seemed to rise up reproachfully before the face of Mrs. Chattaway, and say, "The money to procure all this is not yours and your husband's; it is wrenched from Rupert." And she could do nothing to remedy it; she could only wage ever-continued battle with the knowledge, and with the sting it brought. There existed no remedy. It was not simply that she could not apply a remedy, but there existed none to apply. They had not come into the inheritance by legal fraud or wrong: they succeeded to it fairly and openly, according to the legally-made will of Squire Trevlyn. Did the whole world range itself on Rupert's side, pressing that the property should be resigned to him, Mr. Chattaway had only to point with his finger to the will, and say, "You cannot act against that."

It may be that this very fact brought the remorse with greater force home to Mrs. Chattaway. It may be that her incessant dwelling upon it caused a morbid state of feeling, which of itself served to increase the malady. Certain it is, that by night and by day the wrongs of Rupert were ever pressing painfully on her mind. She loved him with that strange intensity which brings an aching to the heart. When the baby orphan was brought home to her from its foreign birth-place, the pretty baby with its rosy cheeks and its golden curls—when it put out its little arms to her, and gazed at her with its loving blue eyes, her heart gushed out to it there and then, and she caught it to her with a wail of love more passionately fond than any ever given to her own children. The irredeemable wrong inflicted on the unconscious child, fixed itself on her conscience in that hour, never to be lifted from it.

If ever a woman lived a two-faced life, that woman was Mrs. Chattaway. Her true aspect— that in which she saw herself as she really was— was as different from the one presented to the world as light is from darkness. Do not blame her. It was difficult to help it. The world and her own family saw in Mrs. Chattaway a weak, gentle, apathetic woman, who could not, or might not— at any rate, who did not—take upon herself even the ordinary authority of a family's head, a household's mistress. They little thought that that weak woman, remarkable for nothing but indifference, passed her days in inward distress, in care, in thought. The inherent timidity (it had existed in her mother) which had been her bane in former days, was her bane still. She had not dared to rise up against her husband when the great injustice was inflicted upon Rupert Trevlyn; she did not dare openly to rise up now against the petty wrongs daily dealt out to him. There may have been a latent consciousness in her mind that if she did rise up it would not alter things for the better, and it might make them worse for Rupert.   Probably it would have been found so ; and that the non-interference was for the best.

There were many things she could have wished done for Rupert, and she went so far as to hint at some of them to Mr. Chattaway.   She wished he could be relieved entirely of going to Blackstone ; she wished more indulgences might be his at home ; she wished he could be transported to a warmer climate.   A bare suggestion of one or other of these things she dropped, once in a way, to Mr. Chattaway.   They fell unheeded on his ear, as must be supposed, by their not being answered.   He replied to one : the hint of the warm climate—replied to it with a prolonged stare and a demand to know what romantic absurdity she could be thinking of.   Mrs. Chattaway had never mentioned it again ; in these cases of constitutional timidity of mind, a rebuff, let it be ever so slight, is sufficient to close the lips for ever.   Poor lady ! she would have sacrificed her own comfort to give peace and comfort to the unhappy Rupert.   He was miserably put upon, he was treated with less consideration than were the servants, he was made to feel his dependent state daily and hourly by sundry petty annoyances ; and yet she could not interfere openly to help him !

Even now, as she sat watching the deepening shades of the coming night, she was dwelling on this ; resenting it in her heart, for his sake. It was the evening of the day when the young ladies had met George Ryle in the lane. She could hear the sounds of merriment down-stairs from her children and their visitors, and she felt sure that Rupert did not make one amongst them. It had long been the pleasure of Cris and Octave to exclude Rupert from the general society, the evening gatherings of the family, so far as they could exclude him ; and if, through the presence of herself or of Miss Diana, they could not absolutely deny his entrance, they took care to treat him with cavalier indifference. She sat on, revolving these bitter thoughts in the gloom succeeding to the departed day, until roused by the entrance of an intruder.

It was Rupert himself. He approached Mrs. Chattaway, and she fondly threw her arm round him, and drew him down to a chair by her side. Only when they were alone could she show him these marks of affection, or prove to him that he did not stand in the world entirely isolated from all ties of love.

"Do you feel better to-night, Rupert ?"

"Oh, I am a great deal better. I feel quite well. Why are you sitting by yourself in the dark, Aunt Edith?"

"It is not dark yet. What are they doing below, Rupert? I hear plenty of laughter."

"They are playing at some game, I think."

"At what?"

"I don't know. I was taking a place with them, but Octave, as usual, said they were enough without me; so I came away."

Mrs. Chattaway made no reply. She never spoke a reproachful word of her children to Rupert, whatever she might feel; she never, by so much as a breath, cast a reproach on her husband to living mortal. Rupert leaned his head on her shoulder, as if he were weary. Sufficient light was left to show how delicate were his features, how attractive was his face. The lovely countenance of his boyhood characterised him still—the suspiciously bright cheeks and the silken hair. Of middle height, his frame slender and fragile, he scarcely looked his twenty years. There was a resemblance in his face to Mrs. Chattaway's: and it was not surprising, for Joe Trevlyn and his sister Edith had been remarkably alike when they were young.

"Is Cris come in?" asked Mrs. Chattaway.

"Not yet."

Rupert rose as he spoke, and stretched himself.
The verb *s'ennuyer* was one he often felt himself
obliged to conjugate, in his evenings at Trevlyn
Hold.

"I think I shall go down for an hour to Trevlyn
Farm."

Mrs. Chattaway started. She, as it seemed,
shrunk from the words. "Not to-night, Rupert!"

"It is so dull at home, Aunt Edith."

"They are merry enough down stairs."

"*They* are. But Octave takes care that I shall
not be merry with them."

What could she answer to it?

"Well, then, Rupert, you will *be sure* to be
home," she said, after a while. And the pained
emphasis with which she spoke the words "be
sure," no pen could express. Some meaning, understood by Rupert, was evidently conveyed by
them.

"Yes," was all he answered; the tone of his
voice telling of resentment, not disguised.

Mrs. Chattaway caught him to her, and hid her
face upon his shoulder. "For my sake, Rupert,
darling! for my sake!"

"Yes, yes, dear Aunt Edith: I'll be sure to be
in time," he reiterated. "I'll not forget the hour,
as I did the other night."

She stood at the window, and watched him

away from the house and down the avenue, pray-
ing that he might *not* forget the hour. It had
pleased Mr. Chattaway lately to forbid Rupert's
entrance to the house, unless he returned to it by
half-past ten. That his motive was entirely that
of ill-naturedly crossing Rupert, there could be
little doubt. Driven out by unkindness from the
Hold, Rupert had taken to spending his evenings
with George Ryle; sometimes at the houses of
other friends; now and then he would invade old
Canham's. Rupert's hour for coming in from
these visits was about eleven; he generally had
managed to be in by the time the clock struck;
but the master of Trevlyn Hold suddenly issued
a peremptory mandate that he must be in by
half-past ten; failing strict obedience as to time,
he was not to be let in at all. Rupert resented
it, and one or two unpleasant scenes had been the
result. The like rule was not applied to Cris
who might come in any hour he pleased.

Mrs. Chattaway descended to the drawing-room.
Two young ladies, the daughters of neighbours,
were spending the evening there, and they were
playing at proverbs with intense relish: Maude
Trevlyn, the guests, and the Miss Chattaways.
Octave alone joined in it listlessly, as if her
thoughts were far away. Her restless glances
towards the door seemed to say that she was

watching for the entrance of one who did not come.

By-and-by Mr. Chattaway came home, and they sat down to supper. Afterwards, the young ladies departed, and the younger children went to bed. Ten o'clock struck, and the time went on again.

"Where's Rupert?" Mr. Chattaway suddenly asked of his wife.

"He went down to Trevlyn Farm, James," she said, unable, had it been to save her life, to speak without deprecation.

He gave no answer by word or look to his wife; but he rang the bell, and ordered the household to bed. Miss Diana Trevlyn was out upon a visit.

"Cris and Rupert are not in, papa," observed Octave, as she lighted her mamma's candle and her own.

Mr. Chattaway took out his watch. "Twenty-five minutes past ten," he said, in his hard, impassive manner—a manner which imparted the idea that he was utterly destitute of sympathy for the whole human race. "Mr. Rupert must be quick if he intends to come inside to-night. Give your mamma her bed candle."

It may appear almost incredible that Mrs. Chattaway should meekly take her candle and follow her daughter up the stairs without remonstrance, when

she would have given the world to sit up longer.
She was getting quite in a fever on Rupert's
account, and she would have wished to wait in
that room until his ring was heard. But to set
up her own will against her husband's was a
thing she had never yet done; in small things
as in great, she had bowed to his mandates without making the faintest shadow of resistance.

Octave wished her mamma good night, went
into her room, and closed the door. Mrs. Chattaway was turning into hers when she saw Maude
creeping down the upper stairs. She came noiselessly along the corridor, her face pale with agitation, and her heart beating.

"Oh, Aunt Edith, what will be done?" she murmured. "It is half-past ten, and he is not home."

"Maude, my poor child, you can do nothing,"
was the whispered answer, the tone as full of pain
as Maude's. "Go back to your room, dear; your
uncle may be coming up."

The great clock in the hall struck the half-
hour; its sound came booming up like a knell.
Hot tears were dropping from the eyes of Maude.

"What will become of him, Aunt Edith? Where
will he sleep?"

"Hush Maude! Run back."

It was time for her to run; and Mrs. Chattaway
spoke the words in a tone of startled terror. The

heavy foot of the master of Trevlyn Hold was
heard crossing the hall to ascend the stairs.
Maude stole noiselessly back, and Mrs. Chattaway
passed into her dressing-room.

She sat down on a chair, and pressed her hands
upon her bosom to still the beating. Her sus-
pense and agitation were terrible. A sensitive,
timid nature, such as Mrs. Chattaway's, feels
emotion in a most painful degree. Every sense
was strung to its utmost tension. She listened
for Rupert's footfall outside; she waited with a
sort of horror for the ringing of the house-bell
that should announce his arrival, her whole frame
feeling sick and faint.

At last, one came running up the avenue at a
fleet pace, and the echoes of the bell were heard
resounding through the house.

Not daring to defy her husband by going down
to let him in, unless she had permission, she
passed into the bed-room, where Mr. Chattaway
was undressing.

"Shall I go down and open the door, James?"

"No."

"It is only five minutes over the half-hour."

"Five minutes are the same in effect as five
hours," answered Mr. Chattaway, taking off his
waistcoat. "Unless he can be in before the
half hour, *he does not come in at all.*"

"It may be Cris," she resumed.

"Nonsense! You know it is not Cris. Cris has his latch-key."

Another alarming peal.

"He can see the light in my dressing-room," she urged, with parched lips. "Oh, James, let me go down."

"I tell you—No."

There was no appeal against it. She knew there might be none. But she clasped her hands together in agony, and gave utterance to the chief distress at her heart.

"Where will he sleep? Where can he go, if we deny him entrance?"

"Where he chooses. ·He does not come in here."

And Mrs. Chattaway went back to her dressing-room, and listened in despair to the continued appeals from the bell. Appeals which she might not answer.

CHAPTER XIII.

OPINIONS DIFFER.

THE nights were chilly in the early autumn, and a blazing fire burnt in the drawing-room grate at Trevlyn Farm. On a comfortable sofa, drawn close to it, sat Mrs. Ryle, a warm shawl thrown over her black silk gown—warm cushions of eider down heaped around her. A violent cold had made an invalid of her for some days past, but she was getting better. Her face was softened by a white cap of delicate lace; but its lines had grown haughtier and firmer with her years. She wore well, and was handsome still.

Trevlyn Farm had prospered. It was a lucky day for Mrs. Ryle when she decided upon her step-son's remaining on it. He had brought energy and goodwill to bear on his work; he had brought a clear head and calm intelligence; and time had contributed judgment and experience. Mrs. Ryle knew that she could not have been better served than she had been by George, and

she gradually grew to feel his value. Had they
been really mother and son, they could not have
been better friends. In the onset she was inclined
to discountenance sundry ways and habits which
George favoured. He did not make himself into
a *working* farmer, as his father had done, and as
Mrs. Ryle deemed he ought to do. George
objected. A man who worked on his own farm
must necessarily give to it less of general super-
vision, he urged : were his hands engaged on one
spot, his eyes could not be using themselves to
advantage a mile or two off; and after all, it was
but the cost of an additional day-labourer. His
argument carried reason with it; and that keen
farmer and active man, Farmer Apperley, who
deemed idleness the greatest sin (next, perhaps, to
going out hunting) that a young farmer could be
guilty of, nodded his approval. George did not
put aside his books; his classics, and his studies
in general literature : quite the contrary. In
short, George Ryle appeared to be going in for a
gentleman—as Cris Chattaway chose to term it—
a great deal more than Mrs. Ryle considered
would be profitable for him or for her. But
George had held on his course, in a quiet, unde-
monstrative way; and Mrs. Ryle had at length
fallen in with it. Perhaps she now saw its
wisdom. That he was essentially a gentleman, in

person as in manners, in mind as in conduct, she could but acknowledge, and she felt a pride in him which she had never thought to feel in any one, save Treve.

Could she feel pride in Treve? Not much, with all her partiality. Trevlyn Ryle was not turning out in quite so satisfactory a manner as was desirable. There was nothing very objectionable to be urged against him; but Mrs. Ryle was accustomed to measure by a high standard of excellence; and of that Treve fell uncommonly short. She had not deemed it well that George Ryle should be too much of a gentleman, but she had determined to make Trevlyn into one. Upon the completion of his school life, he was sent to Oxford. The cost of this might have been imprudently heavy for Mrs. Ryle's pocket, had she borne it unassisted; but Trevlyn had gained a valuable scholarship at the Barmester Grammer School where he had been educated, and this had rendered the additional cost light. Treve, once at Oxford, did not get on quite so fast as he might have done. Treve spent; Treve seemed to have plenty of wild oats to sow; Treve thought he should like a life of idleness better than one of farming. His mother had foolishly whispered to him the fond hope that he might some time be the Squire of Trevlyn Hold, and Treve reckoned upon its fulfil-

ment more confidently than was good for him.
Meanwhile, until the lucky chance befel which
should give him the inheritance (though by what
miracle the chance should fall was at present
hidden in the womb of mystery), Treve, upon the
completion of his studies at college, was to assume
the mastership of Trevlyn Farm, in accordance
with the plan originally fixed upon by Mrs. Ryle.
He would not be altogether unqualified for this :
he had been out and about on the farm since he
was a child, and had seen how it should be worked.
Whether he would give sufficient personal attention to it, was another matter.

Mrs. Ryle expressed herself as not being too
confident of him—whether of his industry or his
qualifications she did not state. George had
given one or two hints that when Treve came
home for good, he must look out for something
else ; but Mrs. Ryle had waived away the hints
as if they were unpleasant to her. Treve must
be proved yet, what metal he was made of, before
assuming the full management, she briefly said.
And George suffered the subject to drop.

Treve had now but one more term to keep at
the university. At the conclusion of the previous
term he had not returned home : he remained on
a visit to a friend, who had an appointment in one
of the colleges. But Treve's demands for money

become somewhat inconvenient to Mrs. Ryle, and she had begged George to pay Oxford a few days' visit, that he might see how Treve was really going on. George complied, and proceeded to Oxford, where he found Treve absent—as you heard him, in the last chapter, say to Maude Trevlyn.

Mrs. Trevlyn sat by the drawing-room fire, enveloped in her shawl, and leaning on her pillows. The thought of these things was bringing a severe look to her proud face. She had scarcely seen George since his return; had not exchanged more than ten words with him. But those ten words had not been of a cheering nature; and she feared things were not going on satisfactorily with Treve. With that severely hard look on her features, how wonderfully her face resembled that of her dead father!

Presently George came in. Mrs. Ryle looked eagerly up at his entrance.

"Are you better?" he asked, advancing to her, and bending down with a kindly smile. "It is a long while since you had a cold such as this."

"I shall be all right in a day or two," she answered. "Yesterday, I thought I was going to have a long bout of it, my chest was so sore. Sit down, George. What about Treve?"

"Treve was not at Oxford. He had gone to London."

"You told me that much. What had he gone to London for?"

"A little change, Ferrars said. He had been gone a week."

"A little change? In plain Eglish, a little pleasure, I suppose. Call it what you will, it costs money, George."

George had seated himself opposite to her, his arm resting on the centre table, and the red blaze of the fire lighting up his frank and pleasant face. In figure he was tall, slight, gentlemanly; his father, at his age, had been so before him.

"Why did you not follow him to London, George?" resumed Mrs. Ryle. "It would have been but a two hours' journey from Oxford. Not so much as that."

George turned his large dark eyes upon her, some surprise in them. "How was I to know where to look for him, if I had gone?"

"Could Mr. Ferrars not give you his address?"

"No. I asked him. Treve had not told him where he should stop. In fact, Ferrars did not think Treve knew where, himself. Under those circumstances, my going to town might have been only a waste of time and money."

"I *wish* you could have seen Treve!"

" So do I. But I might have been looking for him a week without finding him, in a place like London. And the harvest was not all in at home, you know, mother."

" It is of no use your keeping things from me, George," resumed Mrs. Ryle, after a pause. " Has Treve contracted fresh debts at Oxford ? "

" I fancy he has. A few."

" A ' few !'—and you ' fancy !' George, tell the truth. That you know he has, and that they are not a few."

" That he has, I believe to be true : I gathered so much from Ferrars. But I do not think they are many; I do not indeed."

" Why did you not inquire ? I would have gone to every shop in the town, but what I would have ascertained. If he is contracting more debts, who is to pay them, George ? "

George was silent.

" When shall we be clear of Chattaway ? " she abruptly resumed. " When will the last payment be due ? "

" In a month or two's time. Principal and interest will all be paid off then."

" It will take all your exertions to get the sum up."

" It will be got up, mother. It shall be."

" Yes ; I don't doubt it. But it will not be got

up, George, if a portion is to be taken from it for Treve."

George knitted his brow. He was falling into thought.

" I *must* get rid of Chattaway," she resumed. " He has been weighing us down all these years like an incubus ; and now that the emancipation has nearly come, were anything to frustrate it, I should—I should—George, I think I should go mad."

" I hope and trust nothing will frustrate it," answered George. " I am more anxious to get rid of Chattaway than, I think, even you can be. As to Treve, his debts must wait."

" But it would be more desirable that he should not contract them," observed Mrs. Ryle.

" Of course. But how are we to prevent his contracting them ? "

" He ought to prevent himself. *You* did not contract these miserable debts, George."

" I ! " he rejoined, in surprise. " I had no opportunity of doing it. Work and responsibility were thrown upon me before I was old enough to think of pleasure : and they served to keep me steady."

" You were not naturally inclined to spend, George."

" There's no knowing what I might have ac-

quired an inclination for, had I been sent out into
the world, as Treve has," he rejoined.

"It was necessary that Treve should go to the
university," said Mrs. Ryle, quite sharply.

"I am not saying that it was not," George
answered, quietly. "It was right that he should
go, as you wished it."

"George, I shall live—I hope I shall live—I
pray that I may live—to see Trevlyn the lawful
possessor of Trevlyn Hold. A gentleman's education was therefore essential to him : hence I sent
him to Oxford."

George made no reply. Mrs. Ryle felt chafed
at it. She knew that George did not approve her
policy in regard to Trevlyn. She charged him
with it now, and George would not deny it.

"What I think unwise," he said, "is your
having led Treve to build hopes upon the succession to Trevlyn Hold."

"Why ?" she haughtily asked. "He will come
into it."

"I do not see how," quietly remarked George.

"He has far more right to it than he who is
looked upon as its successor—Cris Chattaway,"
she said, with flashing eyes. "You know that."

George could have answered that neither of
them had a right to it, in fair justice, while Rupert
Trevlyn lived ; but Rupert and his claims had

been so completely ignored by Mrs. Ryle, as by others, that his urging them would have been waived away as idle talk. Mrs. Ryle resumed, her voice unsteady in its tones. It was most rare that she suffered herself to speak of these past grievances; but when she did, her vehemence amounted to agitation.

"When my boy was born, the news that Joe Trevlyn's health was failing had come home to us. I knew the squire would never leave the property to Maude, a girl, and I looked then for my son to inherit it. Was it not natural that I should?—was it not his right?—I was the squire's eldest daughter. I had him named Trevlyn; I wrote a note to my father, saying that he would not now be at fault for a male heir, in the event of poor Joe's not leaving one——"

"He did leave one," interrupted George, speaking probably in impulsive thoughtlessness.

"Be still. Rupert was not born then, and his succession was afterwards barred by my father's will. Through deceit practised on him, I grant you: but I had no hand in that deceit. I named my boy Trevlyn; I regarded him as the certain heir; and when the squire died and his will was opened, it was found that he had bequeathed all to Chattaway. If you think I have ever once faltered since in my hope—my *resolve*—to see

Trevlyn some time displace the Chattaways, George, you do not know much of human nature."

"I grant what you say," replied George, "that of the two, Trevlyn has more just right to it than Cris Chattaway. But has it ever occurred to you to ask, *how* Cris is to be displaced?"

Mrs. Ryle did not answer. She sat beating her foot upon the ottoman, as one whose mind is not at ease. George continued—

"It appears to me to be the wildest possible fallacy, the bare idea of Trevlyn's being able to displace Cris Chattaway in the succession. If we lived in the barbarous ages, when inheritances were wrested away from their possessors by force of arms, when the turn of a battle decided the ownership of a castle, then there might be a chance of Trevlyn Hold being taken from Cris Chattaway. As it is, there is none. There is not the faintest shadow of a chance that it can go to any beside Cris. Failing his death —and he is strong and hearty—he *must* succeed. Why, even were Rupert—forgive my alluding to him again—to urge *his* claims, there would be no hope for him. Mr. Chattaway holds the estate by the sure tenure of legality; he has willed it to his son; and that son cannot be displaced in the succession by any extraneous efforts of others."

Her foot beat the velvet more impatiently; a heavier line settled on her brow. Often and often had the very arguments now put into words by her step-son, brought their weight to her aching brain. George spoke again.

"And therefore, the very improbability—I may almost say the impossibility—of Treve's ever succeeding to Trevlyn Hold, renders it unwise that he should have been taught to build upon it. Far better, mother, that the contingency had never been so much as whispered to him."

"Why do you look at it in this unfavourable light?" she burst forth.

"Because it is the correct light," answered George. "The property is Mr. Chattaway's—legally his, and it cannot be taken from him. It will be Cris's after him."

"Cris may die," said Mrs. Ryle; her sharpness of tone proving that she was vexed at having no better argument to urge.

"And if he were to die? If Cris died to-morrow, Treve would be no nearer the succession. Chattaway has daughters, and he would will it to each of them in rotation, rather than to Treve. He can will it away as he pleases. It was left to him absolutely."

Mrs. Ryle lifted her hands. "My father was mad when he made such a will in favour of Chattaway! He could have been nothing less. I have thought so many times."

"But it was made, and it cannot now be altered. Will you pardon me for saying that it would have been better had you accepted the state of affairs, and endeavoured to reconcile yourself to them?"

"It would have been *better!*"

"Yes;" he decisively reiterated. "The rebelling against what cannot be remedied never brings anything but dissatisfaction. I would a great deal rather see Treve succeed to Trevlyn Hold than Cris Chattaway: but I know that Treve never will succeed: and, therefore, it is a great pity that he has been led to think of it. He might have shown himself more ready to settle down to steadiness, had he never become possessed with the notion that he might some time supersede Cris Chattaway."

"He *shall* supersede him, George. He ——"

The door opened to admit a visitor, and Mrs. Ryle could not finish her sentence. For he who entered was Rupert Trevlyn. Ignore his dormant claims as she would, Mrs. Ryle felt that it would be scarcely seemly to discuss before him Treve's chance of succession to Trevlyn Hold. She had in truth completely put out of her mind all thought of the claims of Rupert. He had been deprived of his right by Squire Trevlyn's will, and there was an end to it. Mrs. Ryle rather liked Rupert ; or, it may be better to say, she did not *dis*like him ; really to like any one save Treve, was not in her nature. She liked Rupert in a cold, negative sort of a way ; but she would not have helped him to his inheritance by the lifting of a finger. In the event of her possessing no son to be jealously covetous for, she might have taken up the wrongs of Rupert. There's no telling—just to thwart Chattaway.

"Why, Rupert," said George, rising, and cordially taking his hand, " I heard you were ill again. Maude told me so to-day."

"I am better to-night, George. Aunt Ryle, they said you were in bed."

"I am better, too, Rupert," she answered. " What has been the matter with you ?"

"Oh, it was my chest again ;" said Rupert, pushing the waving hair from his bright and delicate face. " I could hardly breathe this morning."

"Ought you to have come out to-night ?"

"I don't think it matters," carelessly answered Rupert. " For all I see, I am as well when I go out as when I don't. There's not much to stop in for, there."

He edged himself closer in to the hearth with

a slight shiver. He was painfully susceptive to the feeling of cold. George took the poker and stirred the fire, and the blaze went flickering aloft, playing on the familiar objects of the handsome room, lighting up the slender figure, the well-formed features, the large blue eyes of Rupert, and bringing out to view all the suspicious signs of latent constitutional delicacy. The transparent fairness of complexion and the rich bloom of the cheeks, might alike have whispered a warning.

"Octave thought you were going up there to-night, George."

"Did she?"

"The two Beecroft girls are there, and they turned me out of the drawing-room. Octave told me 'I wasn't wanted.' Will you play at chess to-night, George?"

"If you like; when I have had my supper."

"I must be home by half-past ten, you know. I was a minute over the half hour the other night, and one of the servants opened the door for me. Chattaway pretty nearly rose the roof off, he was so angry; but he could not decently turn me out again."

"Chattaway is master for the time being of Trevlyn Hold," remarked Mrs. Ryle. "Not squire; never squire"—she broke off, straying abruptly from her subject, and as abruptly resuming it. " You will do well to obey him, Rupert. When I make a rule in this house, Rupert Trevlyn, I *never permit it to be broken.*"

A valuable hint, if Rupert had but taken it for his guidance. He meant well : he never meant, for all his light and careless speaking, to be disobedient to Mr. Chattaway's mandate as to the time of his returning. And yet the disobedience happened that very night !

The chess-board was attractive, and the time slipped on to half-past ten. Rupert said a hasty good night, snatched his hat, tore through the entrance-room at a pace to frighten Nora, and made the best speed his lungs allowed him to Trevlyn Hold. His heart was beating, his breath was panting as he gained it, and he rang that peal at the bell which had sent its echoes through the house; through the trembling frame, the weak heart of Mrs. Chattaway.

He rang—and rang. There came back no answering sign that the ring was heard. A light shone in Mrs. Chattaway's dressing-room ; and Rupert took up some gravel, and gently threw it against the window. No response was accorded in answer to it ; he saw not so much as the form of a hand on the blind : the house, in its utter stillness, might have been taken for the house of the dead.   Rupert threw up some more gravel as silently as he could.

He had not to wait very long this time.   Cautiously, slowly, as though the very movement feared being heard, the blind was drawn aside, and the face of Mrs. Chattaway, wet with streaming tears, appeared, looking down at him.   He could see that she had not begun to undress.   She shook her head ; she raised her hands and clasped them with a gesture of deprecating despair ; and her lips formed themselves into the words, "I may not let you in."

He could not read the words ; but he read the expression of the whole all too clearly—that Chattaway would not suffer him to be admitted.   Mrs. Chattaway, dreading possibly that her husband might cast his eyes inside her dressing-room, quietly let fall the blind again, and removed her shadow from the window.

Now what was Rupert to do ?   Lie down on the level grass there that skirted the avenue, and take his night's rest under the trees, with the cold air freezing him, and the night dews wetting him?   A strong frame, revelling in superfluous health might risk that ; but not Rupert Trevlyn.

He walked round the house, and tried its back entrance.   It was quite fast.   He knocked at it, but no answer came. He looked up at the windows; lights shone in one or two of the upper rooms; but there came no sign that anybody meant to let him in.

A momentary thought came over him that he would go back to Trevlyn Farm, and crave a night's shelter there. He would have done it, but for the recollection of Mrs. Ryle's stern voice and sterner face when she remarked to him that, as he knew the rule made for his going in, he need not break it. Rupert had never got on too cordially with Mrs. Ryle. He remembered shrinking from her haughty face when he was a little child : and somehow he shrank from it still. No; he would not knock them up at Trevlyn Farm.

What must he do? Should he walk about until morning? Should he sit down on the upper step of the door-sill, inside the portico, and cower in the angle for the night ? Suddenly a thought came to him—were the Canhams in bed? If not, he could get in there, and lie on their settle. The Canhams never went to bed very early. Ann Canham sat up to lock the great gate—it was Chattaway's pleasure that it should not be done until after ten o'clock ; and old Canham liked to sit up, smoking his pipe.

With a brisk step, now that he had decided on a course, Rupert walked down the avenue. At the first turning he ran against Cris Chattaway, who was coming leisurely up it.

"O, Cris! I am so glad! You'll let me in. They have shut me out to-night."

"Let you in!" repeated Cris. "I can't."

Rupert's blue eyes opened in the starlight. "Have you not your latch-key?"

"What should hinder me?" responded Cris. "*I'm* going in; but I can't let you go in."

"Why not?" hotly asked Rupert.

"I don't choose to fly in the face of the squire's orders. He has commanded you to be in before half-past ten, or not to come in at all. It has gone half-past ten long ago: is hard upon eleven."

"If you can go in after half-past ten, why can't I go in?" cried Rupert.

"It's not my affair," said Cris, with a yawn. "Don't bother. Now look here, Rupert! It's of no use your following me to the door, for I shall not let you in."

"Yes you will, Cris."

"*I will not,*" responded Cris, speaking emphatically, but with the same plausible suavity that he had spoken throughout. Rupert's temper was getting up.

"Cris, I'd not show myself such a hang-dog sneak as you to be made King of England. If

everybody had their rights, Trevlyn Hold would
be mine, to shut you out of it if I pleased. But I'd
not please. If but a dog were turned out of his
kennel at night, I'd let him come into the Hold
for shelter."

Cris put his latch-key in the lock. "*I* don't
turn you out. You must battle that question
with the squire. Keep off, Ru. If he says you
may be let in at eleven o'clock, all well and
good : but I'm not going to encourage you in
disobeying his orders."

He opened the door a few inches, wound himself in, and shut it in Rupert's face. He made a
great noise in putting up the bar, which noise
was not in the least necessary. Rupert had given
him his true appellation—sneak. He was one :
a false-hearted, plausible-mannered, cowardly
sneak. As he stood at a marble table in the hall,
and struck a match to light his candle, his puny
face and his dull light eyes betrayed the most
complaisant enjoyment.

He went up the stairs smiling. He had to pass
the angle of the corridor where his mother's
rooms were situated. She glided silently out as
he was going by. Her dress was off then, and
she had apparently thrown a shawl over her
shoulders to come out to Cris. It was an old-
fashioned spun silk shawl, with a grey border, its

middle white : not so white, however, as the face
of Mrs. Chattaway.

"Cris!" she said, laying her hand upon his arm,
and speaking in the faintest, most timorous of
whispers, "why did you not let him in ?"

" I thought we had been ordered not to let
him in," returned he of the deceitful nature. " *I*
have been ordered. I know that."

" You might have done it just for once, Cris,"
his mother answered. " I know not what will
become of him, out of doors on this sharp night."

Cris disengaged his arm, and continued his
way up to his room. He slept on the upper floor.
Maude was standing at the door of her chamber
when he passed—as Mrs. Chattaway had been.

" Cris—wait a minute," she said, for he was
hastening by. " I want to speak a word to you.
Have you seen Rupert ?"

" Seen him and heard him too," boldly avowed
Cris. " He wanted me to let him in."

" Which, of course, you would not do?" answered Maude, bitterly. " I wonder if you
ever performed a good-natured action in your
life ?"

" Can't remember," mockingly retorted Cris.

" Where is Rupert ? What is he going to do ?"

" You know where he is as well as I do : I suppose you could hear him. As to what he is going

to do, I didn't ask him. Roost in a tree, perhaps, with the birds."

Maude retreated into her room and closed the door. She flung herself on a chair, and burst into a flood of passionate tears. Her heart ached for her brother with an aching that amounted to agony: she could have forced down her proud spirit and knelt to Mr. Chattaway to beg clemency for him : she could have almost sacrificed her own life if it might bring comfort to Rupert, whom she loved so well.

He—Rupert—stamped off from the door when it was closed against him by Oris Chattaway, feeling as if he would like to stamp upon Cris. Arrived in front of the lodge, he stood and whistled, and presently Ann Canham, who was undressing in the dark to save candle, looked from the upper casement in her night-cap.

" Why, it's never you, Master Rupert ! " she exclaimed, in the intensity of her surprise.

" They have locked me out, Ann Canham. Can you manage to come down and open the door to me without disturbing your father? If you can, I'll lie on the settle for to-night."

Once inside, there ensued a contest. In her humble way, begging pardon for the presumption, Ann Canham proposed that Master Rupert should go up to her bed, and she'd make herself contented with the settle. It was but a flock, and very small, she said ; but it would be rather better than the settle. Rupert would not. He threw himself on the hard narrow bench that they called the settle, and protested that if Ann Canham said another word about giving up her bed, he'd go outside and stop the night in the avenue. So she was fain to go back to it herself.

A dreary night it was for him, that wearying bench ; and the morning found him with a cold frame and stiffened limbs. He was stamping one foot on the floor to stamp the cramp out of it, when old Canham entered, leaning on a crutch. Ann had told him the news, and it got the old man up before his time.

" But who shut you out, Master Rupert ? " he asked.

" Chattaway."

" Ann says that Mr. Cris went in pretty late last night. After she had locked the big gate."

" Cris came up while I was ringing to be let in. He went in himself, but would not let me enter."

" He's a reptile," said old Canham in his anger. " Eh me ! " he added, sitting down with difficulty in his arm chair, and extending the crutch out before him, " what a mercy it would have been if poor Mr. Joe had lived ! Chattaway would never have been stuck up in authority then. Better that the squire had left Trevlyn Hold to Miss Diana."

"They say he would not leave it to a woman."

"That's true, Master Rupert. And of his children there were but his daughters left. The two sons had gone. The heir Rupert first : he died on the high seas ; and Mr. Joe, he went next."

"I say, Mark Canham, why did the heir, Rupert, go on the seas?"

Old Canham shook his head. "Ah, it was a bad business, Master Rupert. It's as well not to talk of it."

"But *why* did he go?" persisted Rupert.

"It was a bad business, I say. He, the heir, had fallen into wild ways, had got to like bad company, and that. He went out one night with some poachers—just for the fun of it. It wasn't on these lands. He meant no harm, but he was young and random, and he went out and put a gauze over his face as they did,—just, I say, for the fun of it. Master Rupert, that night they killed a gamekeeper."

A shiver of dismay passed through Rupert's frame. "*He* killed him, do you mean?—my uncle, Rupert Trevlyn?"

"No, it wasn't he that killed him—as was proved a long while afterwards. But you see at the time it wasn't known exactly who had done it : they were all in league, as may be said ; all in the mess. Any way, the young heir, whether in his fear or his shame, perhaps both, went off in secret, and before many months had gone over, the bells here were tolling for him. He had died far away."

"But people never could have believed that he, a Trevlyn, killed a man?" said Rupert, indignantly.

Old Canhau paused. "You have heard of the Trevlyn temper, Master Rupert?"

"Who hasn't?" returned Rupert. "They say I have got a touch of it."

"Well, those that believed it laid it to that temper, you see. They thought the heir had been overtook by a fit of passion that wasn't to be governed, and might have done the mischief in it. In them attacks of passion, a man is mad."

"Is he," abstractedly remarked Rupert, falling into a reverie. He had never before heard this episode in the history of the uncle whose name he bore—Rupert Trevlyn.

CHAPTER XIV.

NO BREAKFAST FOR RUPERT.

OLD Canham stood at the door of his lodge, his bald head stretched out. He was gazing after one who was winding through the avenue, in the direction of Trevlyn Hold, one whom it was old Canham's delight to patronise and make much of in his humble way; whom he encouraged in all sorts of vain and delusive notions—Rupert Trevlyn. Could Mr. Chattaway have divined that bitter treason was talked against himself nearly every time Rupert dropped into the lodge, he might have tried hard to turn old Canham out of it. Harmless treason, however; consisting of rebellious words only. There was neither plotting nor hatching; old Canham and Rupert never glanced at that; both were perfectly aware that Chattaway held his place by a sure tenure, which could not be shaken.

Many years ago, before Squire Trevlyn died, Mark Canham had grown ill in his service. In

his direct service he had caught the violent cold
which ended in an incurable rheumatic affection.
The squire settled him in the lodge, then just
vacant, and allowed him five shillings a week.
When the squire died, Chattaway would have
undone this. He wished to turn the old man out
again (but it must be observed in a parenthesis
that, though universally styled old Canham, the
man was less old in years than in appearance),
and to place some one else in the lodge. I think,
when there is no love lost between people, as the
saying runs, each side is conscious of it. Chattaway disliked Mark Canham, and he had a
shrewd suspicion that Mark returned the feeling
with interest. But he found that he could not
dismiss him from the lodge, for Miss Trevlyn put
her veto upon it. She openly declared that
Squire Trevlyn's act in placing his old servant
there should be reverenced ; she promised Mark
that he should not be turned out of it as long
as he lived. Chattaway had no resource but to
bow to it ; he might not cross Diana Trevlyn ;
but he did succeed in reducing the weekly allow-
ance by just half. Half-a-crown per week was
all the certain money enjoyed by the lodge since
the time of Squire Trevlyn. Miss Diana sometimes gave a trifle from her private purse ; and
the gardener was allowed to make an occasional

present of vegetables that were in danger of spoiling : at the beginning of winter, too, a load of·wood would be stacked in the shed behind the lodge, through the kind forethought of Miss Diana. But it was not much altogether to keep two people upon : and Ann Canham was glad to accept of a day's hard work offered her at any of the neighbouring houses, or to do a little plain sewing at home. Very fine sewing she could not do, for she suffered from her eyes, which were generally more or less inflamed.

Old Canham watched Rupert until the turnings of the avenue hid him from view, and then drew back into the room. Ann was busy with the breakfast. A loaf of oaten bread was on the clothless table, and a basin of skim milk, which she had just made hot, was placed before her father. A smaller cup of it served for her own share : and that constituted their breakfast. Three mornings a week Ann Canham had the privilege of fetching a quart of skim milk from the dairy at the Hold. Chattaway growled at the extravagance of the gift, but he did no more, for it was Miss Diana's pleasure that it should be supplied.

"Chattaway 'll go a bit too far, if he don't mind," observed Old Canham to his daughter, in relation to Rupert. "He must be of a bad nature, to lock him out of his own house. For the matter of that, however, he is of a bad one; and it's knowed he is."

"It is not his own, father," Ann Canham ventured to say in dissent. "Poor Master Rupert haven't got no right to it now."

"It's a shame but what he had. Why, Chattaway has got no more moral right to that there fine estate than I have!" added the old man, holding out his left arm straight in the heat of argument, the arm that was not helpless. "If Master Rupert and Miss Maude were dead,—if Joe Trevlyn had never left a child at all,—there's others would have a right to it before Chattaway."

"But Chattaway has got it, father, and nobody can't alter it, or hinder his having it," sensibly returned Ann Canham. "You'll have your milk cold."

The breakfast hour at Trevlyn Hold was early, and when Rupert entered, he found most of the family downs-tairs. Rupert ran up-stairs to his bed-room, where he washed and refreshed himself as much as was possible after his hard night. He was one upon whom only a night's lack of bed would seriously tell. When he descended to the breakfast-room, they were all assembled except Oris and Mrs. Chattaway. Cris was given to lying in bed in a morning, and the self-indulgence was winked at. Mrs. Chattaway also was apt to be behind-hand, coming down generally when the breakfast was nearly over.

Rupert took his place at the breakfast table. Mr. Chattaway, who was at that moment raising his coffee cup to his lips, put it down and stared at him. As he might have stared had some stranger from the outside intruded and sat down amongst them.

" What do you want ? " asked Mr. Chattaway.

" Want ? " repeated Rupert, not understanding. " Only my breakfast."

" Which you will not get here," calmly and coldly returned Mr. Chattaway. " If you cannot come home to sleep at night, you shall not get your breakfast here in the morning."

" I did come home," said Rupert ; " but I was. not let in."

" Of course you were not. The household had retired."

" Cris came home after I did, and was allowed to enter," objected Rupert again.

" That is no business of yours," said Mr. Chat-taway. " All you have to do is to obey the rules I lay down. And I will have them obeyed," he added, more sternly.

Rupert sat on, unoccupied. Octave, who was

presiding at the breakfast table, did not give him
any coffee ; nobody attempted to hand him anything to eat.   Maude was seated opposite to
him: he could see that the unpleasantness was
agitating her painfully ; that her colour went and
came ; that she toyed with her breakfast, but
could not swallow it : least of all, dared *she* interfere to give even so much as a bit of dry bread to
her ill-fated brother.

"Where did you sleep last night, pray ?" inquired Mr. Chattaway, pausing in the midst of
helping himself to some pigeon-pie, as he looked
at Rupert to put the question.

"Not in this house," curtly replied Rupert.
The unkindness seemed to be changing his very
nature.   It had continued long and long ; it had
been shown in many and various forms.

The master of Trevlyn Hold finished helping
himself to the pie, and began eating it with great
apparent relish.   He was about half-way through
the plateful when he again stopped to address
Rupert, who was sitting in silence, nothing but
the table-cloth before him.

"You need not wait.   If you stop there until
mid-day, you'll get no breakfast.   Gentlemen who
sleep outside do not break their fast in my
house."

Rupert pushed back his chair, and rose.   Hap-

pening to glance across at Maude, he saw that her
tears were dropping silently.   Oh, it was an unhappy home for them both !   Rupert crossed the
hall to the door : he thought he might as well
depart at once for Blackstone.   Fine as the morning was, the air, as he passed out, struck him with
a chill, and he turned back to get an overcoat.
Sitting up does not impart a sense of additional
warmth to the frame.

It was in his bed-room.   As he came down with
it on his arm, Mrs. Chattaway was crossing the
corridor to descend.   She drew him inside her
sitting-room.

"I could not sleep," she murmured ; " I was
awake nearly all night, grieving and thinking of
you.   Just before daylight I dropped into a sleep,
and then I dreamt that you were running up to
the door from the rising waves of the sea, which
were rushing onwards to overtake you.   I thought
you were knocking at the door, and we could not
get down to it in time, and the waters came on
and on.   Rupert, darling, all this is telling upon
me.   Why did you not come in ? "

" I meant to be in, Aunt Edith ; indeed, I did ;
but I was playing at chess with George Ryle, and
did not notice the time.   It was but just turned
half-past when I got here ; Mr. Chattaway might
have let me in without any great stretch of indul-

gence," he added, his tone one of bitterness. "So might Cris."

"What did you do?" she asked.

"I got in at old Canham's, and lay on their settle. Don't repeat this, or it may get the Canhams into trouble."

"Have you had breakfast yet?"

"I am not to have any."

The words startled her. "Rupert!"

"Mr. Chattaway ordered me from the table. The next thing, I expect, he will be ordering me from the house. If I knew where to go, I'd not stop in it another day. I would not, Aunt Edith."

"Have you had nothing—nothing?"

"Nothing. I'd go round to the dairy and get a draught of milk, but that I expect I should be told upon. I'm off to Blackstone now. Goodbye."

The tears were filling her eyes as she lifted them in their sad yearning. He stooped and kissed her.

"Don't grieve, Aunt Edith. You can't make it better for me. I have got the cramp like anything," he carelessly observed as he went off. "It is through lying in the cold on that hard settle."

"Rupert! Rupert!"

He turned back, half in alarm. The tone was one of painful, wild entreaty.

"You will come home to-night, Rupert?"

"Yes. Depend upon me."

She remained a few minutes longer, to watch him down the avenue. He had put on his coat then, and went along with slow and hesitating steps; they did not seem like the firm, careless steps of a hearty frame, springing from a happy heart. Mrs. Chattaway pressed her hands upon her brow, lost in a painful vision. If his father, her once dearly-beloved brother Joe, could be looking on at the injustice done on earth, what would he think of the portion of it meted out to Rupert?

She descended to the breakfast-room. Mr. Chattaway had finished his breakfast and was rising. She kissed her children one by one; she sat down patiently and silently, smiling with outward cheerfulness. Octave passed her a cup of coffee, which was cold; and they asked her what she would take to eat. But she said she was not hungry that morning, and would eat nothing.

"Rupert's gone away without his breakfast, mamma," cried Emily. "Papa would not let him have it. Serve him right! He stayed out all night."

Mrs. Chattaway stole a glance at Maude. She

was sitting pale and quiet, and her bread-and-butter uneaten before her; her air that of one who has to bear some long, wearing pain.

"If you have finished your breakfast, Maude, you can be getting ready to take the children for their walk," said Octave, speaking with her usual assumption of authority—an assumption which Maude at least might not dispute.

Mr. Chattaway left the room, and ordered his horse to be got ready. He was going to ride over his land for an hour before proceeding to Blackstone. While the animal was being saddled, he rejoiced his eyes with his rich stores; the corn heaped in his barns, the fine ricks of hay in his rick-yard. All very satisfactory, very consoling to the covetous mind of the master of Trevlyn Hold.

He went out, riding hither and thither. Half an hour afterwards when in the lane, spoken of previously, which skirted Mrs. Ryle's lands on the one side and his on the other, he saw another horseman before him. It was George Ryle. Mr. Chattaway touched his horse with the spur, and rode up to him at a hand gallop. George turned his head, saw it was Mr. Chattaway, and continued his way. That gentleman had been better pleased that George had stopped.

"Are you hastening on to avoid me, Mr. Ryle?"

he called out, in his sullen temper. "You might have seen that I wished to speak to you, by the pace to which I urged my horse."

George reined in, and turned to face Mr. Chattaway. "I saw nothing of the sort," he answered. "Had I known that you wanted me, I should have stopped; but it is no unusual circumstance for me to see you riding fast about your land."

"Well, what I have to say is this: that I'd recommend you not to get Rupert Trevlyn to your house at night, and to keep him there to unreasonable hours."

George paused. "I don't understand you, Mr. Chattaway."

"Don't you?" retorted that gentleman. "I'm not talking Dutch. Rupert Trevlyn has taken to frequent your house of late; it's not altogether good for him."

"Do you fear that he will get any harm in it?" quietly asked George.

"I think it would be better for him that he should stay away. Is the Hold not sufficient for him to spend his evenings in, but he must seek amusement elsewhere? I shall be obliged to you not to encourage his visits."

"Mr. Chattaway," said George, his face full of earnestness, as he turned it to that gentleman's, "it appears to me that you are labouring under some mistake, or you would certainly not speak to me as you are now doing. I do not encourage Rupert to my mother's house, in one sense of the word; I never press for his visits. When he does come, I show myself happy to see him and make him welcome—as I should do by any other visitor. Common courtesy demands this of me."

"You do press for his visits," said Mr. Chattaway.

"I do not," firmly repeated George. "Shall I tell you why I do not? I have no wish but to be open in the matter. An impression has seated itself in my mind that his visits to our house displease you, and therefore I have not encouraged them."

Perhaps Mr. Chattaway was rather taken aback at this answer. At any rate, he made no reply to it.

"But to receive him courteously when he does come, I cannot help doing," continued George. "I shall do it still, Mr. Chattaway. If Trevlyn Farm is to be a forbidden house to Rupert, it is not from our side that the interdict shall come. So long as Rupert pays us these visits of friendship—and what harm you can think they do him, or why he should not pay them, I am unable to conceive—so long he will be met with a welcome."

" Do you say this to oppose me ? "

" Far from it. If you will look at the case in an unprejudiced light, you may perhaps see that I speak in accordance with the commonest usages of civility. To shut the doors of our house on Rupert when there exists no reason why they should be shut—and most certainly he has given us none—would be a breach of good feeling and good manners that we might blush to be guilty of."

" You have been opposing me all the later years of your life, George Ryle. From that past time when I wished to place you with Wall and Barnes, you have done nothing but act in opposition to me."

" I have forgiven that," said George, pointedly, a glow rising to his face at the recollection. " As to any other opposition, I am unconscious of it. You have given me advice occasionally respecting the farm ; but the advice has not in general tallied with my own opinion, and therefore I have not taken it. If you call that opposing you, Mr. Chattaway, I cannot help it."

" I see you have been mending that fence in the three-cornered paddock," remarked Mr. Chattaway, passing to another subject, and speaking in a different tone. Possibly, he had had enough of the last.

" Yes," said George. " You would not mend it,

and therefore I have had it done. I cannot let my cattle get into the pound. I shall deduct the expense from the rent."

"You'll not," said Mr. Chattaway. "I won't be at the cost of a penny piece of it."

"Oh, yes, you will," returned George, equably. "The damage was done by your team, through your wagoner's carelessness, and the cost of making it good lies with you. Have you anything more to say to me?" he asked, after a pause. "I am very busy this morning."

"Only this," replied Mr. Chattaway, in a significant tone. "That the more you encourage Rupert Trevlyn, by making him a companion, the worse it will be for him."

George lifted his hat in farewell salutation: he could but be a gentleman, even to Chattaway. The master of Trevlyn Hold replied by an ungracious nod, and turned his horse back down the lane. As George rode on, he met Edith and Emily Chattaway—the children, as Octave had styled them—running towards him at full speed. They had seen their father, and were hastening after him. Maude came up more leisurely. George stooped to shake hands with her.

"You are looking pale and ill, Maude," he said, his low voice full of sympathy, his hand retaining hers. "Is it about Rupert?"

"Yes," she replied, striving to keep down her tears. "He was not allowed to come in last night. He has been sent away without breakfast this morning."

"I know all about it," said George. I met Rupert just now, and he told me. I asked him if he would go to Nora for some breakfast—I could not do less, you know," added George, musingly, as if debating the question with himself. "But he declined. I am almost glad he did."

Maude was surprised. "Why?" she asked.

"Because I have a notion in my mind—I have felt it for some time—that any attention shown to Rupert, no matter by whom, only makes his position worse with Chattaway. And Chattaway has now confirmed it, Maude, by telling me as much."

Maude's eyelids drooped over her eyes; she was trying to hide the gathering tears. "Oh, how sad it is!" she exclaimed, with emotion—"and for one in his weak state! If he were but strong as the rest of us are, it would be of less vital import. I fear—I do fear that he must have slept under the trees in the avenue," she continued, lifting her eyes now in her distress, and forgetting what was in them. "Mr. Chattaway inquired where he had passed the night, and Rupert answered——"

"I can relieve your fears so far, Maude," interrupted George, glancing round, as if to make doubly sure that no undesirable ears were near. "He was at old Canham's."

Maude heaved a deep sigh in her relief. "You are sure, George?"

"Yes, yes. Rupert told me so just now. He said how hard he found the settle. Here come your charges back, Maude; so I will say good-bye."

She suffered her hand to linger in his, but her heart was too full to speak. George bent lower.

"Do not make the grief heavier than you can bear, Maude. It *is* grief—real grief; but happier times may be in store for Rupert—and for you."

He released her hand, and cantered down the lane; and the two girls came up, telling Maude that they should go home now, for they had walked long enough. And Maude might not attempt to oppose her will to that of her pupils.

CHAPTER XV.

THERE appeared to be no place on earth for Rupert Trevlyn. Most people have some little nook that they ·can fit themselves into and call their own; but he had none. He was but suffered at the Hold : he was made to feel stranger and stranger in it day by day.

What could be the true source of this ill feeling towards Rupert? Did there exist some latent dread in the heart of Mr. Chattaway, and from thence penetrating to that of Cris, whispering that he, Rupert, the true heir of Trevlyn Hold, might at some future day, through some unforeseen and apparently impossible chance, come into his rights? No doubt it was so. There are no other means of accounting for it. It may be, they deemed that the more effectually he was kept under, treated as an object to be despised, lowered from his proper station, the less chance would there be of that covert dread growing into

a certainty.   Whatever may have been its cause,
Rupert was shamefully put upon.   It is true that
he sat at their table at meals—that he sat in the
same sitting-room.   But at the table he was placed
below the rest, at any inconvenient corner, where
there was no room for his legs or his plate ; where
he was served last, and from the plainest dish.
If two dishes were on the table—boiled mutton
and roast turkey, let us say—while Mr. Chattaway's children revelled to their content in the
turkey and its sauces, Rupert had the mutton
dealt out to him.   Mrs. Chattaway's heart would
ache ; but she could not alter it ; it had ached
from the same cause for many a year.   Maude's
ached : and Maude would decline the rich viands
and eat the poor ones, that it might seem less hard
to Rupert.   There were times, indeed, when Miss
Trevlyn would speak up.   " Rupert, don't you
prefer turkey ? "   " Yes, Aunt Diana "—and Miss
Diana would call down the table, "Mr. Chattaway,
give Rupert some turkey ; he prefers it."   But
this did not happen often : perhaps Miss Diana
was unobservant.   In their evenings, when the
rest were gathered round the comfortable fire,
Rupert would be pushed back with the remote
chairs and tables, and left there to make the best
of the cold.   Nothing in the world, of petty
wants, was so coveted by Rupert **Trevlyn** as a

warm seat by the fire. It had been coveted by his father when he was Rupert's age, and perhaps Miss Diana remembered this, for she would call Rupert forward to the fire, and sharply rebuke those who would have kept him from it.

But Miss Diana was not always in the room; not often, in fact. She had her private sitting-room up-stairs, as Mrs. Chattaway had hers; and both ladies more frequently retired to them in an evening, leaving the younger ones to enjoy themselves, with their books and their work, their music and their games, unrestrained by their presence. And poor Rupert was condemned to the remote, cold, unsocial quarters of the room, where nobody noticed him.

In that point alone, the cold, it was a bitter trial. Of spare, thin frame, weakly of constitution, shivery by nature, a good fire and a place close to it was to Rupert Trevlyn almost an essential of existence. And it was what he rarely got at Trevlyn Hold. No wonder he was driven out. Even old Canham's wood fire, that he might get right into if he pleased, was an improvement upon the drawing-room at Trevlyn.

But this digression is not getting on with the story, and you will not thank me for it. After parting with George Ryle, Maude Trevlyn, in obedience to the imperious mandates of her pupils,

turned her steps homewards. Emily was a bois-
terous, troublesome, disobedient girl; Edith was
more gentle, more amiable, in looks and disposition resembling her mother; but the example' of
her sisters was infectious, and spoiled her. There
was another daughter, Amelia, older than they
were, and at school at Barmester: a very disagreeable girl indeed.

"What was George Ryle saying to you, Maude?"
somewhat insolently asked Emily.

"He was talking of Rupert," she incautiously
answered, her mind buried in thought.

When they reached the Hold, Mr. Chattaway's
horse was being led about by a groom, waiting for
its master, who had returned, and was in-doors.
As they crossed the hall, they met him coming
out of the breakfast-room. Octave was with
him, talking.

"Cris would have waited, no doubt, papa, had
he known you wanted him. He ate his breakfast
in a hurry, and went out. I suppose he has gone
to Blackstone."

"I particularly wanted him,' grumbled Mr.
Chattaway, who never was pleasant-tempered at
the best of times, but would show himself unbear-
able if put out. "Cris knew I should want him
this morning. First Rupert, and then Cris! Are
you all going to turn disobedient?"

He made a halt at the door when he came to it, putting on his riding-glove. They stood grouped around him—Octave, Maude, and Emily. Edith had run out, and was near the horse.

"I would give a crown piece to know what Mr. Rupert did with himself last night," he savagely uttered. "John," exalting his voice, "have you any idea where Rupert Trevlyn hid himself all night?"

The locking-out had been known to the household; had afforded it considerable gossip. John had taken part in it; had joined in its surmises and its comments; therefore he was not at fault for a ready answer.

"I don't know nothing certain, sir. It ain't unlikely as he went down to the 'Sheaf 'o' Corn,' and slep' there."

"No, no, he did not," involuntarily burst from Maude.

It was not a lucky admission, for its tone was confidently decisive, implying that she knew where he did sleep. She spoke in the moment's impulse. The "Sheaf of Corn" was the nearest public house; it was notorious for its irregular doings, and Maude felt shocked at the bare suggestion that Rupert would enter such a place.

Mr. Chattaway turned to her. "Where *did* he sleep? What do you know about it?"

Maude's face turned hot and cold. She opened
her lips to answer, but closed them again without
speaking, the words dying away in her nucer-
tainty and hesitation.

Mr. Chattaway may have felt surprised. He
knew perfectly well that Maude had held no communication with Rupert that morning. He had
seen Rupert come in ; he had seen him go out ;
and Maude, the whole of the time, had not stirred
from his presence. He bent his cold grey eyes
upon her.

" From whom have you been hearing of Rupert's
doings ?"

It is very probable that Maude would have been
quite at a loss for an answer. To say, " I know
nothing of where Rupert slept," would have vio-
lated the rules of truth ; but to avow that the
lodge had sheltered him would not be expedient,
for its inmates' sake. Maude, however, was saved
a reply, for Emily spoke up before she had time
to give one, ill-nature in her tone, ill-nature in
her words.

" Maude must have heard it from George Ryle.
You saw her talking to him, papa. She said he
had been speaking of Rupert."

Mr. Chattaway did not ask another question.
It would have been superfluous to do so, in the
conclusion he had come to. He believed that

Rupert had slept at Trevlyn Farm. How else could George Ryle have had cognisance of his movements ?

"They'll be hatching a plot to try to overthrow me," he muttered to himself, as he went out to his horse : for his was one of those mean, suspicious natures which are always fancying the world is putting itself in antagonism against them. "Maude Ryle has been wanting to get me out of Trevlyn Hold ever since I came into it. From the very hour when she heard the squire's will read, and found I had inherited, she has been planning and plotting for it. She'd rather see Rupert in it than me ; and she'd rather see her pitiful son Treve in it than any. Yes, yes, Mr. Rupert, we know what you frequent Trevlyn Farm for. But it won't answer. It's waste of plans and waste of time ; it's waste of wickedness. They must do away with the executive of England's laws, before they can upset Squire Trevlyn's will. I'm safe in the estate. But it's not less annoying to know that my tenure is continually plotted against ; hauled over and peered into with their tongues and brains, and turned and twisted about, to see if they can't find a flaw in it, or insert one of their own manufacture."

It was a most strange thing that these suspicious fears should hold perpetual place in the

mind of the master of Trevlyn Hold. Not the
suspicion touching the plotting and the hatching ;
that came natural to him ; but the latent fears
lest his ownership should be shaken. A man who
holds an estate by means of a legal will, on which
no shade of a suspicion can be cast, need not
dread its being wrested from him. It was in
Squire Trevlyn's power to leave the Hold and its
revenues to whom he would. Had he chosen to
bequeath it to an utter stranger, one taken at
hazard from the list of names in the London
Directory, it was in his power so to do : and he
had bequeathed it to James Chattaway. Failing
direct male heirs, it may be thought that Mr.
Chattaway had as much right to it as any one
else ; at any rate, it had been the Squire's pleasure to bequeath it to him ; the bequest was made
in all due and legal and proper form, and there
the matter was at an end. *It was looked upon
as at an end by everybody except Chattaway.*
Except Chattaway ! Why, I say, should it not
have been looked upon as at an end by him ?
Ay, there's the strange mystery. None can fathom
the curious depths of the human heart. That the
master of Trevlyn Hold was ever conscious of a
vague dread that his tenure was to be some time
disturbed, was indisputable. He never betrayed
it to any living being by so much as a word ;

he strove to hide it even from himself; he pretended to ignore it altogether : but there it was, down deep in his secret heart. There it remained, and there it tormented him ; however unwilling he might have been to acknowledge that fact.

Could it be that a prevision of what was really to take place was cast upon him ?—a mysterious, not-to-be-accounted-for foreshadowing of the future. There are people who tell us that such warnings come.

The singularity of the affair was, that no grounds, or possible suspicion of grounds, could exist for this latent fear. Why, then, should it show itself ? In point of right, of justice, there's no question that Rupert Trevlyn was the true heir ; but right and justice cannot contend against law, as we know by the instances presented to our notice every day; and there was no more chance that Rupert could succeed in the face of the Squire's will, than that old Canham at the lodge could succeed. Had the Squire's two sons been living, he could have willed the estate to Chattaway, had he chosen. Whence, then, arose the fear ? Why, from that source whence it arises in many people—a bad conscience. It was true the estate had been legally left to him; that he was secure in it by the power of law ; but he

knew that his own nefarious handiwork, his deceit,
had brought it to him; he knew that when he
suppressed the news of the birth of Rupert, and
suffered Squire Trevlyn to go to his grave unin-
formed of the fact, he was guilty of nothing less
than a crime in the sight of God.   Mr. Chattaway
had heard of that inconvenient thing, retribution,
and his fancy suggested that it might possibly
overtake *him*.

If he had but known that he might have set
his mind at rest as to the plotting and planning,
he would have cared less to oppose Rupert's visits
to Trevlyn Farm.   Nothing could be further from
the thoughts of Rupert, or from George Ryle,
than any hatching of plots against Chattaway.
Their evenings, when together, were spent in
harmless conversation, in chess, in other rational
ways, without so much as a reference to Chattaway.   But that gentleman did not know it, and
tormented himself perpetually.

He got on his horse, and rode away.   As he
was passing Trevlyn Farm, buried in his unpleasant thoughts, which of course turned upon
that terrible bugbear of his life, hatching and
plotting, he saw Nora Dickson at the fold-yard
gate.   A thought struck him, and he turned his
horse's head towards her.

"How came your people to give Rupert Trevlyn

a bed last night?   They must know it would very much displease me."

"Give Rupert Trevlyn a bed!" repeated Nora, regarding Mr. Chattaway with the uncompromising stare which she was fond of according that gentleman.   "He did not have a bed here."

"No!" replied Mr. Chattaway.

"No," reiterated Nora.   "What should he want with a bed here?   Has he not got his own at Trevlyn Hold?   One bed there isn't much for him, when he might have expected to own the whole of the place; but I suppose he can at least count upon that."

Mr. Chattaway turned his horse short round, and rode away without another word.   He always got the worst of it with Nora.   A trifling explosion of his private sentiments with regard to her was spoken to the air, and he again became absorbed on the subject of Rupert.

"Where, then, *did* he pass the night?"

CHAPTER XVI.

MR. CHATTAWAY'S OFFICE.

IT was Nora's day for churning. The butter was made twice a-week at Trevlyn Farm, and the making of it fell to Nora. She was sole priestess of the dairy: it was many and many a long year since anybody but herself had interfered in it: except, indeed, in the churning. One of the men on the farm did that for her in a general way: and the words above, with which this chapter commences, "It was Nora's day for churning," would be looked upon by anybody familiar with the executive of Trevlyn Farm as a figure of speech.

In point of fact, however, they would have proved to be literally true as to this particular day. When Nora was detected at the fold-yard gate by Mr. Chattaway, idly staring up and down the road, she was looking for Jim Sanders, to order him in to churn. Not the Jim Sanders whom you heard mentioned in the earlier portion of our history, but Jim's son. Jim the elder was dead : he had brought on rather too many attacks of inward inflammation (a disease to which he was predisposed) with his love of beer ; and at last one attack worse than the rest came, and proved too much for him. The present Jim, representative of his name, was a youth of fourteen, not overdone with brains, but strong of muscle and sound of limb, and was found handy on the farm, where he was required to make himself useful at any work that came uppermost.

Just now he was wanted to turn the churn. The man who usually performed that duty was too busy out of doors to be spared for it to-day : therefore it fell to Jim. But Nora could not see Jim anywhere, and she returned in-doors and commenced the work herself.

The milk at the right temperature—for Nora was too experienced a dairy woman not to know that if she attempted to churn at the wrong one, it would be hours before the butter came—she took out the thermometer, and turned the milk into the churn. As she was doing this, the servant entered : a tall, stolid girl, remarkable for little except her height : Nanny, by name.

"Ain't nobody coming in to churn?" asked she.

"It seems not," answered Nora.

" Shall I do it ? "

" Not if I know it," returned Nora. " You'd like to quit your work for this straightforward pastime, wouldn't you ? Have you got the pota- toes on for the pigs ? "

" No," said Nanny, sullenly.

" Then go and see about it. You know it was to be done to-day. And I suppose the fire's burning and wasting away under the furnace in readiness."

Nanny stalked out of the dairy. She nearly always went about in pattens, which made her look like some great giantess moving in the house. Nora churned steadily away, using her arms alter- nately, and turned her butter on to the making- up board in about three-quarters of an hour. As she was proceeding to make it up, she saw through the wired window George ride into the fold-yard, and leave his horse in the stable. Another minute, and he came in.

" Is Mr. Callaway not come yet, Nora ? "

" I have seen nothing of him, Mr. George."

George took out his watch : the one bequeathed him by his father. It was only a silver one—as it may be in your remembrance. Mr. Ryle remarked —but George valued it as though it had been set in diamonds. He would be sure to wear that watch and no other so long as he should live. His

initials were engraved on it now: G. B. R. standing for George Berkeley Ryle.

"If Callaway cannot keep his appointments
better than this, I shall beg him not to make
any more with me," he remarked. "The last
time he came he kept me waiting three parts of
an hour."

"Have you seen Jim Sanders this morning?"
asked Nora.

"Jim Sanders? I saw him in the stable as I
rode out."

"I should like to find him!" said Nora. "He
is skulking somewhere. I have had to churn
myself."

"Where's Roger, then?"

"Roger couldn't hinder his time in-doors to-
day. I say, Mr. George, what's the matter up at
Trevlyn Hold again about Rupert?" resumed
Nora, turning from her butter to glance at
George.

"Why do you ask?" was his reply.

"Chattaway rode by an hour ago when I was
outside looking after Jim Sanders. He stopped
his horse, and asked how we came to give Rupert
a bed last night, when we knew that it would
displease him. Like his insolence!"

"What answer did you make?" said George,
after a pause.

"I gave him one," replied Nora, significantly. "Chattaway needn't fear he'll get no answer when he comes to me. He knows that."

"But what did you say about Rupert?"

"I said we had not given him a bed. That he he had not slept here. If Chattaway——"

Nora's speech was interrupted by the entrance of Mr. Chattaway's daughter, Octave. She had come to the farm, and, attracted by the sound of voices in the dairy, made her way to it at once. Miss Chattaway had taken it into her head lately to be friendly at Trevlyn Farm, honouring it with frequent visits. Mrs. Ryle neither encouraged nor repulsed her. She was civilly indifferent; but the young lady chose to take that as a welcome. Nora did not show her much greater favour than she was in the habit of showing her father. She bent her head over her butter-board, as if unaware that anybody had entered.

George took off his hat, which he had been wearing, as she stepped on to the cold floor of the dairy, and received her hand, which was held out to him. "Are you quite well, Miss Chattaway?"

"Who would have thought of seeing you at home at this hour?" she exclaimed, in the pretty, winning manner she could put on at times, and which she always did put on to George Ryle.

"And in Nora's dairy, watching her make up the butter!" he answered, in his free, pleasant, laughing tone. "The fact is, I have an appointment with a gentleman this morning, and he is keeping me waiting and making me angry. I can't spare the time to be in-doors."

"You look angry!" exclaimed Octave, laughing at him.

"Looks go for nothing," returned George.

"Is your harvest nearly in?"

"If this fine weather shall only last four or five days longer, it will be all in. We have had a glorious harvest this year. I hope everybody's as thankful for it as I am."

"You have some especial cause to be thankful for it?" she observed.

"I have."

She had spoken lightly, and the strangely earnest tone of the answer struck upon her. George could have said that but for that plentiful harvest they might not quite so soon have got rid of her father's debt.

"When shall you hold your harvest home?"

"Next Thursday; this day week," replied George. "Will you come to it?"

"Thank you very much," said Octave. "Yes, I will."

Had it been to save his life, George Ryle could

not have helped the surprise in his eyes, as he
turned them on Octave Chattaway. He had
asked the question in the light, careless gaiety of
the moment; really not intending it as an invitation; if he had meant it as an invitation, and
proffered it in all earnestness, he never would
have supposed it one to be accepted by Octave.
Mr. Chattaway's family had not been in the habit
of visiting at Trevlyn Farm.

"In for a penny, in for a pound," thought
George. "I don't know what Mrs. Ryle will say
to this; but if *she* comes, some of the rest shall
come."

It almost seemed as if Octave had divined part
of his thoughts. "I must ask my Aunt Ryle
whether she will have me. I shall tell her, by
way of bribe, that I delight in harvest homes."

"We must have you all," said George. "Your
sisters and Maude. Treve will be at home I
expect, and the Apperleys will be here."

"Who else will be here?" asked Octave. "But
I don't know about my sisters and Maude."

"Mr. and Mrs. Freeman. They and the Apperleys always come."

"That starched old parson!" uttered Octave.
"Does *he* come to a harvest home? He is not a
favourite with us at the Hold."

"I think he is with your mamma."

" Oh, mamma's nobody. Of course we are civil
to the Freemans, and exchange dull visits with
them once or twice a-year. You must be passably
civil to the parson you sit under."

There was a pause. Octave advanced nearer
to Nora, who had gone on diligently with her
work, never turning her head, or noticing Miss
Chattaway by so much as a look. Octave drew
close and watched her.

" How industrious you are, Nora!—as if you
enjoyed the occupation. I should not like to
grease my hands, making up butter."

" There are some might make it up in white kid
gloves to save their hands," retorted Nora. " The
butter wouldn't be any the better for it, Miss
Chattaway."

At this juncture Mrs. Ryle's voice was heard,
and Octave quitted the dairy to go in search of
her. George was about to follow when Nora
stopped him.

" What is the meaning of this new friendship
for us here—of these morning calls, and proffered
evening visits?" she asked; her voice full of grave
seriousness, her eyes thrown keenly on George's
face.

" How should I know ? " he carelessly replied.

" If you don't, I do," she said. " Can you take
care of yourself, George Ryle ? "

"I believe I can."

"Then do," said Nora, with an emphatic nod. "And don't despise my caution : perhaps you may want it."

He laughed in his gay light-heartedness : but he did not tell Nora how entirely unnecessary her precautionary warning was.

Later in the day, George Ryle had business which took him to Blackstone. It was no inviting ride. The place, as he drew near, had that flat, dreary, black aspect peculiar to the neighbourhood of mines in work. Rows of black and smoky huts were to be seen, the dwellings of the men who worked in the pits ; and little children ran about with naked legs and tattered clothing, whose thin faces were of squalid whiteness.

"Is it the perpetual *dirt* they live in that makes these children look so unhealthy?" thought George —a question he had asked himself a hundred times. "I believe the mothers never wash them ; perhaps they deem it would be a work of supere-rogation, where all around is so black—even to the very atmosphere."

Black, indeed! Within George's view at that moment might be seen high chimneys congregat-ing in all directions, their tall tops throwing out their volumes of smoke and flame. Numerous works were established around, connected with

iron and other productions of the richly-endowed
mines which abounded in the neighbourhood.
Valuable parts of land for the use of man—for
the furtherance of his civilisation, his comforts—
for the increase of his wealth; but not pleasant
for his eye, as compared with the rich fertilisation
of other spots, with their clear air, their green
meadows, and their blossoming trees.

The office belonging to the colliery of Mr. Chattaway stood in a particularly dreary angle of the
main road. It was a low but not very small
building, facing the road on one side, looking to
those tall chimneys and the dreary flat of country
on two of the others. On the fourth was a sort of
inclosed yard or waste ground, which appeared to
contain nothing but different heaps of coal, a peculiar description of barrow, and some round shal-
low baskets. The building looked like a great
shed; it was roofed over, and divided inside into
partitions.

As George rode by, he saw Rupert standing at
the narrow entrance door, leaning against its side,
as if in fatigue or idleness. Ford, the clerk, a
young man accustomed to take life in an easy manner, and to give himself little concern as to how
it went, was standing near, his hands in his
pockets. To see them thus, doing nothing, was
sufficient to tell George that Chattaway was not

about, and he rode across the strip of waste land
intervening between the road and the office.

" You look tired, Rupert."

" It's what I am," answered Rupert. " If things
are to go on like this, I shall grow tired of life."

" Not yet," said George, cheeringly. " You may
talk of that, perhaps, some fifty years hence."

Rupert made no answer. The sunlight (which
had decidedly a black shade in it) fell on his fair
features, on his golden hair. There was a hag-
gardness in those features, a melancholy look in
the dark blue eyes, that George did not like to
see. Ford, the clerk, who was humming the verse
of a song, cut short the melody in its midst, and
addressed George.

" He has been in this gay state all the afternoon, sir. A charming companion for a fellow !
It's a good thing I'm pretty jolly myself, or we
might both get consigned to the county asylum ;
two cases of melancholy madness. I hope he won't
make a night of it again—that's all. Nothing
wears out a chap for the day like no bed, and no
breakfast at the end of it."

" It isn't that," said Rupert. " I'm sick of it
altogether. There has been nothing but a row
here all day, George—ask Ford. Chattaway has
been on at us all. First, he attacked me : he
demanded where I slept, and I wouldn't tell him :

next, he attacked Cris—a most unusual thing—
and Oris has not got over it yet. He has gone
galloping off, to gallop his ill temper away."

" Chattaway has ? "

" Not Chattaway; Cris. Cris never came here
until one o'clock, and Chattaway had wanted him,
and there ensued a row. Next, Ford came in for
it : he had made his entries wrong. Something
had uncommonly put out Chattaway—that was
certain ; and to mend his temper, the inspector of
collieries came to-day and found fault, ordering
things to be done that Chattaway says he won't do."

" Where's Chattaway now ? "

" Oh, he's gone home. I wish I was there,"
added Rupert, " without the trouble of walking to
it. Chattaway has been ordering a load of coals
to the Hold. If they were going this evening
instead of to-morrow morning, I protest I'd take
my seat upon them, and get home that way."

" Are you so very tired ?" asked George.

" Dead beat."

" It's the sitting up," put in Ford again. " I
don't think much of that kind of thing will do for
Mr. Rupert Trevlyn."

" Perhaps it wouldn't do for you," grumbled
Rupert.

George prepared to ride away. " Have you had
any dinner, Rupert ?" he asked.

" I tried some, but my appetite had gone by. Chattaway was here till past two o'clock, and after that I wasn't hungry."

" He tried at bread-and-cheese," said Ford. " I told him if he'd get a piece of steak I'd cook it for him, if he was too tired to cook it himself; but he didn't."

" I must be gone," said George. " You will not have left in half an hour's time, shall you, Rupert ? "

" No ; nor in an hour either."

George rode off over the black and stony ground, and they looked after him. Then Ford bethought himself of a message he was charged to deliver at one of the pits, and Rupert went in-doors and sat down to the desk on his high stool.

Within the half-hour George Ryle was back. He rode up to the door, and dismounted. Rupert came forward, a pen in his hand.

" Are you ready to go home now, Rupert ? "

Rupert shook his head. " Ford went to the pit, and is not back yet; and I have a lot of writing to do. Why ? "

" I thought we would have gone home together. You shall ride my horse, and I'll walk; it will tire you less than going on foot."

" You are very kind, George," said Rupert. " Yes, I should like to ride. I was thinking just now, that if Cris were worth anything, he'd let me ride his horse back. But he's not worth anything, and he'd no more let me ride his horse and walk himself, than he'd let me ride him."

"Is Cris not gone home?"

"I fancy not. Unless he has gone by without calling in. Will you wait, George?"

"No. I must walk on. But I'll leave you the horse. You can leave it at the Farm, Rupert, and walk the rest of the way."

"I can ride on to the Hold, and send it back."

George hesitated for half a moment before he spoke. "I would prefer that you should leave it at the Farm, Rupert. It will not be far for you to walk after that."

Rupert acquiesced. Did he wonder why he might not ride the horse to the Hold? George would not say to him, "Because even that slight attention must, if possible, be kept from Chattaway."

He fastened the bridle to a hook in the wall's angle, where Mr. Chattaway often tied his horse, where Cris sometimes tied his. There was a stable near; but unless they were going to remain in the office or about the pits, Mr. Chattaway and his son seldom put up their horses.

George Ryle walked away with a hearty step, and Rupert returned to his desk. A quarter of an hour passed on, and the clerk, Ford, did not return. Rupert got impatient for his arrival, and went to the door to look out for him. He did not see Ford; but he did see Cris Chattaway. Cris was approaching on foot, at a snail's pace, leading his horse, which was dead lame.

"Here's a nice bother!" called out Cris. "How I am to get back home, I don't know."

"What has happened?" returned Rupert.

"Can't you see what has happened? *How* it happened, I am unable to tell you. All I know is, the horse fell suddenly lame, and whined out like a child. Something must have run into his foot, I conclude : is there still, perhaps? Whose horse is that? Why, it's George Ryle's," concluded Cris, in the same breath, as he drew sufficiently near to recognise it. "What brings his horse here."

"He has lent it to me, to save my walking home," said Rupert.

"Where is he? Here?"

"He has gone home on foot. I can't think where Ford's lingering," added Rupert, walking into the yard, and mounting on one of the smaller heaps of coal to get a better view of the side road from the colliery, by which Ford might be expected to arrive. "He has been gone this hour."

Cris was walking off in the direction of the stable, carefully leading his horse. "What are you going to do with him?" asked Rupert. "To leave him in the stable?"

"Until I can get home and send the groom for him. *I'm* not going to cool my heels, dragging him home," retorted Cris.

Rupert retired in-doors, and sat down on the high stool. He had some accounts to make up yet. They had to be done that evening; and as Ford did not come in to do them, he must. Had Ford been there, Rupert would have left him to do it, and gone home at once.

"I wonder how many years of my life I am to wear out in this lively place?" thought Rupert; after five minutes of uninterrupted attention given to his work, which in consequence slightly progressed. "It's a shame that I should be put to it. A paid fellow at ten shillings a-week would do it better than I. If Chattaway had a spark of good feeling in him, he'd put me into a farm. It would be better for me altogether, and more fitting for a Trevlyn. Catch him at it! He'd not let me be my own master for——"

A sound as of a horse trotting off from the door interrupted Rupert's cogitations. He flew off his stool to see. A thought crossed him that

George Ryle's horse might have got loose, and be speeding home riderless, at his own will and pleasure.

George Ryle's horse it was, but not riderless. To Rupert's intense astonishment, he saw Mr. Cris mounted on him, leisurely riding away.

"Halloa!" called out Rupert, speeding after the horse and his rider. "What are you going to do with that horse, Cris?"

Cris turned his head but did not stop. "I'm going to ride him home. His having been left here just happens right for me."

"You get off," shouted Rupert. "The horse was lent to me, not to you. Do you hear, Cris?"

Cris heard, but did not stop: he was urging the horse faster. "*You* don't want him," he roughly said. "You can walk, as you always do."

Further remonstrance, further following, was useless. Rupert's words were drowned in the echoes of the horse's hoofs, galloping away in the distance. Rupert stood, white with anger, impotent to stop him, his hands stretched out on the empty air, as if their action could arrest the horse and bring him back. Certainly the mortification was bitter; the circumstance precisely one of those likely to excite the choler of an excitable nature; and Rupert was on the point of going into that dangerous fit of madness known as the Trevlyn passion, when its course was turned aside by a hand being laid upon his shoulder.

He turned, it may almost be said, savagely. Ford was standing there out of breath, his good-humoured face red with the exertion of running.

"I say, Mr. Rupert, you'll do a fellow a service, won't you? I have had a message that my mother's taken suddenly ill; a fit, they say, of some sort. Will you finish what there is to do here, and lock up for once, so that I can go home directly?"

Rupert nodded. In his passionate disappointment about the horse, at having to walk home when he expected to ride, at being put upon, treated as of no account by Cris Chattaway, it seemed of little moment to him how long he remained, or what work he had to do: and the clerk, waiting for no farther permission, sped away with a fleet foot. Rupert's face was losing its deathly whiteness—there is no degree of whiteness like unto that born of passion or of sudden terror; and when he sat down again to the desk, the hectic of reaction was shining in his cheeks and lips.

Well, oh, well for him, could these dangerous fits of passion have been always arrested in their course on the threshold, as this had been arrested

now! The word dangerous is put advisedly :
they brought nothing less than danger in their
train.

But, alas! this was not to be.

CHAPTER XVII.

DEAD BEAT.

NORA was at some business or other in the fold-yard, when the man-servant at Trevlyn Hold, more especially devoted to the service of Cris Chattaway, came in at the gate with George Ryle's horse. As he passed Nora on his way to the stables, she turned round, and the man spoke.

"Mr. Ryle's horse, ma'am. Shall I take it on?"

"You know the way," was Nora's short answer. She did not regard the man with any favour, reflecting upon him, in her usual partial fashion, the dislike she entertained for his master and for Trevlyn Hold in general. "Mr. Trevlyn has sent it, I suppose?"

"Mr. Trevlyn!" repeated the groom, betraying some surprise.

Now, it was a fact that at Trevlyn Hold, Rupert was never called "Mr. Trevlyn." That it was his proper style and title, was indisputable; but Mr. Chattaway had as great a dislike to hear Rupert called by it as he had a wish to hear himself styled " the squire."   At the Hold, Rupert was " Mr. Rupert " only, and the neighbourhood generally had fallen into the same familiar style when speaking of or to him.   Nora supposed the man's repetition of the name had insolent reference to this; as much as to say, " Who's Mr. Trevlyn ? "

" Yes, Mr. Trevlyn," she resumed, in a sharp tone of reprimand.   " He is Mr. Trevlyn, Sam Atkins, and you know that he is, however some people may wish that it should be forgotten.   He is not Mr. Rupert, and he is not Mr. Rupert Trevlyn, but he is Mr. Trevlyn; and if he had his rights, he'd be Squire Trevlyn.   There ! you may go and tell your master that I said it."

Sam Atkins, a civil, quiet young fellow, was overpowered with astonishment at Nora's burst of eloquence.   " I'm not saying aught again it, ma'am," cried he, when he had recovered himself sufficiently to speak.   " But Mr. Rupert didn't send me with the horse at all.   It was young Mr. Chattaway."

" What had he got to do with it ? " resentfully asked Nora.

" He rode it home from Blackstone."

"*He* rode it? Cris Chattaway?"

"Yes," said the groom. "He has just got home now, and he told me to bring the horse back at once."

Nora pointed to the man to take the horse on to its stable, and went in-doors. She could not understand it. When George returned home on foot, and she inquired what he had done with his horse, he told her that he had left it at Blackstone for Rupert Trevlyn. To hear now that it was Cris who had had the benefit of it, and not Rupert, excited Nora's indignation. But the indignation would have increased fourfold had she known that Mr. Cris had rode the horse hard, and made a *détour* of some five miles out of his way, to transact a matter of private business of his own. She went straight to George, who was seated at tea with Mrs. Ryle.

"Mr. George, I thought you said to me that you had left your horse at Blackstone for Rupert Trevlyn, to save his walking home?"

"So I did," replied George.

"Then it's Cris Chattaway who has come home on it. I'd see *him* far enough before he should have the benefit of my horse!"

"It can't be," returned George; "you must be mistaken, Nora; Cris had his own horse there."

"You can go and ask for yourself," rejoined

Nora, in a crusty tone, not at all liking to be told that she was mistaken. "Sam Atkins is putting the horse in the stable, and he says it was Cris Chattaway who rode it from Blackstone."

George did go and ask for himself. He could not understand it at all; and he had no more fancy for allowing Cris Chattaway the use of his horse than Nora had. He supposed they had been exchanging steeds; though why they should do so, he could not imagine: that Cris had used his, and Rupert the one belonging to Cris.

Sam Atkins was in the stable, talking to Roger, one of the men about the farm. George saw at a glance that his horse had been ridden hard.

"Who rode this horse home?" he inquired, as the groom touched his hat to him.

"Young Mr. Chattaway, sir."

"And Mr. Rupert: what did he ride?"

"Mr. Rupert, sir? I don't think he is come home."

"Where's Mr. Cris Chattaway's own horse?"

"He have left it at Blackstone, sir. It fell dead lame, he says. I be going for it now."

George paused. "I lent my horse to Mr. Rupert," he said. "Do you know how it was that he did not use it himself?"

"I don't know nothing about it, sir. Mr. Cris came home just now on your horse, and told me to bring it down here immediate. His orders was, to go on to Blackstone for his, and to mind I led it gently home. He never mentioned Mr. Rupert."

Considerably later—in fact, it was past nine o'clock—Rupert Trevlyn appeared. George Ryle was leaning over the gate at the foot of his garden in a musing attitude, the bright stars above him, the slight frost of the autumn night rendering the air clear, though not very cold, when he saw a figure come slowly winding up the road. It was Rupert Trevlyn. The same misfortune seemed to have befallen him that had befallen the horse, for he limped as he walked.

"Are you lame, Rupert?" asked George.

"Lame with fatigue; nothing else," answered Rupert in that low, half-inaudible voice which a very depressed state of physical energy will induce. Let me come in and sit down half an hour, George, or I shall never get to the Hold."

"How was it that you let Cris Chattaway ride my horse home? I left it for yourself."

"*Let* him! He mounted and galloped off without my knowing—the sneak! I should be ashamed to be guilty of such a trick. I declare I had half a mind to ride his horse home, lame as it was. But that the poor animal is in evident pain, I would have done it!"

"You are very late."

"I have been such a while coming. The truth is, I sat down when I was half way here; I was so dead tired I couldn't stir a step; and I dropped asleep."

"A very wise proceeding!" cried George, in a pleasant, though mocking tone. He did not care to say more plainly how *un*wise—nay, how pernicious, it might be for Rupert Trevlyn. "Did you sleep long?"

"Pretty well. The stars were out when I awoke; and I felt ten times more tired when I got up than I had felt when I sat down."

George placed him in the most comfortable arm-chair they had, and got him a glass of wine. Nora brought some refreshment, but Rupert could not eat it.

"Try it," urged George.

"I can't," said Rupert; "I am completely done over."

He leaned back in the chair, his fair curls falling on its cushions, his bright face—bright with a touch of inward fever—turned upwards to the light. Gradually his eyelids closed, and he dropped into a calm sleep.

George sat watching him. Mrs. Ryle, who was poorly still, had retired to her chamber for the night, and they were alone. Very unkindly, as may be thought, George woke him soon, and told him it was time for him to go.

"Do not deem me inhospitable, Rupert; but it will not do for you to be locked out again to-night."

"What's the time?" asked Rupert.

"Considerably past ten."

"I was in such a nice dream. I thought I was being carried along in a large sail belonging to a ship. The motion was pleasant and soothing to a degree. Past ten! What a bother! I shall be half dead again before I get to the Hold."

"I'll lend you my arm, Ru, to help you along."

"That's a good fellow!" exclaimed Rupert.

He got up and stretched himself, and then fell back in his chair, like a leaden weight. "I'd give five shillings to be there without the trouble of walking," quoth he.

"Rupert, you will be late."

"I can't help it," returned Rupert, folding his arms and leaning back again in the chair. "If Chattaway locks me out again, he must. I'll sit down in the portico until morning, for I shan't be able to stir another step from it."

Rupert was in that physically depressed state which reacts upon the mind. It may be said that he was as incapable of *care* as of exertion: whether he got in or not, whether he passed the night in a comfortable bed, or under the trees in the avenue, seemed of very little moment in his present state of feeling. Altogether, he was some time getting off; and they heard the remote church clock of Barbrook chime out the half-past ten before they were half-way to the Hold. The sound came distinctly to their ears on the calm night air.

"I was somewhere about this spot when the half-hour struck last night, for your clocks were fast," remarked Rupert. "I ran all the way home after that—with what success, you know. I can't run to-night."

"I'll do my best to get you in," said George. "I hope I shan't be tempted, though, to speak my mind too plainly to Chattaway."

The Hold was closed for the night. Lights appeared in several of the windows. Rupert halted when he saw the light in one of them. "Aunt Diana must have returned," he said; "that's her room."

George Ryle rang a loud, quick peal at the bell. It was not answered. He then rang again: a sharp, imperative, urgent peal, and shouted out with his stentorian voice; a prolonged shout that could not have come from the lungs of Rupert; and it brought Mr. Chattaway to the window of his wife's dressing-room in very surprise. One or two more windows in different parts of the house were thrown up.

"It is I, Mr. Chattaway. I have been assisting Rupert home. Will you be so kind as to allow the door to be opened?"

Mr. Chattaway was nearly struck dumb with the insolence of the demand, coming from the quarter it did. He could scarcely speak at first, even to refuse.

"He does not deserve your displeasure to-night," said George, in his clear, frank, ringing voice, which might be heard distinctly ever so far. "He could scarcely get here from fatigue and illness. But for taking a rest at my mother's house, and having the help of my arm thence here, I question if he would have got as far. Be so good as to let him in, Mr. Chattaway."

"How dare you make such a request to me?" roared Mr. Chattaway, recovering himself a little. "How dare you come disturbing the peace of my house at night, George Ryle, as any housebreaker might come—save that you make more noise about it!"

"I came to bring Rupert," was George's clear answer. "He is waiting here to be let in; he is tired and ill."

"I will not let him in," raved Mr. Chattaway. "How dare you, I ask?"

"What *is* all this?" broke from the amazed voice of Miss Diana Trevlyn. "What does it mean? I don't comprehend it in the least."

George looked up at her window. "Rupert could not get home by the hour specified by Mr. Chattaway—half-past ten. I am asking that he may be admitted now, Miss Trevlyn."

"Of course he can be admitted," said Miss Diana.

"Of course he shan't," retorted Mr. Chattaway.

"Who says he couldn't get home in time if he had wanted to come?" called out Cris from a window on the upper story. "Does it take him five or six hours to walk from Blackstone?"

"Is that you, Christopher?" asked George, going a little back that he might see him better. "I want to speak to you. By what right did you take possession of my horse at Blackstone this afternoon, and ride him home?"

"I chose to do it," said Oris.

"I lent that horse to Rupert, who was unfit to walk. It had been more in accordance with generosity—though you may not understand the word —had you left it for him. He was not in bed last night; he has gone without food to-day—you were more capable of walking home than he."

Miss Diana craned forth her neck. "Chattaway,

I must inquire into this. Let that front door be opened."

"I will not," he answered. And he banged down his window with a resolute air, as if to avoid further colloquy.

But in that same moment the lock of the front door was heard to turn, and it was thrown open by Octave Chattaway.

CHAPTER XVIII.

MRS. CHATTAWAY'S "OLD IMPRESSION."

IT was surely a scene to excite some interest, if only the interest of curiosity, that was presented at Trevlyn Hold that night. Octave Chattaway in evening dress—for she had not begun to prepare for bed, although some time in her chamber —standing at the hall-door which she had opened; Miss Diana pressing forward from the back of the hall in a hastily thrown-on dressing-gown; Mr. Chattaway in a waistcoat; Cris in greater dishabille; and Mrs. Chattaway dressed as was Octave.

Rupert came in, coughing with the night air, and leaning on the arm of George Ryle. There was no light, save what was afforded by a candle carried by Miss Trevlyn; but she stepped forward and lighted the lamp.

"Now then," said she. "What is all this?"

"It is this," returned the master of Trevlyn Hold: "that I make rules for the proper regula-

tion of my household, and a beardless boy chooses
to break them. I should think"—turning shortly
upon Miss Diana—"that you are not the one to
countenance that."

"No," said she; "when rules are made they
must be kept. What is your defence, Rupert?"

Rupert had thrown himself upon a bench against
the wall in utter weariness both of mind and
body. "I don't care to make any defence," said
he in his apathy, as he leaned his cheek upon his
hand, and fixed his blue eyes on Miss Trevlyn;
"I don't know that there's much defence to make.
Mr. Chattaway orders me to be in by half-past
ten. I was at George Ryle's last night, and I a-
little exceeded the time, getting here five minutes
or so after it, so I was locked out. Cris let himself in with his latch-key, but he would not let in
me."

Miss Diana glanced at Cris, but she said nothing.
Mr. Chattaway interrupted. George, erect, fear-
less, was standing opposite to the group, and it
was to him that Mr. Chattaway turned.

"What I want to know is this—by what right
you interfere, George Ryle?"

"I am not aware that I have interfered—
except by giving Rupert my arm up the hill, and
by asking you to admit him. No very unjustifiable interference, surely, Mr. Chattaway."

"But it is, sir. And I ask why you presume to do it?"

"Presume?" returned George, making a pause after the word. But there was no answer to it, and he went on. "I saw Rupert to-night, accidentally, as he was coming from Blackstone. It was about nine o'clock. I was at my garden-gate. He appeared terribly tired, and wished to come into the house and rest. There he fell asleep. I awoke him in time, but he seemed to be too weary to get here himself, and I came with him to help him along. He walked slowly—painfully I should say; and it made him arrive later than he ought to have arrived. Will you be so good, Mr. Chattaway, as to explain what part of this interference was unjustifiable? I do not see that I could have done less."

"You will see that you do less for the future," growled Mr. Chattaway. "I will have no interference of yours between the Hold and Rupert Trevlyn."

"Oh, Mr. Chattaway, you may make yourself perfectly easy," returned George, some sarcasm in his tone. "Nothing could be farther from my intention than to interfere in any way with you, or with the Hold, or with Rupert in connection with you and the Hold. But, as I told you this morning, until you show me any good and sufficient reason for the contrary, I shall certainly observe common courtesy to Rupert when he comes in my way."

"Nonsense!" interposed Miss Diana. "Who says you are not to show courtesy to Rupert, George? Do you?" she asked, wheeling sharply round on Chattaway.

"There's one thing requires explanation," said Mr. Chattaway, turning to Rupert, and drowning Miss Diana's voice. "How came you to stop at Blackstone till this time of night? Where had you been lagging?"

Rupert answered the questions mechanically, never lifting his head. "I didn't leave until late. Ford wanted to go home, and I had to stop. After that I sat down on the way and dropped asleep."

"Sat down on your way and dropped asleep!" echoed Miss Diana. "What made you do that?"

"I don't know. I had been tired all day. I had no bed, you hear, last night. I suppose I can go to mine now?" he added, rising. "I want it badly enough."

"You can go—for this time," assented the master of Trevlyn Hold. "But you will understand that it is the last night I shall suffer my rules to be set at nought. You shall be in to time, or you do not come in at all."

Rupert shook hands with George Ryle, spoke a general "Good night" to the rest collectively, and went towards the stairs. At the back of the hall, lingering there in her timidity, stood Mrs. Chattaway. "Good night, dear Aunt Edith," he whispered.

She gave no answer. She only laid her hand upon his as he passed, and so momentary was the action that it escaped unobserved, save by one pair of eyes—and those were Octave Chattaway's.

George was the next to go. Octave put out her hand to him. "Does Caroline come to the harvest home?" she inquired.

"Yes, I think so. Good night."

"Good night," replied Octave, amiably. "I am glad you took care of Rupert."

"She's as false as her father," thought George, as he commenced his strides down the avenue.

They were all dispersing. There was nothing now to stay up for. Chattaway was turning to the staircase, when Miss Diana stepped inside one of the sitting-rooms, carrying her candle with her, and beckoned to him.

"What do you want, Diana?" he asked, in not a pleasant tone, as he followed her in.

"Why did you shut out Rupert last night?"

"Because I chose to do it!"

"But suppose I choose that he should not be shut out," returned Miss Diana.

"Then we shall split," angrily rejoined the master of Trevlyn Hold. "I say that half-past ten o'clock is quite late enough for Rupert to enter. He is younger than Cris; you and Edith say he is not strong; *is* it too early?"

Mr. Chattaway was right in this. It was a sufficiently late hour; and Miss Diana, after a pause, pronounced it to be so. "I shall talk to Rupert," she said. "There's no harm in his going to spend an hour or two with George Ryle, or with any other friend, but he must be home in good time."

"Just so; he must be home in good time," acquiesced Chattaway. "He shall be home by half-past ten. And the only way to ensure that, is to lock him out at first when he transgresses it. Therefore, Diana, I shall follow my own way in this, and I beg you will not interfere."

Miss Diana went up to Rupert's room. He had taken off his coat, and thrown himself on the bed, as if the fatigue of undressing were too much for him.

"What's that for?" asked Miss Diana, as she entered. "Is that the way you get into bed?"

Rupert rose and sat down on a chair. "Only the coming up stairs seems to tire me," he said, in a tone of apology. "I should not have lain a minute."

Miss Diana threw her head a little back, and looked fully at Rupert. The determined will of the Trevlyns shone out from every line of her face.

"I have come to ask where you slept last night. I mean to know it, Rupert."

"I don't mind your knowing it," replied Rupert; "I have told Aunt Edith. I decline to tell Chattaway, and I hope that nobody else will tell him."

"Why?"

"Because he might lay blame where no blame is due. Chattaway turned me from the door, Aunt Diana, and Cris, who came up just after, turned me from it also. I went down to the lodge, and got Ann Canham to let me in; and I lay part of the night on their hard settle, and part of the night I sat upon it. That's where I was. But if Chattaway knew it, he'd be turning old Canham and Ann from the lodge, as he turned me from the door."

"Oh, no, he'd not," said Miss Diana, "if it were my pleasure to keep them in it. Do you feel ill, Rupert?"

"I feel middling. It is that I am tired, I suppose. I shall be all right in the morning."

Miss Diana descended to her own room. Inside it, waiting for her, was Mrs. Chattaway. Mrs. Chattaway had a shawl thrown over her shoulders now, and seemed to be shivering. She slipped the bolt of the door—what was she afraid of?—and turned to Miss Trevlyn, her hands clasped.

"Diana, this is killing me!" she wailed. "Why should Rupert be treated as he is? I know I am but a poor creature, that I have been one all my life—a very coward; but sometimes I think that I must speak out and protest against the injustice, though I should die in the effort."

"Why, what's the matter?" uttered Miss Diana, whose intense composure formed a strange contrast to her sister's agitated words and bearing.

"Oh, you know!—you know! I have not dared to speak out much, even to you, Diana; but it's killing me—it's killing me! Is it not enough that we despoiled Rupert of his inheritance, but we must also——"

"Be silent!" sharply interrupted Miss Diana, glancing around and lowering her voice to a whisper. "Will you never have done with that folly, Edith?"

"I shall never have done with its remembrance. I don't often speak of it; once, it may be, in

seven years, not more. Better for me that I
could speak of it; it would prey upon my heart
less!"

"You have benefited by it as much as anybody
has."

"Yes: I cannot help myself. Heaven knows
that if I could retire to some poor hut, and live
upon a crust, and benefit by it no more, I should
do so—oh, how willingly! But there's no escape. I am hemmed in by its consequences;
we are all hemmed in by them—and there's no
escape."

Miss Diana looked at her. Steadfastly, keenly;
not angrily, but searchingly and critically, as a
doctor looks at a patient supposed to be afflicted
with mania.

"If you do not take care, Edith, you will become insane upon this point, as I believe I have
warned you before," she said with composed calm-
ness. "I am not sure but you are slightly
touched now!"

"I do not think I am," replied poor Mrs. Chattaway, passing her hand over her brow. "I feel
confused enough here sometimes for madness, but
there's no fear that it will really come. If thinking could have turned me mad, I should have
been mad years ago.

"The very act of your coming here in this

state of excitement, when you should be going to your bed, and of saying what you do **say,** must be nothing less than a degree of madness."

"I would go to bed if I could sleep," said Mrs. Chattaway. "I lie awake night after night, thinking of the past; of the present; thinking of Rupert and of what we did for him; thinking of the treatment we deal out to him now. I think of his father, poor Joe; I think of his mother, Emily Dean, whom we once so loved; and I—and I—I cannot sleep, Diana!"

There really did seem something strange in Mrs. Chattaway to-night. For once in her life, Diana Trevlyn's heart beat a shade faster.

"Try and calm yourself, Edith," she said, soothingly.

"I wish I could! I should be more calm if you and my husband would let me be. If you would but allow Rupert to be treated with common kindness——"

"He is not treated with unkindness," interrupted Miss Diana.

"It appears to me that he is treated with nothing but unkindness. He——"

"Is he beaten?—is he starved?"

"The system pursued towards him is altogether unkind," persisted Mrs. Chattaway. "Indulgences dealt out to our own children are denied to him. When I think that he might be the true master of Trevlyn Hold——"

"Edith, I shall not listen to this," interrupted Miss Diana. "What has come to you to-night?"

A shiver passed over the frame of Mrs. Chattaway. She was sitting on a low toilette chair covered with white drapery, her elbow on her knee, her head bent on her hand. By her reply, which she did not look up to give, it appeared that she took the question literally.

"I feel the pain more than usual; nothing else. I do feel it so sometimes."

"What pain?" asked Miss Diana.

"The pain of remorse: the pain of the wrong dealt out to Rupert. It seems to be greater than I can bear. Do you know," she added, raising her bright, feverish eyes to Miss Diana, "that I scarcely closed my eyelids once last night? All the long night through I was thinking of Rupert. I fancied him lying outside on the damp grass; I fancied him——"

"Stop a minute, Edith. Are you seeking to blame your husband to me?"

"No, no; I don't blame him—I don't seek to blame any one. But I wish it could be altered."

"If Rupert knows the hour for coming in—and it is not an unreasonable hour—it is he who is to blame if he exceeds it."

Mrs. Chattaway could not gainsay this. In point of fact, though she found that things were grievously uncomfortable, wrong altogether, she had not the strength of mind to say *where* the system was deficient, or how it should be altered. On this fresh agitation, the coming in at half-past ten at night, she could only judge as a vacillating woman. The hour, as Miss Diana said, was not an unreasonable one, and Mrs. Chattaway would have fallen in with it with all her heart, and approved her husband's judgment in making it, if Rupert had only obeyed its mandate. If Rupert did not obey it—if he somewhat exceeded its bounds—she would have liked that the door should still be open to him, and no scolding given. It was the discomfort that worried her; it was mixing itself up with the old feeling of wrong done to Rupert, rendering things, as she aptly expressed it, more miserable than she could bear.

"I'll talk to Rupert to-morrow morning," said Miss Diana. "I shall add my authority to Chattaway's, and tell him that he *must* be in."

It may be that a shadow of the future was casting itself over the mind of Mrs. Chattaway, dimly and vaguely pointing to the terrible events hereafter to arise—events which would throw their consequences on the remainder of Rupert's future life, and which had their origin in this new and ill-omened mandate, touching his entrance into the Hold at night.

"Edith," said Miss Diana, "I would recommend you to get less sensitive on the subject of Rupert. It is growing with you into a morbid feeling."

"I wish I could! It does grow upon me. Do you know," she added, sinking her voice and looking feverishly at her sister, "that old impression has come again! I thought it had worn itself out: I thought it might have gone away for ever."

Miss Diana nearly lost her patience. Her own mind was a very contrast to her sister's; the two were as widely opposite in their organisation as are the north 'and the south pole. Fanciful, dreamy, vacillating, and weak, the one; the other strong, practical, very matter-of-fact.

"I don't know what you mean by the 'old impression,'" she rejoined, with a contempt she did not seek to disguise. "Is it not some new folly?"

"I have told you of it in the old days, Diana. I used to feel certain—certain—that the wrong which we inflicted on Rupert would avenge itself —that in some way he would come into his inheritance, and we should be despoiled of it. I felt so certain of it that every morning of my life when I got up I seemed to look for its fulfilment before the day should close. But the time went on and on, and it never was fulfilled ;—it went on so long that the impression wore itself out of my mind, and I ceased to expect it. But now it has come again. It is stronger than ever. For some weeks past it has been growing more palpable to me day by day, and I cannot shake it off."

"The best thing you can do now is to go to bed, and try and sleep off your folly," cried Miss Trevlyn, with the stinging contempt she allowed herself at rare times to show to her sister. "I feel more provoked with you, Edith, than I can express. A child might be pardoned for indulging in such absurdities of mind ; a woman, never !"

Mrs. Chattaway rose. "I'll go to bed," she meekly answered, "and get what sleep I can. I remember that you cast ridicule on this feeling of mine in the old days——"

"Pray did anything come of it then ?" interrupted Miss Diana, sarcastically.

"I have said it did not. And the impression left me. But it has come again now. Good night, Diana."

"Good night, and a more sensible frame of mind to you !" was the retort of Miss Diana Trevlyn.

Mrs. Chattaway crept softly along the corridor

to her own dressing-room. She was in hopes
that her husband by that time was in bed and
asleep. What was her surprise, then, to see him
sitting at the table when she entered, not un-
dressed, and as wide awake as she was.

"You have business with Diana late," he
remarked.

Mrs. Chattaway felt wholly and entirely subdued : she had felt so since the previous night,
when Rupert was denied admittance. The painful timidity, clinging to her always, seemed
partially to have left her for a time—not to be
putting itself so palpably foremost. It was as
though she had not the strength left to be shy;
almost as Rupert felt in his weariness of body,
she was past caring for anything in her utter
weariness of mind. Otherwise, she might not
have spoken to Miss Diana as she had just done :
most certainly she could never have spoken as she
was about to speak to Mr. Chattaway.

"What may your business with her have
been ?" he resumed.

"It was not much, James," she answered. "I
was saying how ill I felt."

"Ill ! With what ?"

"Ill in mind, I think," said Mrs. Chattaway,
putting her hand to her brow. "I was telling her
that the old fear had come upon me ; the impres-

sion that used to cling to me always that some change was at hand regarding Rupert. I lost it for a great many years, but it has come again."

" Try and speak lucidly, if you can," was Mr. Chattaway's answer. " What has come again ?"

" It seems to have come upon me in the light of a warning," she resumed, so lucidly that Mr. Chattaway, had he been some steps lower in the social grade, might have felt inclined to beat her. "I have ever felt that Rupert would in some manner regain his rights—I mean what he was deprived of," she hastily added, in deprecation of the word " rights," which had slipped from her. " That he will regain Trevlyn Hold, and we shall lose it."

Mr. Chattaway listened in consternation, his mouth gradually opening in his bewilderment. " What makes you think that ?" he asked, when he had found his tongue.

" I don't exactly *think* it, James. Think is not the right word. The feeling has come upon me again within the last few weeks, and I cannot shake it off. I believe it to be a presentiment; a warning."

Paler and paler grew Mr. Chattaway. He did not understand. Like Miss Diana Trevlyn, he was very matter-of-fact, comprehending nothing but what could be seen and felt ; and his wife might as well have spoken to him in an unknown language as of "presentiments." He drew a rapid conclusion that some unpleasant fact, bearing upon the dread which *he* had long felt, must have come to his wife's knowledge.

"What have you heard?" he gasped.

"I have heard nothing; nothing whatever. I——"

"Then what on earth are you talking of?"

"Did you not understand me, James? I say that the impression was once firmly seated in my mind that Rupert would somehow be restored to what—to what "—she scarcely knew how to frame her words with the delicacy she deemed due to her husband's feelings—"to what would have been his but for his father's death. And that impression has now returned to me."

"But you have not heard anything? Any plot? —any conspiracy that's being hatched against us?" he reiterated.

"No, no."

Mr. Chattaway stared searchingly at his wife. Did he fancy, as Miss Diana had done, that her intellects were becoming disordered?

"Why, then, what do you mean?" he asked, after a pause. "Why should such an idea arise?"

Mrs. Chattaway was silent. She could not

to him the truth : could not say to him that she
believed it was the constant dwelling upon the
wrong and the injustice, which had first suggested
the notion that the wrong would inevitably recoil
on them, the workers of it. They had broken
alike the laws of God and man; and those who
do so cannot be sure in this world of immunity
from punishment. That they had so long enjoyed
unmolested the inheritance gained by fraud, gave
no certainty that they would enjoy it to the end.
She felt it, if her husband and Diana Trevlyn did
not. Too often there were certain verses of Holy
Writ spelling out their syllables upon her brain.
"Remove not the old landmark; and enter not
into the fields of the fatherless : for their
Redeemer is mighty; he shall plead their cause
with thee."

All this she could not say to Mr. Chattaway.
She could give him no good reason for what she
had said; he did not understand imaginative
fancies, and he went to rest after bestowing upon
her a sharp lecture for indulging in such.

Nevertheless, in spite of her denial, the master
of Trevlyn Hold could not divest himself of the
impression that she must have picked up some
scrap of news, or heard a word dropped in some
quarter, which had led her to say what she did.
And it gave him terrible discomfort.

Was the haunting shadow, the dread lying latent in his heart, about to be changed into substance? He lay on his bed, turning uneasily from side to side until morning light, and wondering from what quarter the first glimmer of the mischief would come.

CHAPTER XIX.

A FIT OF AMIABILITY IN CRIS.

RUPERT came down to breakfast the next morning. He was cold, sick, shivery; little better than he had felt the previous night; his chest was sore, his breathing painful. A good fire burnt in the grate of the breakfast-room—Miss Diana was a friend to fires, and caused them to be lighted as soon as the heat of summer had passed—and Rupert bent over it. He cared for it more than for food; and yet it was no doubt the having gone without food the previous day which was causing the sensation of sickness within him now. Miss Diana glided in, erect and majestic. "How are you this morning?" she asked of Rupert.

"Pretty well," he answered, as he warmed his thin white hands over the blaze. "I have got the old pain here a bit"—touching his chest. "It will go off by-and-by, I dare say."

Miss Diana had her eyes riveted on him. The extreme delicacy of his countenance—its lines of

fading health—struck upon her greatly. Was he
looking worse? or was it that her absence from
home for three weeks had caused her to notice it
more than she had done when seeing him daily?
She asked herself the question, and she could not
decide.

"You don't look very well, Rupert."

"Don't I? I have not felt well for this week
or two. I think the walking to Blackstone and
back is too much for me."

"You must have a pony," she continued, after
a pause.

"Ah! that would be a help to me," he said, his
countenance brightening. "I might get on better
with what I have to do when there. Mr. Chattaway grumbles, and grumbles, but I declare to you,
Aunt Diana, that I do my best. The walk there
seems to take away all my energy, and, by the
time I sit down, I am unfit for work."

Miss Diana went nearer to him, and spoke in
a lower tone. "What was the reason that you
disobeyed Mr. Chattaway with regard to coming
in?"

"I did not do it intentionally," he replied.
"The time slipped on, and it got late without my
noticing it. I think I told you so last night,
Aunt Diana."

"Very well. It must not occur again," she

said, peremptorily and significantly. "If you are locked out in future, I shall not interfere."

Mr. Chattaway came in, settling himself into his coat, with a discontented gesture and blue face. He was none the better for his night of sleeplessness, and the torment which had caused it. Rupert drew away from the fire, leaving the field clear for him: as a schoolboy does at the entrance of his master.

"Don't let us have this trouble with you repeated," be roughly said to Rupert. "As soon as you have breakfasted, you make the best of your way to Blackstone: and don't lag on the road."

"Rupert's not going to Blackstone to-day," said Miss Diana.

Mr. Chattaway turned upon her: no very pleasant expression on his countenance. "What's that for?"

"I shall keep him at home for a week," she said, "and let him be nursed. After that, I dare say he'll be stronger, and can attend better to his duty in all ways."

Mr. Chattaway could willingly have braved Miss Diana, if he had only dared. But he did not dare. He strode to the breakfast-table and took his seat, leaving those who liked to follow him.

It has been remarked that there was a latent

antagonism ever at work in the hearts of George
Ryle and Octave Chattaway; and there was certainly ever perpetual, open, and visible antagonism
between the actions of Mr. Chattaway and Miss
Diana Trevlyn, in so far as they related to the
ruling economy at Trevlyn Hold. She had the
open-heartedness of the Trevlyns—he, the miserly
selfishness of the Chattaways; she was liberal on
the estate and in the household—he would have
been niggardly to a degree. Miss Diana, however,
was the one to reign paramount, and he was
angered every hour of his life by seeing some
extravagance—as he deemed it—which might have
been avoided. He could indemnify himself at the
mines; and there he did as he pleased.

Breakfast over, Mr. Chattaway went out. Cris
went out. Rupert, as the day grew warm and
bright, strolled into the garden, and basked on
the bench there in the sun. He very much
enjoyed these days of idleness. To sit as he was
doing now, feeling that no exertion whatever was
required of him; that he might stay where he
was for the whole day, and gaze up at the blue
sky as he fell into thought; or watch the light
fleecy clouds that rose above the horizon, and form
them in his fancy into groups of animals—of
mountains, of many fantastic things—constituted
one of the pleasures of Rupert Trevlyn's life.

Not for the bright blue of the sky, not for the wreathing and ever-changing clouds, not even for the warm sunshine and the balmy air—it was not for all these he cared, but for the *rest*. The delightful consciousness that he might be as still as he pleased ; that no Blackstone or any other far-to-be-reached place would demand him ; that for a whole day he might be at rest—there lay the charm. Nothing could possibly have been more suggestive of his want of strength—as anybody might have guessed who possessed sufficient penetration.

No. Mr. Chattaway need not have feared that Rupert was engaged hatching plots against him, whenever he was out of his sight. Had poor Rupert possessed the desire to hatch such, he would have lacked the energy.

The dinner hour at Trevlyn Hold, nominally early, was frequently regulated by the will or the movements of the master. When he said he could only be home by a given hour—three, four, five, six, as the case might be—then the cook had her orders accordingly. It was fixed on this day for four o'clock. At two (the more ordinary hour for it) Cris came in.

Strictly speaking, however, it was ten minutes past two, and Cris burst into the dining-room with a heated face, afraid lest he should come in for

the tail of the meal. Whatever might be the
hour fixed, the dinner was required to be on the
table to the minute; and it generally was so.
Miss Diana was an exacting mistress. Cris burst
in, hair untidy, hands unwashed, desperately afraid
of losing his share.

A long face drew he. Not a soul was in the
room, and the dining-table showed its bright
mahogany, nothing upon it. Cris pulled the
bell.

"What time do we dine to-day?" he asked, in
a sharp tone, of the servant who answered it.

"At four, sir."

"What a nuisance! And I am as hungry as a
hunter. Get me something to eat. Here—stop,
you!—where are they all?"

"Madam's at home, sir; and I think Miss
Octave's at home. The rest are out."

Cris muttered something which was not heard,
which perhaps he did not intend should be
heard; and when his luncheon was brought in,
he sat down to it with great satisfaction. After
he had finished, he went to the stables, and by-
and-by came in to find his sister.

"I say, Octave, I want to take you for a drive.
Will you go?"

The unwonted attention on her brother's part
quite astonished Octave. Before now she had

asked him to drive her out, and been met with rough refusal. Cris was of that class of young gentlemen who see no good in overpowering their sisters with politeness.

"Get your things on at once," said Cris.

Octave felt dubious. She was engaged writing letters to some particular friends with whom she kept up a correspondence, and did not much care to be interrupted.

"Where is it to go, Cris?"

"Anywhere. We can drive through Barmester, and so home by the cross roads. Or we'll go down the lower road to Barbrook, and go on to Barmester that way."

The suggestion did not offer sufficient attraction to Octave. "No," said she; "I am busy, Cris, and shall not go out this afternoon. I don't care to drive out when there's nothing to go for."

"You may as well come. It isn't often I ask you."

"No, that it is not," returned Octave, with emphasis. "You have some particular motive in asking me to go now, I know. What is it, Cris?"

"I want to try my new horse. They say he'll go beautifully in harness."

"What! that handsome horse you took a fancy to the other day?—that papa said you should not buy?"

Cris nodded. "They let me have him for forty-five pounds."

"Where did you get the money?" wondered Octave.

"Never you mind. I have paid ten pounds down, and they'll wait for the rest. Will you come?"

"No," said Octave. "I shan't go out to-day."

The refusal perhaps was somewhat softened by the dashing up to the door of the dog-cart with the new purchase in it; and Cris ran out. A handsome animal certainly, but apparently a remarkably sprightly one, for it was executing a dance on its hind legs. Mrs. Chattaway came through the hall, dressed for walking. Cris seized upon her.

"Mother, dear, you'll go for a drive with me," cried he, caressingly. "Octave won't—an ill-natured thing!"

It was so unusual a circumstance to find herself made much of by her son, spoken to affectionately, that Mrs. Chattaway, in very surprise and gratitude, ascended the dog-cart forthwith. "I am glad to accompany you, dear," she softly said. "I was only going to walk in the garden."

But before Cris had gathered the reins in his hand and taken his place beside her, George Ryle came up, and somewhat hindered the departure.

"I have been to Barmester to see Caroline this morning, Mrs. Chattaway, and have brought you a message from Amelia," he said, keeping his hold on the side of the dog-cart as he spoke—as much of a hold as he could keep on it, for the dancing horse.

"That she wants to come home, I suppose?" said Mrs. Chattaway, smiling.

"The message I was charged with was, that she *would* come home," he said, smiling in answer. "The fact is, Caroline is coming home for a few days: and Amelia thinks she will be cruelly dealt by, unless she is allowed the holiday also."

"Caroline is coming to the harvest home?"

"Yes. I told Amelia——"

The holding on became impossible; and George drew back, and took a critical survey of the new horse. "Why, it is the horse Allen has had for sale!" he exclaimed. "What brings him here, Cris?"

"I have bought him," shortly answered Cris.

"Have you? Mrs. Chattaway, I would not advise you to venture out behind that horse. I do not think he has been broken in for harness."

"He has," returned Cris. "You mind your own business. Do you think I should drive him if he were not safe? He's only skittish. I understand horses, I hope, as well as you."

George turned to Mrs. Chattaway. "Do not go with him," he urged, "Let Cris try him first alone."

"I am not afraid. George," she said, in a loving accent. "It is not often Cris finds time to drive me. Thank you all the same."

Cris gave the horse his head, and the animal dashed off. George stood watching until the angle in the avenue hid them from view, and then gave utterance to an involuntary exclamation :—

"Cris has no right to risk the life of his mother."

Not very long afterwards, the skittish horse was flying along the road, with nothing of the dog-cart left behind him, except its shafts.

CHAPTER XX.

AN INVASION AT THE PARSONAGE.

On the lower road, leading from Trevlyn Farm to Barbrook, was situated Barbrook rectory. A pretty house it was, covered with ivy, standing in the midst of a productive garden, and surrounded by green fields. An exceedingly pretty place for its size, that parsonage—it was never styled anything else—but very small. A good thing that the parsons inhabiting it had none of them owned large families, or they would have been at fault for room.

The present incumbent was the Rev. John Freeman. Incumbent of the parsonage house, you understand : not of the living. The living was in the gift of a neighbouring cathedral; it was held by one of the chapter; and he delegated his charge (beyond an occasional sermon) to a curate. It had been so in the old time when Squire Trevlyn flourished, and it was so still. Whispers were abroad that when the death of this canon should take place—a very old man, both as to his years and to his occupancy of his prebendal stall—changes would be made, and the next incumbent of the living would have to live on the living. But this has nothing to do with us, and I don't know why I mentioned it.

Mr. Freeman had been curate of the place for more than twenty years. He succeeded the Rev. Shafto Dean, of whom you have heard. Mr. Dean had remained at Barbrook but a very short time after his sister's marriage to Joe Trevlyn. That event had not tended to allay the irritation existing between Trevlyn Hold and the parsonage, and on some promotion being offered to Mr. Dean, he embraced it. The promotion given him was in the West Indies: he would not have chosen to undertake a residence there under happier auspices; but he felt sick of the continual contention with Squire Trevlyn. Mr. Dean went out to the West Indies, and died: carried off by fever within six months of his arrival. Mr. Freeman had succeeded him at Barbrook, and Mr. Freeman was there still: a married man, without children.

The parsonage household was very modest. One servant only was kept; and if you have the pleasure of forcing both ends to meet yearly upon the moderate sum of one hundred pounds sterling, you will wonder how even that servant could be retained. But a clergyman has advantages in some points over the rest of the world : at least, this one had ; his house being held rent free, and his garden supplying more vegetables and fruit than his household could consume. Some of the choicer fruit, indeed, he sold : I hope you won't think any the worse of him for doing so. His superfluous vegetables he gave away ; and many and many a cabbage leaf full of gooseberries and currants did the little parish children look out for, and get. He was a quiet, pleasant little man of fifty, with a fair face and fat double chin : never an ill word had he had with anybody in the parish since he came into it. His wife was pleasant, too, and talkative ; and would as soon be caught by visitors making puddings in the kitchen, or shelling the peas for dinner, as sitting up in state, looking out for company.

At the back of the parsonage house, detached from it, was a flagged room called the brewhouse, where sundry abnormal duties, quite out of the regular routine of things, were performed. A furnace was in one corner, a large board or table which would put up or let down at will was underneath the casement, and the floor was flagged. On the morning of the day when Mr. Cris Chattaway contrived to separate his dog-cart from its shafts, or to let his new horse do it for him, of which you will hear further presently, this brewhouse was so filled with steam, that it could not be seen across. A tall, strong, rosy-faced woman, looking about thirty years of age, was standing over a washing-tub, rubbing away; and in the furnace, bubbling and boiling, the white linen heaved up and down like the waves of the sea in a ground swell. Altogether, an immense mass of steam congregated, and made itself at home.

You have seen the woman before, though the chances are that you have forgotten all about her. It is Molly, who once lived at Trevlyn Farm. Some five years ago she came to an issue with the ruling potentates at the farm, Mrs. Ryle and Nora, and the result was a parting. Since then Molly had been living at the parsonage, and had grown to be valued by her master and mistress. She looks taller than ever, but you see she has pattens on, to keep her feet off the wet stones of the brewhouse. Indeed, it was much the fashion in that neighbourhood for the servant-maids to go about in pattens, let the flags be wet or dry.

Molly was rubbing vigorously at her master's surplice—which shared the benefits of the wash with more ignoble things, when the striking out of the church clock caused her to pause, and glance up through the open casement window. She was waiting to count the strokes.

"Twelve o'clock, as I'm alive! I knew it must have gone eleven, though I hadn't heard it strike; but I never thought it was twelve yet! And nothing out but them handful o' coloured things and the flannels! If missis was at home, she'd say I'd been wasting all my morning, gossiping."

An accusation which Mrs. Freeman might have made with great truth. There was not a more inveterate gossip than Molly in the parish: and the waste of time her propensity caused, had lost her her last place.

She turned to the furnace, seized hold of the rolling-pin which lay on its edge, and poked down the rising clothes with a fierceness which seemed as if it wished to make up for the lost hours. Then she dashed open the little iron door underneath, threw on a shovel of coal to the fire, and shut it again.

"This surplice is wearing as thin as anything in front," soliloquised she, recommencing her work vehemently over the tub. "I'd better not rub it too much. But it's just in the very place where master gets 'em most dirty. If I were missis, I should line 'em in front. His other one's going worse than this. They must cost a smart penny, these surplices: the linen is—— Now, who's that?"

Molly's interjection was caused by a flourishing knock at the front door. It did not please her. She was too busy to answer useless visitors: useless because her master and mistress were out.

"I won't go to the door," decided she, in her vexation. "Let 'em knock again, or go away."

The applicant preferred the former course, for a second knock, louder than the first, sent its echoes through the house. Molly jerked her wet arms out of the water, gave them a dab upon a towel lying handy, just to keep the soap-suds from dropping on the floor, and then went on her way, grumbling.

"It's that bothering Mother Hurnall, I know! And ten to one but she'll walk in, under pretence of resting, and poke her nose into my brewhouse, and see how my work's getting on. She's a interfering, mischief-making old toad, and if she *does* come in, I'll——"

Molly had drawn the door open, and her words came to an abrupt conclusion. Instead of the meddlesome lady she had expected to see, there stood a gentleman, a stranger: a tall, oldish man, with a white beard and white whiskers, jet-black eyes, a kindly but firm expression on his sallow face, a carpet-bag in one hand, and a large red umbrella in the other.

Molly dropped a curtsey, but a dubious one. Beards were not much in fashion in that simple country-place, neither were red umbrellas, and her opinion vacillated. Was the gentleman before her some venerable much-to-be-respected patriarch; or was he one of those conjurors that went about to fairs in a caravan? Molly had had the gratification of seeing the one perform who came to the last fair, and he wore a white beard.

"I have been directed to this house as being the residence of the Rev. Mr. Freeman," began the stranger. "Is he at home?"

"No, sir, he's not," replied Molly, dropping another and a more self-assured curtsey. There was something about the stranger's voice, his straightforward glance, which insensibly calmed her fears. "My master and mistress are both gone out for the day, and won't be home till night."

This appeared to be a poser to the stranger. He looked at Molly, and Molly looked at him. "It is very unfortunate," he at length said. "I came—I have come a great many hundred miles, and I reckoned very much upon seeing my old friend Freeman. I shall be going away again from England in a few days."

Molly had opened her eyes. " Come a great many hundred miles, all to see master !" she exclaimed.

" Not to see him," answered the stranger, with a half-smile at Molly's simplicity—not that he looked like a smiling man in general, but a very sad one. " I had to come to England on business, and I travelled a long way to get here, and shall have to travel the same long way back again. I have come down from London on purpose to see Mr. Freeman. It is many years since we met, and I thought, if quite agreeable, I'd sleep a couple of nights here. Did you ever happen to hear him mention an old friend of his, named Daw ?"

The name struck on Molly's memory : it was a somewhat peculiar one. " Well, yes, I have, sir," she answered. " I have heard him speak of a Mr. Daw to my mistress. I think—I think," she added, putting her soapy fingers to her temple in consideration, " that he lived somewhere over in France, that Mr. Daw. I think he was a clergy-man. My master lighted upon a lady's death a short time ago in the paper, while I was in the parlour helping my missis line some bed furni-ture, and he exclaimed out and said it must be Mr. Daw's wife."

"Right—right to all," said the gentleman. "I am Mr. Daw."

He took a small card-case from his pocket, and held out one of its cards to Molly; deeming it well, no doubt, that the woman should be convinced he was really the person he professed to be. "I can see but one thing to do," he said, "you must give me house-room until Mr. Freeman comes home this evening."

"You are welcome, sir. But my goodness! there's nothing in the house for dinner, and I'm in the midst of a big wash."

He shook his head as he walked into the parlour—a sunny apartment, redolent of the scent of mignonette, boxes of which grew outside the windows. "I don't care at all for dinner," he carelessly observed. "A crust off a loaf and a bit of fresh butter, with a cup of milk, if you happen to have it, will be as well for me as dinner."

Molly left him, to see about what she could do in the way of entertainment, and to take counsel with herself. "If it doesn't happen on purpose!" she ejaculated. "Anything that upsets the order of the house is sure to come on a washing day! Well, there! it's of no good worrying. The wash must go, that's all. If I can't finish it to-day, I must finish it to-morrow. Bother! There'll be the trouble and expense of lighting the furnace

over again! I think he's what he says he is:
I've heard them red umberellas is used in France."

She carried in the tray of refreshment—bread,
butter, cheese, milk, and honey. She had pulled
down the sleeves of her grown, and straightened
her hair, and put on a clean check apron, and
taken off her pattens. Mr. Daw detained her
while he served himself, asking divers questions;
and Molly, nothing loth, ever ready for a gossip,
remembered not her exacting brewhouse of work.

"There is a place called Trevlyn Hold in this
neighbourhood, is there not?"

"Right over there, sir," replied Molly, extending
her hand in a slanting direction from the window.
"You might see its chimblies but for them trees."

"I suppose the young master of Trevlyn has
grown to be a fine man?"

Molly turned up her nose. She never supposed
but the question alluded to Cris, and Cris was no
favourite of hers. She had caught the prejudice,
possibly, during her service at Trevlyn Farm.

"I don't call him so," said she, shortly. "A
weazened-faced fellow, with a odd look in his
eyes as good as a squint! He's not much liked
about here, sir."

"Indeed! That's a pity. Is he married? I
suppose not though, yet. He is young."

"There's many a one gets married younger

than he is. But I don't know who'd have him,"
added Molly, in her prejudice. "*I* wouldn't, if I
was a young lady."

"Who has acted as his guardian?" resumed
Mr. Daw.

Molly scarcely understood the question. "A
guardian, sir? That's somebody that takes care
of a child's money, who has got no parents, isn't
it? *He* has no guardian that I ever heard of,
except it's his father."

Mr. Daw laid down his knife. "The young
master of Trevlyn has no father," he exclaimed.

"But indeed he has," returned Molly. "What
should hinder his having one?"

"My good woman, you cannot know what I am
talking of. His father died years and years ago.
I was at his funeral."

Molly opened her mouth in very astonishment.
"His father is alive now, sir, at any rate," cried
she, after a pause. "I saw him ride by this house
only yesterday."

They could but stare at each other, as people at
cross purposes frequently do. "Of whom are you
speaking?" asked Mr. Daw, at length.

"Of Cris Chattaway, sir. You asked me about
the young master of Trevlyn Hold. Cris will be
its master after his father. Old Chattaway's its
master now."

"Chattaway? Chattaway?" repeated the stranger to himself, as if recalling the name. "I remember. It was he who—— Is Rupert Trevlyn dead?" he hastily asked.

"Oh no, sir."

"Why, then, is he not the master of Trevlyn Hold?"

"Well, I don't know," replied Molly, after some consideration. "I suppose because Chattaway is."

"But surely Rupert Trevlyn inherited it on the death of his grandfather, Squire Trevlyn?"

"No, he didn't inherit it, sir. It was Chattaway."

So interested in the argument had the visitor become, that he pushed his plate from him, and was looking at Molly with astonished eyes, his elbows on the table. "Why did he not inherit it? He was the heir."

"It's what folks can't rightly make out," answered the woman. "Chattaway came in for it, that's certain. But folks have never called him the Squire, though he's as sick as a dog for it."

"Who is Mr. Chattaway? What is his connection with the Trevlyns? I forget."

"His wife was Miss Edith Trevlyn, the squire's daughter. There was but three of 'em.—Mrs.

Ryle, and her, and Miss Diana. Miss Diana was never married, and I suppose won't be now."

"Miss Diana?—Miss Diana? Yes, yes, I recollect," repeated the stranger. "It was Miss Diana whom Mrs. Trevlyn—— Does Rupert Trevlyn live with Miss Diana?" he broke off again.

"Yes, sir; they all live at the Hold. The Chattaways, and Miss Diana, and young Mr. Rupert. Miss Diana has been out on a visit these two or three weeks past, but I heard this morning that she had come home."

"There was a pretty little girl—Maude—a year older than her brother," proceeded the questioner. "Where is she?"

"She's at the Hold, too, sir. They were brought to the Hold quite little babies, those two, and they have lived at it ever since, except when they've been at school. Miss Maude's governess to Chattaway's children.'

Mr. Daw looked at Molly doubtingly. "Governess to Chattaway's children?" he mechanically repeated.

Molly nodded. She was growing quite at home with her guest; quite familiar. "Miss Maude has had the best of edications, they say: plays and sings first-rate; and so they made her the governess."

"But has she no fortune—no income?" re-iterated the stranger, lost in wonder.

"Not a penny-piece," returned Molly, deci-sively. "Her and Mr. Rupert haven't got a half-penny between 'em of their own. He's clerk, or something of that, at Chattaway's coal mine, down yonder."

"But they were the heirs to the estate," the stranger persisted. "Their father was the son and heir of Squire Trevlyn, and they are his children! How is it? How can it be?"

The words were spoken in the light of a remark. Mr. Daw was evidently debating the wonder with himself. Molly thought the question was put to her.

"I don't know the rights of it, sir," was all she could answer. "All I can tell you is, that the Chattaways have come in for it, and the inherit-ance is theirs. But there's many a one round about here calls Mr. Rupert the heir to this day, and will call him so, in spite of Chattaway."

"He is the heir—he is the heir!" reiterated Mr. Daw. "I can prove——"

Again came that break in his discourse which had occurred before. Molly resumed—

"Master will be able to tell you better than me, sir, why the property should have went from Master Rupert to Chattaway. It was him that

buried the old squire, sir, and he was at the Hold
after, and heard the squire's will read. Nora told
me once that he, the parson, cried shame upon it
when he come away. But she was in a passion
with Chattaway when she said it, so perhaps it
wasn't true. I asked my missis about it one day
that we was folding clothes together, but she said
she knew nothing of it. She wasn't married then."

"Who is Nora?" inquired Mr. Daw.

" She's the housekeeper and manager at Trevlyn
Farm; she's a sort of relation to 'em. It was
where I lived before I come here, sir; four year,
turned, I was at that one place. I have always
been one to keep my places a good while," added
Molly, with pride.

Apparently the boast was lost upon him; he
did not seem to hear it. "Not the heir to
Trevlyn!" he muttered; "not the heir to Trevlyn!
It's a puzzle to me."

" I'm sorry master's out," repeated Molly, with
sympathy. " But you can hear all about it to-
night. They'll be home by seven o'clock. Twice
a year, or thereabouts, they both go over to stop
a day with missis's sister. Large millers they be,
fourteen mile off, and live in a great big handsome
house, and keep three or four in-door servants.
The name's Whittaker, sir."

Mr. Daw did not show himself very much interested in the name, or in the worthy millers them-selves. He was lost in a reverie. Molly made a movement amidst the plates and the cheese and butter; she insinuated the glass of milk under his very nose. All in vain.

"Not the heir!" he reiterated again; "not the heir! And I have been picturing him in my mind as such all through these long years!"

END OF VOL. I.

BRADBURY AND EVANS, PRINTERS, WHITEFRIARS.

NEW WORKS.

NEW NOVEL BY THE AUTHOR OF "EAST LYNNE."

This day is published, in 3 vols.,

REVLYN HOLD. By Mrs. WOOD, Author
"East Lynne," "Danesby House," &c.

TINSLEY BROTHERS, 18, Catherine Street.

NEW WORK BY CAPTAIN BURTON.

*Ready this day, in 2 vols., with Portrait of the Author, Map, and
Illustrations,*

BEOKUTA; and an Exploration of the Cameroo
Mountains. By Capt. R. F. BURTON, Author of "A Pilgrimage t
Mecca," &c.

"A book which is as instructive as it is pleasant,—as significant and suggestiv
o the watchful statesman as it is full of amusement for the veriest idler."—*Time*

TINSLEY BROTHERS, 18, Catherine Street.

NEW NOVEL BY THE AUTHOR OF "GUY LIVINGSTONE."

On April 11th will be published, in 2 vols.,

IAURICE DERING; or, The Quadrilateral. B_.
the Author of "Guy Livingstone."

TINSLEY BROTHERS, 18, Catherine Street.

NEW WORK BY MR. SALA.

This day, in 2 vols., at all the Libraries,

FTER BREAKFAST; or, Pictures done with
Quill. By G. A. SALA.

TINSLEY BROTHERS, 18, Catherine Street.

Ready this day, in 3 vols., at all the Libraries,

RUTH RIVERS. By KENNER DEENE, Author o
"The Schoolmaster of Alton."

TINSLEY BROTHERS, 18, Catherine Street.

NEW WORK BY THE AUTHOR OF "ENGLAND UNDER THE
STUARTS."

In the press, in 3 vols. 8vo.,

HE LIFE OF GEORGE THE THIRD. Fron
Published and Unpublished Letters and Documents. By J. HENEAG
JESSE, Author of "England under the Stuarts." [*In May*

TINSLEY BROTHERS, 18, Catherine Street.

In the Press,

NEW NOVEL, BY THE AUTHOR OF "ABEL DRAKE'S WIFE,'
entitled

Lightning Source UK Ltd.
Milton Keynes UK
UKHW012149301118
333276UK00010B/936/P